MIDNIGHT PLUS ONE

Also by
GAVIN LYALL

★

THE WRONG SIDE OF THE SKY
THE MOST DANGEROUS GAME

MIDNIGHT
PLUS ONE

*

GAVIN LYALL

THE COMPANION BOOK CLUB
LONDON

This edition is issued by arrangement with
Hodder & Stoughton Ltd., London

Made and printed in Great Britain
for The Companion Book Club (Odhams Books Ltd.)
by Odhams (Watford) Limited
Watford, Herts.
S.366.V.O.

It was April in Paris, so the rain wasn't as cold as it had been a month before. But still too cold for me to walk through it just to see a fashion show. I wouldn't find a taxi until it had stopped raining, and when it stopped I wouldn't need one: I only had a few hundred yards to go. Impasse.

That left me sitting in the Deux Magots getting wet only on the inside and listening to the evening traffic making angry Grand Prix starts from the lights on the Boulevard St Germain outside.

The café claimed it was the *Rendez-vous de l'élite intellectuelle,* but it was the quiet time when most of the *élite* had gone off to wave their arms and egos over dinner. The only other customer I could see without turning my head was a young gent in a green corduroy suit and mauve denim shirt, but he obviously wasn't really *intellectuelle* because he was reading the continental edition of the *Daily Mail.* The front page was getting excited about the setting up of another inquiry into British security leaks. I stayed calm; all it meant was that another half-dozen retired civil servants and judges were going to be told secrets they wouldn't have known otherwise.

The loudspeaker on the wall said: *"Monsieur Caneton, Monsieur Caneton. Téléphone, s'il vous plâit."*

Ask me what my wartime code-name was and I'd need a moment to remember. Broadcast it over a café loudspeaker in Paris and I know immediately who you mean. The back of my neck felt cold, as if somebody had touched it with a gun muzzle.

I finished taking a sip of Pastis, which I found I'd been in the middle of, and started thinking what to do. In the end, I did the only thing possible: went to answer it. Whoever-it-was must already know I was there. He couldn't have been ringing the Deux Magots twice a day since 1944 on an off-chance.

The telephones are downstairs, near the *toilettes*; two wooden booths with small porthole windows. I could see somebody's back view in one; I picked up the other phone and said: *"Allo?"*

"C'est Monsieur Caneton?" said whoever-it-was.

"Non," I said. *"Je ne connais pas Monsieur Caneton. Qui est là?"* If he wanted to play by the old rules, he'd get 'em. You never admitted to knowing anybody, let alone being them.

All he did was chuckle. Then he said, in English: "I am an old friend. If you meet Monsieur Caneton, please you tell him that Henri *l'avocat* wishes to talk with him."

"And where would he find Henri the lawyer?"

"In the next telephone box."

I dumped the phone, stepped out, and yanked open the next door. And there he was, wearing a malicious grin that stretched from side to side of the booth.

"You bastard," I said. "You sadistic bastard." I wiped the back of my neck.

The grin flowed out of the booth towards me. Behind it was a shortish tubby man in a crisp white raincoat, curly grey hair, a deep fat face with bright grey eyes behind rimless glasses, and the sort of moustache that could have been just a moment's forgetfulness in shaving.

Henri Merlin, Paris lawyer. And one-time Resistance pay-master.

We shook hands, using all four of them. It was ten years since we'd met and I hadn't seen much of him since the end of the war. He'd aged—he was well into his fifties—but elegantly and, it seemed, prosperously.

"You have not forgotten everything, then," he beamed. "Even the accent is not too horrible."

"The accent's bloody good." Good enough to keep me alive in France for three years in the war—and a sight better than his English. But on a second thought, I wondered if his English might not be deliberately stagey. American and British businessmen or lawyers might ease up a little once

6

they had him spotted as that familiar type, the gay, flippant musical-comedy boulevardier. Top Paris lawyers are as gay and flippant at work as the men who cut diamonds for a living.

Then I remembered I had a living to make, too. "Can't stop now, Henri. Can I see you later?"

He stretched a fat hand towards the stairs. "We go together. We are enemies." He grinned again.

"You're in on this case?"

"Naturellement. You see how determined *le Maître* is this time?—he now has the best of all Paris lawyers. This time we *prove* your Mercedes Melloney is stealing the—the *modèles"*—he held out his raincoat like a skirt while he searched for the word—"the dress designs (you see? in England you do not even have a word for it)—the designs of *le Maître.* We prove it. You pay us one million francs. Then we have dinner—and we talk about a job I have for you."

"We'll take it to court," I said. But he was already bouncing up the stairs.

He stopped halfway and looked down at me. "You are not perhaps Caneton any more? Not with *l'Intelligence* now?"

"Not Caneton. Just Lewis Cane."

"Louis." He gave it the French pronunciation. "With all these years, I did not know your real name. We go to see the horrible fashions of Mercedes Melloney." He accelerated upstairs.

★ 2 ★

As far as I know there had never been anyone called
Mercedes Melloney, which doesn't surprise or sadden me. It
was just Ron Hopkins' idea of the sort of name he needed to
sell the sort of dresses he made. He had another, and better,
idea of how to sell them, of course; that was why he needed
the sort of advice I specialized in.

It sounds crazy, an English mass-production dress manu-
facturer giving fashion shows in Paris, but Ron didn't haul
a plane-load of clothes and models across the Channel for
anything but the health of his bank balance. According to
him, the French had stuck to the *haute couture* from the big
fashion houses, or the tailor-made stuff from the little-
woman-round-the-corner. Which left themselves wide open
for somebody doing cheap up-to-date mass-production
clothes. And since he'd been doing this for three years now,
I suppose he was right. Always taking into account his little
gimmick, of course.

The show was in the dining-room of a big hotel in Mont-
parnasse, probably because Ron thought Paris was more
Parisian on the left bank. It was a long, narrow room done
up in white and gold and long scarlet drapes that did a fine
job of recalling a pre-1914 era that it had never known. It
also gave a good excuse for the hard little gilt chairs you had
to sit on.

As Merlin and I came in Ron zoomed down at us, under
the impression that we were French cabinet ministers or
some such leaders of fashion, saw who I was, and said
sharply: "You're late, boy."

"So's the opposition." I did the introductions. "Henri
Merlin, Monsieur Ron Hopkins. *A vrai dire, c'est Mercedes
Melloney.*"

Merlin smiled politely. *"Enchanté."* Ron was wearing a
dark-green dinner jacket with light-green silk lapels and a
pink orchid which was his idea of how to look as pansy

8

as he thought the Paris dress trade was. Behind it, he
looked as English as roast beef and as homosexual as a
tomcat.

He gave Merlin a fast up-and-down, then nodded at the
cat-walk down the middle of the room. "There's a front seat
for you over there, boy, and your pal next to you. Don't go
selling me out, now."

I leered at him, and we kicked our way past a row of legs
to our places; the audience seemed to be mostly women, and
mostly either those who had got old without getting fat or
got fat without getting old. A couple of trumpeters in
plumed brass helmets let out a toot to announce a new range
of dresses and half a dozen models floated out from an arch
of roses. Somewhere along the way Merlin had picked up a
programme. "*Numéro* 37," he read. "It is called *Printemps
de la Vie*. Springtime of life—a most enchanting title. When
he first designed it, *le Maître* named it only *au Printemps*.
Your Hopkins shows a most accurate understanding of that
somewhat decayed age of woman to which it is supposed to
sell. When I decide that it is also exactly the same dress, it
will cost him one million francs."

"It won't be exactly the same," I said.

He was looking at his programme again. "And these
frightfulnesses are supposed to be for *le cocktail*."

A model in a black sheath dress twittered her feet up the
catwalk and paused to despise the air over our heads.

Merlin looked up and said firmly: "Of what sex is that
creature?"

The girl's negligent smile froze on her face.

I winced. She was thin, all right, but not that thin. "Very
sexy," I said loud and clear. "I could rape her myself, here
and now." She didn't seem encouraged.

Merlin shrugged his fat shoulders. "For Englishmen,
always sex. Sex and fashion are not even connected. In
England, you think if a woman gets raped her dress must be
fashionable. You have forgotten all you knew about France,
Caneton." He slid me a sideways look.

I knew about the look without meeting it. "Wait until
after this case. What's this job you want me to do?"

Merlin said quickly and quietly: "A client wishes to go

from Brittany to Liechtenstein. Others wish him not to go. Shooting is possible. You wish to help him get there?"

I pulled out a cigarette and lit it and blew smoke at a model's ankles. "How was he planning to get there? Plane? Train? And what are you paying for this?"

"I would say twelve thousand francs—nearly one thousand pounds. I would suggest by car; it is more simple, more— more flexible. And there are frontiers to cross—or you have forgotten where Liechtenstein is?"

"The far side of Switzerland, between it and Austria. And what's this lad doing in Brittany if he should be in Liechtenstein?"

The trumpets tooted again and the models drifted away. Next scene: dress *sportif*.

Henri said: "He is not in Brittany now. He is on a yacht in the Atlantic. He cannot reach Europe before tomorrow night, and the nearest point he can reach is Brittany. *C'est très simple*. You take him from there to Liechtenstein. The problem is the others who know also where he is and that he must be in Liechtenstein very soon."

It didn't sound like just the only problem to me—not like twelve thousand francs'-worth of problem, anyway.

"I've only heard of two good reasons for going to Liechtenstein," I said. "One is to collect the new postage stamps they do every year. The other is to set up a tax-dodging company. Your man doesn't sound like a stamp collector."

He chuckled gently. "His name is Maganhard."

"I recognize the fortune. Not the face."

"Nobody knows the face. There is one passport photograph only—just one—taken eight years ago. And not in France."

"I'd heard he was something to do with Caspar AG."

He spread his hands. "One hears anything about such men. I cannot tell you much, you understand—perhaps he himself will tell you more—but he will lose much if he does not reach Liechtenstein quickly."

"Lawyer's confidences, eh? Now let's get this straight: I pick up Maganhard in Brittany, in a car, and drive him to Liechtenstein, fighting off gunmen all the way. Very simple.

Only why doesn't he go by plane or train and ask for French police protection?"

"Ah, yes." He nodded and looked at me with a sad smile. "There is of course the other problem. He is also wanted by the police of France."

"Oh yes?" I said casually. "And what would that be for?"

"An *affaire* of rape. Last summer—on the Côte d'Azur."

"They notice such things down there?"

He smiled again. "Fortunately the woman did not complain until after Maganhard had left France. I had to advise him not to return."

"It didn't get much space in the papers; I never saw it."

"As you say"—he shrugged—"in summer on the Côte d'Azur rape is merely a variation on a theme. But still illegal."

"I might not be too keen on helping a rapist escape justice."

"*C'est possible.* But the police would be no problem—they will not know he is in France. Only his rivals know he must get to Liechtenstein."

"On the other hand, rape is about the best frame-up charge I know."

"Ah." He gazed sunnily up at the models and said quietly: "I had hoped the great Monsieur Caneton had not forgotten everything he once knew."

A model stalked past, hips and head shoved well forward as if she was auditioning for the Hunchback of Notre Dame, and wearing a tartan cloak where the Campbell-Macdonald war was still going on.

"All right. Why don't you fix a private plane for him?—then he wouldn't have to show his face at the frontiers."

He sighed. "Airfields are carefully watched these days, *mon Caneton.* And it could not be a small aeroplane to fly all the way from Brittany to Liechtenstein, not one that can land just in a field anywhere. And all the good pilots are honest—and the bad pilots"—he shrugged again—"a man like Maganhard does not fly with bad pilots."

That all added up. I nodded. "So where can I get a car?—not hired or stolen."

11

"The police have not confiscated the Paris cars of Maganhard—and I do not think they know I have the keys. Would you wish the Fiat President or the Citroën DS?"

"If it's not a fancy colour, the Citroën."

"Black. Nobody will notice it."

I nodded. "Are you coming with us?"

"No. But I meet you in Liechtenstein." He smiled up at the girl in the Glencoe Massacre cloak and asked out of the side of his face: "Do you want also a gunman?"

"If there's likely to be shooting, yes: I'm not a professional. I hear that Alain and Bernard are still the best men. And the American, Lovell, is the next best. Can I have any of them?"

He glanced at me. "You know such people?" He hadn't expected me to be able to name the top three bodyguard-gunmen in Europe.

"I also have clients, Henri—and some of *them* are worried about getting shot in the back, too." Perhaps I was exaggerating. I certainly had clients who were liable to get shot, but most of them—rightly—didn't value their own lives at as much as a good bodyguard costs. Still, one tries to keep in touch.

He nodded. "I forgot—you knew Alain and Bernard in the war, I think."

I had. They'd been a couple of good Resistance men, further south, who hadn't wanted to lay down their guns when the war ended. So they hadn't. I'd heard that they always worked together—and also that not all of their work was bodyguarding. But if I could get them on my side, I was ready to skip moral questions.

Merlin said: "I am afraid I cannot contact them. But I can get Lovell. You know him?"

"Never met him. He was in the American Secret Service, wasn't he?"

Over there, "Secret Service" doesn't mean what it does in Europe. In America, the Secret Service specializes in providing bodyguards for presidents and their families. That all meant that Lovell was a well-trained man—but what did his leaving the service mean? Well, maybe some people just don't like being organization gunmen.

Merlin said: "I will fix for Lovell to meet you at Quimper."

"If that's where we're starting. Can you get the car to meet me there, too? I can drive to Liechtenstein inside twenty-four hours, but I don't want to do any driving the day before."

"I fix it."

The trumpets called the models home across the sands of Dee.

Merlin gave me a satisfied but slightly curious look. "It seems, Caneton, that you are doing this job. Do you know why?"

"Twelve thousand francs is why." Perhaps I'd said that a little too quickly. I said more slowly: "Provided I get eight thousand in advance—and double if I land in jail."

Merlin nodded.

"And one more thing," I said. "You're Maganhard's lawyer: I want your promise that he didn't do this rape—and that he's going to Liechtenstein to save his own investment, not pinch somebody else's."

He smiled a sleepy, cat-like smile. "So Caneton is a moralist—you wish to be on the side of truth and justice now, *hein*?"

"I have the impression," I said sharply, "that I was on the right side when you first knew me—in the war."

"Wars are so simple, morally." He sighed. "But I promise: Maganhard is no rapist—and he is not trying to steal another's money. You will believe that when you meet him."

The trumpets blew a complicated fanfare: Big Scene—evening dresses, including number 37. The models flooded out through the arch of roses.

Merlin waggled his backside to get more comfortable on the stiff little chair, and said: "I ring you at your hotel, later. Now—we become the enemies. *Voici*."

He had spotted number 37.

To me, number 37—*Printemps de la Vie*—was just a bolt of bottle-green silk wrapped around the girl to give a lot of horizontal creases up top and vertical creases below, and dragging a short train behind. But I got Henri's point about

13

the age of the women who'd wear it: under those thick creases you could be any shape at all. The only idea the dress put across was that you were rich enough to afford a lot of bottle-green silk.

I leaned over to Merlin and whispered: "Far better than anything *le Maître* could have done."

"*La mode n'existe qu'à Paris*," he said firmly. "If it is good—it is stolen." He had a photograph in his hand and was glancing from it to the model and back again.

She knew what he was doing; she slowed up as she went past us, groping around her waist for a pocket or belt to hook her hands into. I don't know why models do that; if a girl hooked her hands into her belt in real life you'd think she was a tart.

Merlin exploded. "It is the dress of *le Maître*! It is—*c'est un vol! Votre Hopkins, il est un larron, un espion . . .*"

I stopped listening. I knew where we were, now.

When he'd finished, I said mildly: "I agree there are similarities. But there are differences, too——" If that was true, I couldn't spot them. But Merlin had.

"They are very small. It is the dress of *le Maître*. Many years your Hopkins has done this. Now Henri Merlin has caught him."

I said thoughtfully: "I doubt Hopkins will give in without a fight."

"Then we will fight." He stood up and shoved back along the front row. The model had turned and was floating along the catwalk, keeping level with us. I winked up at her and she winked down at me. She'd given up trying to find a belt or pockets and just had one hand on her hip. It didn't make her look less like a tart. Only like a cheaper one.

At the door, Hopkins and Merlin were standing pretending not to look at each other.

I smiled at both and said to Merlin: "Excuse me—I have some advice to give to my client."

"Advise him to be rich tomorrow or cut his throat tonight." He gave me a fat grin. "I ring you." And he marched out.

Hopkins said: "Well, boy—does he think he's got a case?"

"No. He started getting angry in French. If he'd had a

case, he'd have explained it to me in English. But I acted worried enough so that he'll push it a bit." I looked at my watch. "He'll probably leak the story to the Press tonight. He's got time."

"Marvellous." He thumped my shoulder, grinning hard. "You'll go too far one of these days, Ron. They'll nick you."

"I'll ruddy well *have* to go too far. I can't pull this stunt much longer: they'll get fed up and stop making a fuss. And then what'll happen?"

"Nobody in Paris'll buy your clothes."

"Dead right, boy. Unless they think I'm pinching the big Paris ideas, I'm finished."

"La mode n'existe qu'à Paris."

"Ay?"

"Something Merlin said. Roughly translated, there's no fashion but Paris fashion."

"Right again, boy." Then he turned mournful. "Put *Paris* on the label and you could sell 'em a sack that still smelled of manure. Don't get me wrong—I'm not knocking Paris. It's a bleeding miracle how good most of their stuff is. But it don't need to be. Most of the old cows haven't got no more taste than a sixpenny hamburger. That's why just being good ain't enough." He waved a hand at the models titupping past us.

I shrugged. "Why not change your name—call yourself Ron Paris? Then you could put *Mode de Paris* on the label."

He stared at me. Then he thumped my shoulder again.

"You're a marvel, boy. Knew I was on to a good thing when I got you instead of one of them lawyers. Too much bloody law with them."

I smiled weakly at him. "I'll ring you in a few days, Ron."

He shook my hand, a cool firm grip that had nothing to do with his fancy dinner jacket. "What you doing now, boy?"

"Spending a few days over here. Might be doing a little shooting."

"Shooting—in April? You can't shoot anything now."

I shrugged again. "I've been told you can find something."

15

★ 3 ★

I GOT off the train at Quimper at half past ten the next night. By then I was wearing a lightweight grey-blue raincoat over a new brown sports-coat with brass buttons, a blue shirt of that Swiss cotton that looks like silk, buttoned up to the neck without a tie, dark-grey trousers, and a short haircut.

I wasn't playing at being a fashion model. I just wanted to look French enough so that if the gendarmes got the word to look out for a tall, thin, forty-year-old Englishman, they might pass over me—but not so French that if they *did* stop me, they'd get suspicious at a Frenchman carrying a British passport; there hadn't been time to get a false identity card.

It was a fairly subtle line I was trying to draw, and I could be wrong several ways. But I thought the brass buttons might just do it. They were the size and thickness of dog-biscuits and stamped with a heraldic crest that could only have belonged to a dog. I was very proud of them. They were just the sort of thing the French wear because they think it's an English fashion.

The night had a heavy ceiling of cloud, low enough to reflect the lights of the town, and the Place de la Gare was still wet from the last rain. Facing the station there was a row of restaurants. I picked the one I wanted and went in.

Only five of the tables still had anybody at them, and all at the coffee and cognac stage. A waiter gave me a sour look and came forward to explain that they were closing.

I picked a character sitting alone and asked him: *"Je m' excuse, mais n'avez-vous pas vu une jeune fille avec——"*

He said: "Pass, friend, all's well. Harvey Lovell."

"Lewis Cane." I sat down. The waiter hovered off my starboard bow.

"Like a drink?" Lovell asked.

"Marc, if they've got one."

He snapped his fingers. *"Un marc."*

"Aren't you?" I asked.

16

He shook his head quickly. "Not tonight." We waited and looked each other over.

He was solidly built, a few years younger and maybe a couple of inches shorter than me. He had wiry fair hair, cut rather short, and was wearing a grey sports-coat with a faint red check, dark trousers, a knitted black tie. None of this told you anything about him once you'd met his face.

It might have been a haunted face, but if so, it was used to its ghosts by now. He had a wide mouth, held set, and light-blue eyes that moved quickly or stayed very still. The rest was lines: two sharp trenches carved from his nose down past his mouth, deep creases beside his eyes, permanent lines along his forehead. But they didn't express anything; they were just there. Not tired or hungry or haggard. Not a face that had seen hell—but perhaps one that expected to.

I grabbed for a cigarette. Maybe I was imagining things. I hoped so: I wanted a sensitive gunman as much as I wanted one with two tin hands.

He shook his head at my cigarettes and lifted one out of a packet of Gitanes on the table, using his left hand.

"So what's the plan?" he asked.

"I'm collecting the car at midnight. Two o'clock we're down at the Baie d'Audierne flashing a torch at the sea. They row Maganhard ashore—and we get rolling."

"What route are we going?"

"We've pretty well got to go through Tours, anyway; after that, I'd pick the southern route: Bourges, Bourg, Geneva. I reckon we should be in Geneva by the middle of the afternoon. Then it's only about six hours to Liechtenstein."

He nodded thoughtfully. "You know anything about the characters who are supposed to be trying to stop us?"

"Merlin couldn't say much. They're something to do with Maganhard's Liechtenstein business—it sounds as if they're trying to take it over. He's something to do with Caspar AG."

"AG?"

"*Aktiengesellschaft*—means 'corporation', roughly. Caspar's a big holding and marketing company: controls a lot of electronics firms in this end of Europe, France, Germany, Italy, so on. The firms make the stuff, then sell it at cost to

Caspar. They don't make any profit, so they don't pay any tax. Caspar markets the stuff, takes all the profit—but there's no real profits tax in Liechtenstein. So they don't pay tax anywhere. It's not a new idea."

The waiter came up with my *marc*.

When he'd gone, Harvey said, "I don't see what Liechtenstein gets out of all this."

"Some stamp duty, a small capital tax, a lot of work for Liechtenstein lawyers." I sipped. "They get a small cut of businesses they wouldn't even get a smell of otherwise. The last I heard, there were six thousand foreign firms registered in Liechtenstein."

He smiled. It was a slow, twisted movement that used up only one side of his face. "And I thought they lived by printing new mail stamps every year." He crushed his cigarette out. "I hear the cops are also after us."

"If they know Maganhard's in the country. According to Merlin, they shouldn't know. But if they do—let's get one thing straight." I looked at him. "There's no shooting policemen."

He looked back at me, rubbing one finger slowly up and down the side of his bony nose. "Well, well, well," he said softly. "And I was just going to say the same thing. Okay." His voice got brisker. "So we don't kill cops. But we could have a problem—if Maganhard's business pals remember they could fix him just by tipping off the cops that he's around. No bother, no risk—to them."

I nodded. "I'd thought of that. Maybe they haven't. Or maybe they want him dead."

He smiled his sideways smile again. "Or maybe there's a lot we don't know about this job yet?"

It was about eleven o'clock when we left the restaurant and it had started raining again: a slow, steady drizzle that looked as if it could keep up for hours.

"You book a room?" Harvey asked.

"No. I didn't want to go filling out forms and leaving my name around here."

"Better come up to mine."

I looked at him sharply in the lamplight. He smiled

18

lopsidedly back. "I brought a different passport. This one doesn't say Harvey Lovell."

We went to his hotel, just north of the river, and got up to his room without anybody seeing me. It was a small, clean, worn room with as much personality as a dead mouse. He sat on the bed, leaving me a choice of the bedside table or a chair, neither of which had been built for sitting on. While I was still making up my mind, he reached an old fabric Air France suitcase out from under the bed, and took out a rolled black wool shirt. He unwrapped it, and had a stubby revolver in a holster with some complicated-looking straps.

"Sorry I don't have a drink to offer," he said shortly. Then he pulled up his right trouser leg and started fitting the holster on to his calf and ankle. I walked across and picked the gun off the bed.

It was a Smith and Wesson with a two-inch barrel, loaded with five .38 Specials. It was a perfectly ordinary-looking little gun except that he'd added a little more wood to the butt, to improve the grip. But even that wasn't fancy: no careful carving so that every finger fitted exactly into the right place—and took five minutes to get fitted. Fully carved grips are strictly for the Saturday afternoon gunmen.

I glanced quickly at him. He'd frozen with the holster still half-strapped to his ankle, his eyes on my hand. He didn't like somebody else holding a gun, and especially not his. Gunmen never do.

I tossed it back on the bed and nodded at the holster. "Why're you wearing it down there?"

He relaxed and went back to strapping the holster on. "Easiest place to get it, in a car. Stick it in your belt, or under your arm and it'll take you a week to pull it."

That made sense to me. "You planning to wear it there when you get out of the car?" I asked.

"Nope." He went on fixing the holster.

I waited a moment, then said: "You've only got five rounds in that thing. Why not an automatic?"

"You need a thirty-eight round to have any punch," he said, with careful calmness. "Thirty-eight automatic would be a sight heavier and a sight bigger. Automatics can jam, too." But by now I was hardly listening. I wasn't really interested in his opinions on guns—only that he had some. To a man who bets his life on his choice of guns there's only one True Belief about guns—his own—and the only True Prophet is himself. Every one has a different belief, of course, which is why there are still so many gunmakers in business.

"Anyway—you think they'll come at us more than five at a time?" he ended up.

I shook my head. He finished strapping on the holster and, still sitting on the edge of the bed, dropped the revolver in. Then snatched it out again. And again—and again. There was nothing smooth and graceful about it, the way it is in the cowboy books. It came out in a vicious grab. I liked that, too.

Then he stood up and slid the gun into a small open-sided spring-clip holster on his belt just forward of his left hip.

"You bringing a gun on this trip?" he asked.

"Yes."

"Merlin said you probably wouldn't."

"He didn't ask me. I borrowed one off some friends in Paris."

He was about to ask me what type. I said: "Mauser 1932."

For him, it was probably an expression of intense surprise: his face just went utterly still.

"The big job? The thing with a change lever that'll fire full automatic?"

"That's the one."

He slanted his eyebrows slightly, one up, one down. He had me now: I'd betrayed a bit of my own True Belief— and what a belief.

"You towing it behind us on a trailer?" he asked. "Or sending it ahead by freight train?"

I grinned. There are a lot of snags to the old "broom-handle" Mauser, particularly the 1932 model converted to real automatic fire. It weighs three pounds, is a foot long, has one of the worst grips going, and fired on full automatic it's as easy to aim as an angry cat. But it has its advantages —and the hell with anybody who doesn't agree.

I said: "I've always thought the best place to wear a gun is in your hand. If you're fast in your thinking you won't have to be all that fast with a gun."

"Sounds reasonable," he said, in a voice with the reasonableness carefully sprinkled on top.

"So you don't like the Mauser '32?" I asked.

"You could say that. You might also say I don't like you telling me about guns."

I grinned cheerfully. "All I wanted to know. I had to be sure I didn't have to run you as well as everything else on this job."

He slanted his eyebrows again. "This was just to see if I could be pushed around?"

"I didn't know you. I've heard talk of you——" His face suddenly snapped shut, like a blind across a window. I went on: "But they could have been wrong."

He relaxed slowly and looked at the floor. "Yes," he said, "they could have been wrong." He looked up. "I could like working with you. As long as you remember I won't be making applications in triplicate to open fire. You'll know I want to shoot when you hear me shooting."

"That's another thing I wanted to be sure of."

He smiled. "I've worked with people who didn't understand that—at first." Then his face got expressionless again. "Just one thing. We're hired for different jobs: you get him to Liechtenstein—and I keep him alive. Most of the time it'll be the same job. But maybe not always. You might remember that, too."

I nodded and buttoned up my raincoat. "I'm going to pick up the car. I'll meet you down beside the river in twenty minutes."

He smiled again. "I still think you're crazy, bringing that Mauser."

I shrugged. "Call it wartime experience. I started this work when it was mostly Sten-guns and plastic explosive. Doesn't it make you feel better, being backed up by a machine-gun battalion?"

He shook his head firmly. "Not backed up . . . If you ever get around to firing that thing, I want to be *behind* you."

We grinned at each other. I thought of asking him why he'd gone stiff when I said I'd "heard talk" of him. But that isn't the sort of question you ever ask a professional bodyguard-gunman.

Later on, I sometimes wondered if I should have asked it anyway. But I always tell myself that he would never have answered it—and that already it was too late.

★ 4 ★

THE plan for the car was strictly from the old wartime rule
book. Any sort of hand-over—of a car, arms, information—is
the most dangerous time. It implicates two people, perhaps
betrays two groups.

I had the car number. It would be parked in the Cathedral
place, alongside the Cathedral itself. Locked. Keys just
under the left front-wheel arch, held there by a piece of
sticky tape. Simple.

It was still raining, which would cut down any spectators.
Not that it would need much: after half past ten, the only
things on the Quimper streets are the street lamps. Their
light rippled across the wet cobbles in the *place* as I strolled
down the line of cars up against the Cathedral. There were
plenty of them: Quimper is mostly narrow streets, so the
cars pile up in the *places*.

I found it: a black Citroën DS with the streamlined front
end that always reminds me of a partly-opened oyster. I slid
along the left side and dropped a casual hand to grope under
the wheel arch. No keys. I tried again, not so casually.
Definitely none.

I straightened up and looked carefully round the *place*,
making my head move slowly. I had that vague, creepy feeling that's usually pure imagination—except that imagination is the only way to see round corners.

It didn't have to mean anything: people have forgotten
their orders before, or misunderstood them. The keys could
be on the other side, or he'd forgotten his sticky tape, or just
decided to leave them in the dashboard. I reached for the
door handle, just to try it. It eased open.

Then I knew exactly why the driver had forgotten his
orders.

Fifteen minutes later I was cruising west on the Quai de
l'Odet. Harvey Lovell stepped out from under a café awning.
I pulled up, and he peered in to make sure it was me.

"The password is: Let Me Get The Hell In Out Of The Rain," he said. He slammed the door behind him, and slipped his Air France suitcase down on the floor by his feet. He made another quick movement that looked like shifting the gun from his waist to his ankle.

I pulled away and kept going west.

He peeled off a thin plastic mac and threw it on to the back seat. "All go okay?"

"Not quite. We've a problem."

"No gas or something?"

"Petrol's all right. Just look on the floor at the back."

He turned and leaned over. After a few moments he slid back into place. Then he stared at me. "Yes," he said softly. "He does look like a problem. Who is—was he?"

I turned right, away from the river, on the N785 sign-posted for Pont l'Abbé. "I assume he's the man who was sent here to deliver the car."

"You fade him?"

"Not me. I just found him as he was. Whoever it was had just left him there, with the keys in the dashboard."

He thought about it. "This, I don't like. They just left the car and keys and all, hey? Maybe they wanted to see who picked it up."

"I'd thought of that. But if anybody follows us, we'll know."

"D'you know how he got it?"

"Shot. Don't know what by. I was hoping you'd give an expert opinion when we're clear of town."

He didn't say anything. I glanced sideways at him; he was peering ahead with the instrument lighting showing a faint frown on his face.

Then he said: "It isn't the end of the business I'm good at, but I'll try. Then what?"

"We off-load him down at the beach or somewhere."

"And just keep on as we planned?"

"It's what we're being paid for."

After a while he said softly: "Looks like maybe we're going to earn our money."

Once we were clear of the town, I started trying the car

out: shoving on the accelerator, throwing it into bends, stamping on the brakes. I hadn't driven a Citroën DS for a couple of years, and while it's a damn good car it's also a damn peculiar one. It has a manual gear-change but without a clutch; a front-wheel drive—and everything works by hydraulics. Springing, power steering, braking, and gear-change—all hydraulic. The thing has more veins in it than the human body—and when they start to bleed, you're dying.

Also, in the last two years, they'd hotted the engine up a bit. It had always had a top speed good enough for most French roads; now it had some real push in the acceleration as well.

We slipped into the typical fast scurrying motion, a series of small shocks mostly damped out, curling round the bends without a hint of a roll. On high beam, the big yellow headlights lit the road like carnival night.

Harvey said: "Is there a heater in this thing?"

"Somewhere."

"Let's find it."

It didn't feel that cold to me. The rain was the slow, steady drizzle of a warm front, so the temperature was probably rising. On top of that, the thought of our friend on the floor at the back was keeping me fairly warm. But maybe riding with a corpse takes people's temperature different ways.

I fiddled around and switched on the heater and demister. There weren't any big villages or resorts on the big beach for which we were heading, but the local road stayed good and wide, if over-cambered. We wound between dry-stone walls, with occasional disused windmills showing in the headlights.

We passed through Plonéour-Lanvern and headed for Tréguennec, one of a stack of old Cornish-Celtic names in this part of the world. We hadn't seen a person nor a car since leaving Quimper, and if anybody was following us he was doing it by radar and not headlights.

Harvey didn't say anything; just stared ahead through the drizzle being wiped off the windscreen.

As we reached the sign for Tréguennec I slowed down and dipped the lights, then went on to the parking lights. It held us right down in speed, but now we were only a mile or so from the sea, and the road didn't go anywhere else. I didn't want anybody wondering why a Citroén with a Paris number was driving down to the sea on a night like this.

Finally, the road petered out into a wide sprawl of sand and gravel. I stopped, and switched everything off. When I opened the door we could hear the casual crunch of the sea over a slight rise ahead.

"End of the line," I said.

Harvey reached back and got his mac. "What do we do with our new old friend? Plant him somewhere?"

"Something like that. You take a look at him while I explore." I opened the briefcase down by my leg and decanted a bundle of local 200,000-scale Michelin road maps on the front seat. Under them was a big wooden holster. I opened the top, took out the Mauser, fumbled around for the magazine, and rammed it in. Then I reversed the wooden holster and clipped it on the back of the Mauser butt to form a shoulder piece. Then I got hold of the bolt, and cocked it. Then I was ready.

Harvey said: "I should have timed you on that. I don't think you'd have beaten Billy the Kid on a fast draw."

"I haven't been practising. I might get it down to five minutes yet."

"I heard Billy was faster than that even."

"On a night like this we wouldn't either of us hit anything. It's only the sound that matters. *I'll* sound like a machine-gun."

He nodded. "You got a point there. All right, you pick a grave plot."

I stepped out and slammed the door. It takes a long time for your eyes to adjust to real darkness. I blundered forward, working on what I felt under my feet. After a dozen steps, it turned into heavy shingle, and then took a slope upwards.

A few yards got me to the top of the shingle bank, and even in that light I could see the sea about thirty yards down on the other side, the waves coming in with a muscular thump after their long trip from the Bahamas. As an open beach facing into the prevailing wind, it didn't look like a good small-boat landing to me, but maybe Maganhard didn't have much choice. At least its unsuitability meant it was lonely.

I stepped back from the crest of the bank, turned my back on the rain, and squinted off to either side inland. On my right, south, there was a huddle of what looked like huts a few yards off the end of the road. Nothing to the other side except a vague shape maybe two hundred yards away. I tramped down to the huts—one of which was an old bus without wheels and the windows boarded up. No sign of life. I turned and walked back along the inland side of the bank to the north.

The first thing was a faded notice painted with a big skull and the word MINEN! That made it an old German fortification. I stood around for a while trying to convince myself that any mines would have rusted away by now, then realized that they either would or wouldn't, no matter what I thought. I turned away, down towards the sea.

The water was just below the last of the shingle, showing a patch of sand, and the last of the stones were still wet. It looked as if the tide was on its way out. I walked back to the car.

My eyes were getting adjusted to the dark; I could see the interior light of the Citroën glaring like a beacon the moment I topped the shingle bank. It went off as Harvey heard me coming and closed the door.

"Find a place for him?" he asked.

"You find what he died of?"

"More or less. He stopped three of them, and I'd guess from pretty close. Maybe through the window of the car. They're all three still in him, so I'd guess a small calibre gun: something like a 6·35 millimetre. But I ain't no surgeon."

"You can't tell from the size of the wounds?"

He shook his head. "You can't tell a thing. If it goes in straight, the hole shuts up again. I can tell you he didn't bleed much, so he died fast—if that's any help."

"Only to him." I flashed the torch on him. I hadn't had time for any stocktaking back in the Cathedral *place*. He was a short, wide man with smooth dark hair, a sad moustache, and the pale, disinterested expression of being dead. He had on a coarse tweed jacket, and Harvey had opened his shirt to show three neat punctures across his chest.

Without much wanting to, but wanting to make sure, I felt round his back: no exit wounds. Then I started groping in his pocket.

Harvey said: "No score. No identity card, no driver's licence. Either he didn't bring them, or somebody lifted them."

They hadn't cleaned him out, though: he still had some coins in his pocket, a few bills and receipts, a maker's label on the jacket. The police wouldn't have any trouble identifying him. It would just take them a little time; maybe that was all the killer wanted.

I took out his key-ring: a few door and luggage keys, and also, hung by a smaller ring through a drilled hole, an empty brass cartridge case.

I turned it up to the torchlight. The percussion cap in the base showed it had been fired, and by something with a big, rectangular firing pin. The lettering round it had been worn faint by years in a pocket, but I could still read *W.R.A.—9 mm.* I passed the key-ring to Harvey.

He held it under the torchlight. "Winchester Repeating Arms," he interpreted. "Guess they sent them over in the war. What the hell has a firing-pin like that?"

"Sten gun."

"So he was in the Resistance, hey?"

I nodded. That wasn't a surprise: anybody who did this sort of work for Henri Merlin would likely have been in the Resistance with him. But it wasn't so likely he'd have had a Sten. In the movies, everybody in the Maquis has Stens; in the war, they were handed out to people who'd proved they were cool enough to get up close, and shoot only when they knew they were going to hit somebody. For anybody else, a Sten is just the fastest way of wasting ammunition.

So he'd met somebody else who was good at getting up close and shooting only when he knew he would hit. I shrugged: the Resistance was a long time ago and we'd all of us forgotten a lot. But it didn't sound as if the Other Side, whoever they were, had forgotten quite so much.

I stuck the key-ring back in his pocket and stood up into the rain.

Harvey asked: "Where do we take him?"

"We'll throw him in the sea. The tide's on its way out, and we can't dig in shingle or wet sand, anyway."

"He'll probably get picked up."

"Maybe. Or maybe not. Or maybe a long way from here. And after a few days in the sea they won't be able to time his death properly."

He looked at me.

I said: "I'm not trying to do the poor bastard out of a decent burial—it's just that he's a damn nuisance. If anything happens and they back-track us to this beach, I don't want them to find *him* here."

He nodded and we picked him up and started over the shingle bank. He was a hefty weight, making us slow and clumsy, but we finally made it down to the edge of the sea. We got our feet wet up to the knees and threw him a yard further. He floated, of course, and for a moment it looked as if he didn't want to leave us. Then every receding wave dragged him a bit further out than it pushed him in.

I led the way back up to the top of the bank, and looked back. There was no horizon: sea and sky just became a thick blackness at some range you couldn't even guess at—four hundred yards or four miles. On an off-chance, I pulled out my torch and flashed a Morse code OK seawards. Nothing flashed back.

I hadn't expected anything yet; with the rain, and the general confusion of setting up the whole deal, I wasn't going to start worrying until he was at least an hour late. I only hoped he'd got enough sense to keep his yacht outside the three-mile limit, and use only a small boat in French waters.

It was going to be a long, wet wait. But no need for both of us. I said: "You go back to the car. Come out and take over in a quarter of an hour."

He didn't say anything, nor move. I flashed the torch on his face. He jerked his head away. "Turn it off, damn it!"

I turned it off. "Sorry."

"Don't ever blind me like that. I need to *see*." His voice had a raw, jittery edge on it.

"Sorry," I said again. "You want to go and keep dry?"

"Okay." He didn't move. Then he asked: "You got a drink around?"

"Thought you weren't drinking tonight?"

"I didn't think I was carrying stiffs around, either."

Silly of me. I should have remembered that professional gunmen don't like being reminded of the end product of their work. I'd even made him do a post-mortem.

I said: "Sorry," for the third time. "There's some Scotch in my case. Hold on here and I'll get it."

I walked back and got it from the car. It was just a half-bottle of a whisky I didn't much like but all I'd been able to get on the flight from London. I'd opened it on the train as being cheaper than railway prices, but it was still three-quarters full.

I came back up the bank, flashed at the sea, and then handed the bottle to Harvey.

He said: "No thanks. Changed my mind."

I glared at him through the darkness and rain. I was cold and wet and I hadn't exactly enjoyed finding and then dumping that body myself—and *now* I was stuck with a gunman who couldn't even make up his bloody mind about something as simple as whether he wanted a drink or not.

Well, by now I certainly wanted one myself. I took a swig and then held the bottle out again. "Have a sip. It's going to be a long ride."

He took it. Then his arm whipped over and the bottle exploded on the shingle by his feet. *"I don't want a drink!"*

The gulp of whisky was lead on my stomach and the taste sour in my mouth. I asked quietly: "How long have you been off the stuff, Harvey?"

He just sighed, a long resigned sound.

I said: "How long?"

"I'll be all right. Don't you worry."

No. No worries at all. Except for a bodyguard who was a practising alcoholic. But no more than that.

At least I knew now why he hadn't stayed to draw a pension from the American Secret Service.

"How *long*?" I asked grimly.

"Forty-eight hours. About. I've done it before. I can do it."

That's the funny thing: they *can* do it. For forty-eight hours, or a week or weeks.

"You going to get the shakes on me?" I asked.

"No. I've had them. They won't happen again until I'm back on it."

The calm assumption that he'd be going back on it shook me. I opened my mouth to say several severe but well-meant things, then shut it again before too much rain got in. All I wanted was for him to stay sober for twenty hours more. After that, he wasn't my problem.

And in a way, it was cheering that he didn't plan to stay dry for ever. When they suddenly remember how long for ever is, they're back inside the bottle with a rush. But just another day is an easy target. No need for him to crack before then.

I flashed the torch at the sea.

For a few minutes nobody said anything. The waves crashed on the beach below, their echo dulled by the steady rain. Then I asked: "Had your first amnesia yet?"

He made a sound that might have been a chuckle. "The first memory blackout, you mean? Now, how would a man remember *that*?"

I just nodded. I hadn't really expected an answer, but it had been worth asking. The first amnesia, the first time you can't remember what the hell happened the night before, that's the big step. After that, you're over the hill. Nowhere to go but down. Or so the doctors say.

Getting an answer would have helped me guess how committed he was, how likely to crack.

I said: "Just interested."

"If you're that interested, you know a man hates talking about it."

So he'd taken the trouble to check up on the stages and symptoms. They sometimes do. It's a way of standing back, watching themselves go down the slope. Less effort than trying to hold themselves back.

"So you know something about it?" he asked.

"Something. A bit of drinking wasn't exactly uncommon in the war—particularly in our sort of business. I read it all up once. Had to know how much security risk those people'd be."

"And how much were they?"

I shrugged, but he probably couldn't see. "Some were, some weren't. We won the war anyhow."

"So I heard." Then: "You got a light."

"What?"

He waved at the sea. "Out there. You got a light."

I flashed the torch again. A faint light winked back. I looked at my watch: just after two o'clock.

"Can't be him," I said. "He's hardly late yet."

"You ever think a real big-businessman might be efficient? And he might hire efficient people to get him around?"

We looked at each other through the rain and darkness. "No," I said, "looking at you and me, I wouldn't say that thought had occurred to me. But now we're hired, maybe we'd better try."

5

THE boat hit on the beach with a long, grinding crunch. Several people bounced out and grabbed hold to steady it. The next wave swamped them to their waists.

That was what they'd been hired for, and I'd got quite wet enough for one night already; we stood back on the shingle. It was a motorised whaleboat with a good width, which it must have needed coming through that surf, and a clear twenty-five feet long, which told you something about the size of yacht that carried it.

One of the men stumped up to me and said in guttural English: "The fish are biting."

I tried hard to think of the proper password. Passwords are fine in the right place, which means a seemingly casual remark in a crowded street which won't betray anything if the wrong person hears it. Here, they were nonsense. But Merlin had insisted.

Then I remembered. "And the birds are singing."

He grunted and walked back. I glanced at Harvey; he was slipping something back under his mac.

Somebody was stepping off the whaleboat and getting a lot of help from the crew. He walked slowly up to us, and announced: "I am Maganhard."

"Cane."

Harvey said: "Lovell."

Maganhard said: "There are twenty kilos of luggage and two of us. I believe you have the Citroën."

He didn't ask "Is that all right?" or anything. Just telling us. If there was anything we didn't expect, it was up to us to say so. Efficiency—as Harvey had guessed.

And there was something I hadn't expected. "Two of you?"

"My secretary, Miss Helen Jarman." He stood there, waiting for me to say something else. All I could tell of him in the dark was that he was a square, solid man in a dark coat, no hat, and the glint of spectacles. His voice had a flat, metallic tone like a bad dictaphone.

Somebody else crunched up the shingle and stopped beside Maganhard. "Is everything all right?"

A clear, cool, and unmistakably English voice. Nobody could ever imitate that upper-crust-girls'-school accent. Or perhaps nobody ever wanted to.

She looked fairly tall, with dark hair and a dark coat that glistened softly in the rain.

Maganhard said: "I believe so. Has our luggage come?"

She looked back and a sailor arrived carrying two cases. Maganhard tramped past us over the shingle bank. Harvey patted me on the shoulder, and took two fast steps to arrive just behind Maganhard's right shoulder, just where a bodyguard should be.

I tagged on behind the procession, just where a chauffeur should be.

The sailor dumped the two cases, both expensive solid-looking lumps of horsehide, into the boot of the Citroën. He got a nod from Maganhard and headed back over the bank.

Harvey was standing beside Maganhard, looking out into the night but at the same time making sure he was blocking the most likely lines of fire at Maganhard. Shooting back is only the second half of a bodyguard's job: the first half is trying to be in the way of any bullets.

I asked: "Where d'you want to sit, Harvey?"

"Up front."

The girl said: "Mr Maganhard may wish to sit there."

"He might," I agreed, "in which case he'll be disappointed. Harvey arranges the seating."

Maganhard said: "Mr Lovell—you are the bodyguard?"

Harvey said: "Yes."

"I told Monsieur Merlin I did not need a bodyguard. A driver would have been quite enough. I do not like shooting."

"Don't like it myself," Harvey said evenly, still watching outwards. "But just you and me don't make a majority."

"Nobody is trying to kill me," Maganhard said. "That is

just Monsieur Merlin's idea. The only danger is in being stopped by the police."

I said: "I had that theory, too. But when we picked up the car tonight in Quimper, there was a dead man in it."

The rain pattered softly on the roof of the warm, dry car beside us.

Then Maganhard said: "You mean killed?"

"I mean killed. I imagine he was the man who was supposed to deliver the car to us."

The girl said: "Dead in *this* car?"

"Only the front seat. And he isn't even there any more."

"What did you do with him?"

I didn't answer. Maganhard said: "Do you really wish to know what these men do with the bodies, my dear?" But I wasn't sure his heart was in the crack.

Harvey said wearily: "If we're ever getting into the car, I want Maganhard behind me, on the right."

They got in, and even into the right places, without arguing. So maybe Maganhard was a little shaken, at that.

Past Tréguennec I turned on the headlights. But I wasn't even out of second gear yet: I didn't want to leave any impression of hurrying. Merely coming up from the sea was suspicious enough at that time.

We went through Plonéour-Lanvern and I got into third. The rain spattered steadily on the windscreen and was flipped away by the wipers, leaving a small, unswept patch in the middle. I tried to find a comfortable position leaning over to my left, against the door.

After a while, Harvey said: "D'you think they'll be laying for us in Quimper?"

"Don't know. They could be."

"Can we dodge it?"

"Not without a hell of a detour. We've got to cross the river, and there's no bridge below Quimper and nothing for about ten kilometres above it."

From behind us, Maganhard asked: "Why should anybody be waiting for us?"

"I'm thinking about the man in the car, Mr Maganhard. Somebody knew about him. So perhaps they know about us."

35

Maganhard said: "They could have followed you or Mr Lovell from Paris."

"No." I didn't need to consult Harvey on that one.

Maganhard said crisply: "Can you be certain?"

"We know how to be certain."

The Citroën scurried along the wide rough road, empty and lonely between the rough dry-stone walls. The Mauser was back in my briefcase, and I'd changed my shoes for a pair of nasty grey moccasins that would be a lot more comfortable on a long drive than the normal hard-heeled jobs.

After a time, Maganhard said: "I hope you will try to avoid trouble, rather than attempt to defeat it."

"I'll try," I said. "But I don't have much choice of routes until we're out of Brittany—another two hundred kilometres. You were on time, so we may as well make use of that: just move as fast as we can. They may not be quite ready for us."

I wasn't sure I believed that myself: somebody had been ready for the driver of the car more than two-and-a-half hours before. But I still didn't have any choice.

We came down into Quimper. I changed down into second with more of a thump than I'd intended; it takes longer to learn to change down on a strange car than change up. Harvey lifted his elbow off the big arm-rest on the door and felt down by his ankle. We snaked quietly towards the Quai.

Apart from the line of parked cars, it was dead and empty under the rain: a blotchy, shiny tunnel of light from the street lamps half hidden in the trees on the riverside. The Citroën trembled gently across the cobbles.

Then Harvey said: "You should have turned right there. You're on a one-way street the wrong way."

"I know. I hoped they wouldn't expect that."

I snapped off the side lights to darken our number plate and pushed gently on the accelerator. We picked up speed. Then we were at the end of the Quai and swinging right across the river—again wrong way on a one-way bridge. Slight swing right, hard left, and we were legal again accelerating past the station on the N165. I switched on the lights. The town began to dwindle around us.

"Did anybody see anybody?" I asked.

Nobody answered. Then Harvey said: "I wouldn't jump anybody in the middle of town, anyhow. Too much publicity. They must be expecting us to shoot back by now: they know we found the guy who was delivering it."

"They left us the car, too. So perhaps they just wanted us to get clear of this part of the world."

We were out of the town by now, and I was up to ninety-five kilometres an hour. In top gear for the first time. Now, we were starting to run.

Maganhard asked suspiciously: "Why would they do that?"

"Don't know. Maybe they thought one body was enough for one town. You must know more about these people than I do, Mr Maganhard."

His voice went stiff. "You believe I know such people?"

"It's you they're after, not us. We're here because you're here."

"I am sorry: I do not know any hired gunmen socially. I lead a very narrow life."

I glanced at Harvey and caught the quick twist of a smile in the backlash of light from the headlamps.

But perhaps there was still something Maganhard could tell me. "So you think they'll be hired gunmen, do you?"

"I imagine that if, as you and Monsieur Merlin believe, somebody is trying to kill me, then that would be the easiest way."

I shook my head. "Not necessarily. Professional gunmen—real ones—are very rare birds. Most killings are *passionel* or just mistakes; the average crook doesn't like risking a murder charge. You might be able to pick up a pathological case or some doped-up teenager who likes waving a gun around—but they aren't pros and they won't do a pro job. To find somebody you can depend on, you've got to know France pretty well."

"Monsieur Merlin found you," he pointed out.

"Merlin knows France." I thought about saying that even so, he'd ended up picking a driver who hadn't done much of this sort of thing since the war, and a bodyguard who was

37

at least on the edge of alcoholism. But there's no point in apologizing until the customer starts complaining.

"But the people who'd be doing the hiring," I persisted. "Do they know France?"

There was a long pause. Then he said slowly: "I am afraid I do not know who *is* doing the hiring."

I reached down beside my seat and lowered the car's hydraulic springing a couple of notches now we were on a reasonably good road. I was holding one hundred and twenty kilometres an hour with the headlights on high beam and the road to ourselves.

The rain came down with the same weary relentlessness. The front and back seat heaters were both going, and with everybody starting off wet, the atmosphere inside had developed like a cosy Turkish bath. But we were moving.

Coming into Quimperlé I nearly ended the journey right there, on a downhill left-hand curve that was fast but not as fast as it looked. The front wheels had a brief moment of forgetfulness, then I lifted my foot, the wheels took more weight, and gripped again. When we were straight again, I glanced at Harvey. He was sitting comfortably, his hands still and relaxed in his lap, not looking at me. Getting on with his job—and leaving me to mine.

In Quimperlé itself they were celebrating the start of the tourist season by tearing up the cobblestones into big ragged heaps, but once we were through, the road was open and empty again.

I got out my cigarettes and passed them to Harvey. Without saying anything he lit one, gave it back to me, then lit up one of his own Gitanes.

He smoked quietly for a while, then said: "You know, if you don't want our number to show, I could go back and kick in the lamp."

I thought about this. "No. I don't think so. The gendarmes would be likely to chase us just to tell us the lamp was out. We want to look clean and law-abiding on the surface."

He blew smoke into the stream of air from the dashboard fresh-air grille. "Yeah, I noticed that on the one-way street back in Quimper."

"That was what the generals call a 'calculated risk'."

"I thought that was just when they won by accident. But if that's what you want, we should have used a panel truck —a small van. Nobody'd suspect that."

"They'd suspect the number plate. Any cop would get suspicious of a local delivery van wearing a Paris number out in Brittany or on the Swiss frontier."

"Maybe. So we should have got a long-distance truck— a *camion*."

"From where? And I'm no *camion* driver."

For a while he just smoked, using his left hand. He'd got it so that by now he looked naturally left-handed —unless you realized what he was keeping his right free for.

"Maybe," he said, "what I mean is I wish we'd had more time to plan this thing out."

"If there'd been more time, we wouldn't be in it."

"I guess so." He looked across at the dashboard instruments. "When d'you need to get gas?"

"Not yet." The gauge was showing nearly full. "I hope we won't need any until after it gets light—when there's more stuff on the road."

"Sunrise at about five-thirty."

I raised my eyebrows; I hadn't even bothered to check the sunrise time, although I should have done. I had to keep remembering that Harvey had been in this sort of game more often and more recently than I had. He had his own problem, of course, but when that wasn't showing he was a hard, cool, intelligent character.

I looked at him sideways. His face was calm and his hands were still when he wasn't lifting his cigarette. But his eyes were watching ahead, carefully vetting each wall, house, tree as they grew in the headlights and then ran away behind us, proven innocent.

The car seemed to dwindle around me, fitting more closely, feeling more a part of me. Back-seat passengers don't breathe down your neck in a big Citroën, and we hadn't heard a squeak from them in half an hour. They had faded, had become no more weight or individuality than a couple of vague memories. The car was just Harvey and me in a dim

39

cockpit, flickering through the night with the precision of a high-powered bullet.

It was one of those times when you know exactly, can *feel* exactly, what the car will do—and the road also. It felt familiar, although it wasn't. I understood the pattern of it: what it would do next, how tight its bends would be, how steep its slopes.

It happens. And when it happens, you're right and you're safe. But it doesn't last. And you're never more wrong, more dangerous, than when it's stopped lasting and you don't realize it.

The dashboard clock said three-thirty. Two hours to dawn. Sixteen hours to Liechtenstein.

6

AT four o'clock we were running down a tree-lined avenue into Vannes. It was the biggest town we'd meet for another hour.

"There's a Michelin Guide in the pocket in front of you," I told Harvey. "Look up this place and find me the post office. I want to ring Merlin, if there's a phone box there."

"Why?"

"He wanted me to keep him in touch. And he may be able to find out something about the shooting in Quimper. It could help."

After a while he said: "Turn right in a moment. Alongside this square. Post office on your right in a couple of hundred yards."

I drew up and switched off the engine alongside a dark telephone box. The silence was a sudden thing, rushing in on me, making me feel how noisy we must have been moving. Then I shook my head: it was far too early to start getting jumpy on this trip. I stepped out into the rain.

The box was open, and after a while I got the operator to wake up. I asked for Henri's private Paris number.

It rang several times, then a woman's voice said sleepily: *"Allo?"*

"Est il possible de parler à Henri? Voici Caneton."

There was a pause, then: *"Il vous donnera un coup de téléphone dans quelques minutes. Quel est le numéro?"*

I gave her the number, hung up, then went back to the car.

"Didn't get him yet," I told Harvey. "He's ringing back." I slid into the front seat and started lighting a cigarette.

Maganhard asked: "What are you ringing for?"

"To tell him what happened to his boy in Quimper. And see if that means anything to him. He might have some suggestions."

Maganhard's voice got slightly harder, more metallic. "I thought you were an expert?"

41

"An expert is a man who knows when to call in experts."

The phone in the box jangled and I jumped for it.

Henri said: *"Monsieur Caneton?"*

"Hello, Henri. Bad news: your cousin in Brittany is ill, *very* ill."

"That is bad news. How did it happen?"

"Suddenly—very suddenly. Anything you think I should do?"

"Is he—he is well looked after, yes?"

"He's okay where he is for a day or two, anyhow."

"Then, perhaps I think you should go on as you go. You are at Vannes?"

"Yes. I'm just worried that what he's got might be—infectious. You haven't heard of any disease he's been near recently?"

"I have heard nothing. But now—in the morning—I will ask. You will ring me again?"

"Sure. Night, Henri."

"Au 'voir, Caneton."

I got back into the car. "He doesn't know anything." I started the engine again. "We could turn off here and go for Rennes, then Le Mans and the northern route. But the road isn't as good. I think we'll keep going for Nantes." A big yellow Berliet *camion* growled round the corner ahead and trundled past us, shivering the ground.

Harvey said: "Well, let's roll. The road'll be full of those things by breakfast."

The road was straighter and faster now, the farmland around it looked thicker and richer in the headlights. We were almost off the Brittany peninsula.

But the spell had broken. I wasn't feeling the road as I had been before. We were covering ground, but the magic had gone.

There were occasional *camions* and farm lorries, the spray blowing away from their rear wheels like smoke. I realized we must be trailing a wake like a torpedo boat: nobody had a hope in hell of reading our number plate.

Nobody said anything. Just the flicker of light as Harvey or the girl behind me lit a cigarette. It was the last low hour before the dawn. The time when you know you haven't built up strength enough for a new day; the time when sick men decide the night has been too long, and give up and die. The time a good gunman knows to lay an ambush.

But nobody did. Soon after five we were winding through the industrial desert of Nantes, by-passing the centre through the north-west suburbs.

Harvey asked: "How's the gas?"

"Wearing out. But I think we can make Angers. We've only done about two hundred and fifty kilometres so far."

The girl asked: "Can we stop to get some breakfast?"

"We'll get something in Tours."

"Why wait till then?"

"It's more of a tourist town than anything this side of it: they aren't so likely to remember strangers."

We went on. Up the valley of the Loire, on the N23. A good, fast road except where it suddenly twisted into descending turns down to the riverside villages. There was more traffic now; lorries carrying fish up from the sea, others bringing vegetables down from farmlands. And more *camions,* carrying whatever *camions* carry: Berliets, Somurs, Saviems, Unics, and Willeme tankers. All with the square, solid military look of French *Légionnaires*—and the same habit of walking over anything that got in their way.

The night began to wear thin around us; the shapes of trees and houses separated from the sky; the headlights grew pallid. Even the rain was thinning out; with the wind behind us, we were probably out-running the front.

When it was light enough I twisted the rear-view mirror to have my first good look at our passengers.

Maganhard must have been about fifty and in one way he looked it: a heavy square face frozen in a suspicious frown. But the details were missing. The face was quite unmarked, unworn; the hair a thick pure-black mass swept carefully back from a sharp widow's peak. It looked like a metal sculpture from the twenties or thirties when they got the shape exactly right but made everything smooth and stylized to show that it was Really Art.

He wore square glasses with thick black rims, a bronze-coloured raincoat of very simple cut, and his arms were

43

folded across his chest showing a square wristwatch and a pair of angular gold cuff-links by one of those Scandinavian designers who can make stainless steel look like a million dollars and gold look like fifty cents.

The girl, Miss Jarman, was something else.

Her face was both innocent and haughty, which isn't a rare combination, but which rarely looks as good as it did on her. The face was a pure oval, rather pale, with thin arched eyebrows that were mostly pencilwork. Long brown hair in Garbo's Queen Christina cut, curled in under the chin. She was fast asleep, but doing it without letting her mouth come unbuttoned.

She didn't fit at all with Maganhard—or maybe she did, in a way. At least you could see why he wanted her in the front office, and somehow I was pretty sure that was the only place he did want her. She'd be very good at telling minor millionaires to go climb a tree without hurting their feelings. From her, they'd take it.

This had earned her a dark shaved-sealskin coat, probably on Maganhard's money but certainly not his design. It was a casual wrap-around job held with a loose tie belt, as if it was just another coat. Under it, a white blouse.

I glanced at Harvey, twisted the mirror back, and went back to watching the road. We ran into Angers at about six o'clock. Despite the good road, our speed had dropped in overtaking the *camions*.

We drifted down the broad empty streets, past tall old houses with blind, shuttered windows. When a French town goes to sleep, it dies. It was like sneaking a short cut through the graveyard. I kept the speed down, the car as quiet as I could.

From here to Tours I had a choice of routes: the main road looping north or the tourist route alongside the river. In the end I reckoned that there'd be more *camions* on the north route than tourists on the river at this time of day. We stayed alongside the Loire.

"We're stopping for petrol soon," I announced, "and from now on we may be meeting people. Cafés and so on. Better decide what parts we play."

Harvey asked: "You passing as French?"

"Unless anyone asks for my passport. I can do it." The French are so convinced that nobody else can speak the language properly, that once you know it well it never occurs to them that you could be a foreigner. Useful.

Harvey said: "My accent isn't good enough. So maybe I won't know any at all. Just a little old tourist from Moose Droppings, Iowa. First trip to Europe. Sure is a quaint little old place."

I gave him a look, then asked the back seat: "How about you, Mr Maganhard? What passport do you carry?"

"I am an Austrian citizen resident in Switzerland."

"The passport's in your own name?"

"Of course."

I hadn't expected much else, but there still seemed to be a disturbing amount of honesty going on.

"You'd better speak English," I said. His accent wasn't perfect, and he didn't look particularly English—at least to me. But he was probably convincing enough for a French café proprietor. I added: "But if you have to show your passport, don't speak any English or French at all. Not knowing any languages'll make you seem rather small-time."

He grunted. I wasn't sure he liked the idea of seeming small-time, but he must have seen the sense of it.

"Miss Jarman?" I asked.

"I have an English passport, of course, but I believe I can speak French well enough."

"I'd rather you stayed English. You look it. And act as upper-class as you like. If they're looking for a secretary they won't expect a Duchess. Be really snooty."

"I will behave as I want to behave, Mr Cane." And the voice came from a lot further off than just the back seat.

I nodded. "That's perfect."

Which left us as an English businessman, his upper-crust girl friend, an American tourist, and a French friend doing the driving. It wasn't particularly logical, but it was some distance from a couple of hired hands taking an Austrian businessman and secretary on a trip to Liechtenstein.

Probably none of it would help at all. But it was practice at remembering that we only needed to make one mistake to bring the ceiling down on us.

For the same reason, I reversed in a side road and turned so as to come up to a petrol station from the East, as if we were going from Paris to the Atlantic coast.

I asked for forty-five litres, and the attendant wandered off round the back, still half asleep. I got out and stretched. Harvey slid out of his door and took a fast look around, then propped himself on the road side of the car.

I walked round the car, getting my first daylight look at it. As far as I could tell it hadn't got any scrapes or dents, and the tyres were nearly new Michelin X's—so no trouble there.

As I came back Harvey said: "Sure a mighty pretty little place, this France of yours. Only trouble is the Goddamned fancy cooking. What I'd give now for a real deep-frozen chicken and some shrivelled-up black-eye peas. Yes, sir."

I gave him a look that should have sliced his head off, then had to go through with the joke; the attendant was looking at us.

I spread my hands. "You are—making the pleasantry— yes? Or really you are—*que dites vouz?*—are homesick for your little town in Iowa?"

"Where my dear old pappy sits rockin' on his porch and figurin' new ways to cheat the Indians out of their oil-wells. You bet."

I leered at the attendant and nodded at Harvey. *"Ameri-cain . . . Il n'aime pas beaucoup la cuisine Française."*

The attendant stared at Harvey as if he had escaped from the Insect House at the Zoo, then shrugged at me. *"Quarante six."*

I dealt him fifty francs, and hopped into the car. We'd only fooled a sleepy garage hand, but at least it was a start.

I turned into a side road, did a swing round behind the garage and rejoined the main road east of it. The time was six-thirty-five, and the eastern sky was a mass of dirty ragged clouds with a tepid yellow light somewhere behind it. We hadn't seen the sun yet.

The road was a series of fast, gentle curves with just a wall on the right to keep the river off the road and me out of the river. The fields were green and lush; this is some of the finest French farmland.

We passed a couple of U.S. Army trucks keeping non-

46

union hours and the first sign of Tours, a big Eiffel-Tower-shaped power pylon, loomed up. Then the twin towers of the cathedral and the tall blocks of modern flats. Then I was stuck in a swarm of early workers on autocycles, buzzing like bees all over the road.

"Where are we eating?" Harvey asked.

"We'll find a place down by the market; they'll have been open for hours."

I took the first bridge, weaved through more autocyclists, and went straight across into the old town. It was jammed with fruit and fish lorries. Just before the Place des Halles, I turned off into a side street and parked.

Harvey bounced out on to the pavement, holding up his left hand to stop Maganhard and Miss Jarman moving until he'd approved of the view. There were quite a number of people about.

"I could have done without the crowd," he said quietly.

I shrugged. "Or it could be protection."

"*I'm* the protection. Let's not make it a habit, hey?"

Maganhard and the girl got out and I locked up.

We were in a small, cramped square made of blank, scruffy flat-faced buildings, decorated with the gaudy tatters of last year's circus posters. On the far side of the square there was a small café that looked like standing room only. I led the way round the corner.

After a few yards, we found another café: small, dark, but warm and busy. We edged past a group of characters in smudged blue overalls or leather aprons talking about racing and drinking cognac, and found a table in the corner. The waiter zoomed up, bent an ear at me without looking at us, took an order for four coffees and croissants, and vanished.

Miss Jarman said: "I'd've preferred mine white."

"Sorry. It seemed to be a choice between quick service and no service." I handed round my cigarettes; she took one, Harvey shook his head and went on keeping an inconspicuous watch on the door. Without me noticing it, he'd shunted us into the best pattern: himself with his back against the corner, facing the door, Maganhard on his right, me blocking the line from the door to Maganhard, the girl clear of the line.

47

Maganhard asked: "What route are we going now?"

"Geneva, as direct as we can. We've done about four hundred and fifty kilometres; we've got nearly six hundred to go to the Swiss border."

"What time will I be in Liech——"

"*Don't!* Not that name out loud, please."

His mouth twitched. "Aren't you being rather over-cautious, Mr Cane?"

"How do we know? You can't tell me what trouble we'll meet, or where. I'm just trying to cover everything." I looked at my watch. "We should be there by nine or ten tonight—if nothing else happens."

7

THE waiter weaved through the crowd and dealt four large
cups of black coffee and a plastic bowl of croissants. I asked
for cream for Mademoiselle. He jerked his eyebrows to show
how hard I was trying his patience, then asked if I was quite
sure we didn't want cognacs as well.

I could have used a real drink; I'd been awake and active
a lot longer than any of the market porters in the café. But
I reckoned that if Harvey could stay off it, the least I could
do was stay with him.

I glanced round the table. The girl shook her head.
Maganhard didn't bother to look at me. Harvey said: "Not
for me, thanks. But you have one."

I told the waiter No, thanks.

We sipped at the coffee and tore up the croissants, which
were fresh and warm. Somebody at the next table had a
transistor radio pumping out information on the day's
racing, and a keen audience crowded around commenting
on the three-leggedness of the runners.

Miss Jarman asked: "Why didn't you choose a more
northerly route—Orleans, Dijon, and Neuchatel?"

"Because I like this route."

The radio said: *"Maganhard."*

I froze. The radio said: *". . . grand yacht de luxe appar-
tenant à un financier international a été arrété par une
frégate de guerre auprès de la côte . . ."*

Somebody turned the radio off.

I looked at Maganhard: "Oh, you bloody nit," I said.
"You hadn't even got the sense to stay outside the three-mile
limit—and now your crew's singing the whole story in
Brest."

Harvey said: "I mean let's not start fighting out loud in
here, hey?"

I took a deep breath and a firm hold on my common-sense.
"That's right. Nobody heard it, okay? We're still just
tourists."

The waiter banged the cream jug down in front of Miss Jarman.

Harvey said casually: "So what's the new plan?"

"We have to assume the crew talked. So they know Maganhard's ashore, probably where he's heading. They'll know you're with him——" I nodded at the girl. "Would they know who we are?"

Maganhard said: "I don't believe so."

Harvey asked: "What about the car—want to try and switch it?"

I thought about that, then shook my head. "I don't think they'll have the car number yet. It'll take them a few hours to establish it's missing and get that on the teleprinters. We can't hire a car without showing a passport, and if we pinch one, they're likely to have *that* number as soon as they get the Citroën's. Particularly since we'd have to dump the Citroën. No, we'll just keep on. But"—I turned to Maganhard—"you can forget any idea of being in L. tonight. We're on side roads from here on."

"Why?"

"I don't think local cops will worry us. They'll get the news slowly, and they won't take it seriously. A village policeman won't *expect* to catch an international businessman, so he won't really look. It's the *Sûreté Nationale* that'll be looking for us. They're good—but they stick to the main roads. So if we keep off the *routes nationales* we should be clear. But we'll be slow."

Maganhard stared at the last of his coffee, then looked up at me, totally without expression. "All right. If I can send a message some time today, I can waste another night."

Harvey said: "Let's go, then."

I had enough change to cover the bill, so I left it on the table, picked up my briefcase, and we strolled out. We dropped almost naturally into pairs: Maganhard, with Harvey on his outside, then me and Miss Jarman following.

There were more cars parked in the square by now. A grey Mercedes just behind the Citroën, and a little green Renault 4L just in front. Harvey and Maganhard reached the car a couple of yards ahead of us—and kept going. Then I saw why. I slid an arm round Miss Jarman's shoulders, smiled into her face, and said: "Just keep walking. We're in trouble here."

We went round the corner, and the one after that. Harvey and Maganhard were waiting for us, Maganhard tucked into a doorway.

Harvey said: "You're jammed by those two cars, aren't you?"

"Yes. And they've both got Paris numbers."

He nodded. "So no accident. What now?"

"It can't be the cops: they wouldn't do it that way. So it's our business friends. They'll be waiting somewhere with a view of the cars."

"That café in the square."

"That's my guess."

Harvey stretched his fingers and then clenched them. "Okay," he said quietly. "Let's go suggest they shift their cars." He turned to Maganhard. "I don't like leaving you alone, but we don't have a choice. You stick here and we'll pick you up. Okay, Cane?"

I stuck the briefcase in the doorway, blocked the view with my body, and slipped the Mauser under my raincoat and into my waistband. It was about as comfortable as walking around in an iron lung, but not quite as obvious.

We walked back round the first corner. Without needing to talk it over, we went past the street leading to the square, and turned at the next, to come up beside the café without showing ourselves to its windows.

As we reached the square again, Harvey stopped and looked carefully around. A couple of workmen ambled out of sight past the parked cars on the other side of the square.

I looked over my shoulder into the street we'd come up. It was narrow, shadowed, and nobody seemed to be using it to go anywhere. "You know, if I was wanting a quiet talk about borrowing some car keys, I'd take it here rather than in the café."

Harvey moved his head in a very faint nod, and led the way.

We hadn't expected any trouble in finding them, and there wasn't any: in that crowd of market workers, the three of them stood out like crocodiles in a goldfish pond. And they were where they had to be: at a table alongside the window, near the door, with a little stack of francs beside their coffee cups so that they could dive out at any time without the waiter chasing them for payment.

Harvey looked them over and chose the leader: a fat man in his late forties, wearing last year's raincoat and yesterday's beard. Harvey leant down so that his mac hung open to shield his right hand from the rest of the café.

"Venez faire une promenade, mes enfants," he suggested quietly.

The fat man went very still and just rolled his yellowish eyes sideways at Harvey. I moved up between the other two, giving them a confident smile and a good look at the big Mauser in my waistband. Then I faded back out of reach to keep an eye on the café crowd.

Nobody had noticed us yet; the waiter was out of sight and the rest were chattering busily.

Harvey said: *"Marchez."*

The fat man suddenly jabbed both hands against the table to shove himself clear. There was a silver flash and a thump, and his fat face twisted in silent pain. He moved his left hand slowly to comfort his right, still flat on the table edge and beginning to bleed a little.

Harvey drew back the Smith and Wesson close to his body and slowly thumbed the hammer back to full cock. The click was lost in the noise of the café behind us. The fat man opened his eyes and watched sombrely. Harvey turned the gun towards him and pulled the trigger. He was still holding back the hammer, so it didn't fire; the fat man made a gulping sound.

Now anything that dislodged Harvey's thumb would fire the gun: it was about as safe as a grenade with a half-second fuse. No sane man believes he can knock aside a gun in that condition; all he believes is that he can get himself shot accidentally by making too sudden a movement.

We seemed to have been there a long time; the waiter was going to pop up and ask what we wanted—and find out. I began to sweat. But the fat man was sweating a lot harder.

Then he frowned once, just for his own self-respect, and

52

made a very small gesture to show he was ready to get up. Harvey stood back. The five of us marched out in a close line like five trucks on a freight train.

We went round the corner and past a bend that put the square out of sight from our side of the street. Harvey halted the procession and held out his left hand: *"Les clefs de la Mercédes et la Renault."*

The fat man leant against the wall and started to explain that they weren't his cars and, anyway, what the Devil——

Harvey just smiled. He had the sort of face for that sort of smile. It made me think of other walls, pitted with bullet marks, and blindfolds and firing squads. Then he pulled out his gun again, and this time you could hear the click.

He got the keys, and held them up over his shoulder to me.

I moved behind him to take them. "I'll need about a minute to get the Mercedes clear."

"Take all the time you want."

I reached for the keys.

So far, all I knew of our new acquaintances was that they'd set up a situation with the parked cars which could easily have resulted in a gun-battle in the middle of Tours. Which made them fairly stupid, to my mind. But stupid or not, their teamwork was good.

I never saw any signal, but the first to move was the one at the end of the line. He jumped forward, then threw himself flat in the road. As Harvey swung to cover him, the fat man launched himself off the wall, his left hand groping under his coat.

I was behind Harvey, with him blocking my line of fire, and a good chance of getting knocked over by him if the fat man hit him. I left off trying to get the Mauser into action and took a leap backwards.

The fat man hit Harvey with his right shoulder just as he pulled an automatic with his left hand. They started to fall back towards me. Harvey planted his gun neatly on the man's left shoulder and loosed the hammer.

There was a nasty squashy *bang* and the fat man spun in the air and fell on his back, his gun waving feebly towards the wall. Harvey rolled near my feet. The third party started around them to get at me.

I finally got the Mauser untangled from my trousers and jammed my thumb hard on the single/automatic button; if ever I wanted to sound like a machine-gun, now seemed the time.

Harvey shouted: "Don't shoot that thing!"

The third man saw the long magazine on the Mauser, and dropped any idea of drawing a gun. His hands went up before he'd got his feet to stop.

I swung the gun side-to-side. *"Venez chercher, mes amis!"* I felt tensed up and ready to pull the trigger.

Harvey rolled on to his feet. "Jesus Christmas, the war's over. Take it easy, Cane." He flicked his short gun left and right, and the two men backed quickly up to the wall again. The fat man in the gutter let out a sudden moan.

Harvey said: "Go get the car."

Rather reluctantly, I put the Mauser away under my raincoat, and walked back to the square.

Nobody seemed to be looking for the source of a gun going off. It hadn't made much noise; noise, after all, is only energy that's got wasted on the surrounding air, and the fat man's shoulder had got just about all the energy going from that shot. I didn't want to examine that shoulder.

I backed the Mercedes off a couple of yards, checked the tyres of the Citroën in case they'd tried two sorts of funny business, then drove it out to the corner.

Harvey walked slowly up the far side of the street, his right hand tucked under his mac. He slid in and I whipped around the corner.

"What'd you do with them?"

He said: "Told them to pick him up and get him home. I was a damn fool."

"What?"

"He was left-handed; I hadn't thought of that. I knew he was the boss, I knew they wouldn't start anything without him. But I thought I'd fixed him when I banged his right hand in the café. I should have thought of him being left-handed."

I pulled round the next corner and slowed. "Everybody makes mistakes."

54

"Not in my business."

I reached back to open the back-seat doors. Maganhard and the girl and my briefcase jumped in and, thank God, they didn't waste time doing it.

I pulled away and turned left into the Place des Halles, snaking between the last fruit and fish lorries.

Miss Jarman suddenly leant forward and said to Harvey: "You smell of gunpowder."

Harvey nodded. "That's right. I had to shoot a guy. He didn't get killed."

She said coldly: "Bad luck."

"It was intentional."

I said: "We wouldn't have got the same fun out of it, killing him without you watching."

She said: "Why didn't you just throw your joke book at him?"

Harvey chuckled. "I don't think she appreciates us. But Jesus, you scared me."

"Me?" I said.

"You. Waving that machine-gun around and shouting 'Come and Get It!' I thought you were going to loose it off—and me in front of you."

"Well, I told you I learnt this business in wartime."

"That's a long time ago. Fashions have changed."

I started into a zigzag of back streets leading south-east to the main road running south out of town.

"Well," I said, "What did you think of the opposition?"

"They'll never make the First Team."

I nodded. "My own thoughts exactly. D'you know any of them?"

"No."

Maganhard said: "What did they plan to do?"

"I'd guess they were disobeying orders," Harvey said rapidly. "They'd probably been told to pick us up in Tours —and that wouldn't be difficult. We had to cross the river here and there's only two bridges. Then they were told to trail us out to somewhere quiet and jump us there. With that Mercedes, they could have hung on to us. But we stopped at the café and they thought they'd got an easy chance. Crazy."

I nodded; that sounded good sense. "Was that why you didn't kill anybody?"

I felt his quick sideways look. "Didn't seem necessary," he said evenly. "They were so slow, I had time."

Miss Jarman leant forward and said incredulously: "Did you *want* somebody to get killed?"

"No: I can take it or leave it." But that wasn't quite true. I *was* a little worried that nobody had ended up dead.

Being a good bodyguard-gunman isn't being particularly fast with a gun, or even particularly accurate. These are just refinements. The real talent is being ready, at any time and without asking questions, to kill. A gunman can still be as fast as a cat and accurate as Robin Hood—but if he's got to debate with his conscience whether he's ready to kill or not, then he's ready for unemployment pay. Or, quite likely, dead.

Or perhaps drinking too much.

I zipped across the Boulevard Béranger, still heading south-east. I shoved the clump of Michelin local maps across to him. "Pick me a course heading south-east and keeping on only the D roads."

Harvey said: "You want to get off the main line between Brittany and Switzerland?"

"That's right. That's where the roadblocks'll be."

He stared back at a map. "You'll end up in the Auvergne."

I nodded. "That's the idea. I have friends there. Or I did, once."

★ 8 ★

FOR a moment I thought they'd caught us right there, two kilometres out of town on the bridge across the Cher into St Avertin. They were rebuilding the bridge and it was a nasty mess of grey girders, plank surfacing—and a cop staring watchfully at every car.

Then I realized he was just looking out for traffic tangles. I drove across quietly and carefully. A minute later we were heading due south on the D27, through a messy collection of vineyards and bright new suburban houses looking oddly naked as they waited for the neighbours to spring up around them.

We crossed one *Route Nationale*—no road blocks or roaming *Sûreté* cars—and after that we were clear. I pushed the Citroën along the narrow over-cambered road, reaching ninety kilometres on the good straight stretches.

On a job like this the *Sûreté* doesn't block every road everywhere. They pin up a map in headquarters and say: "They started *there* at *that* time, so they should be around *here* by *this* time." And that's where they put the blocks and warn the cars. It's like ripples on a pond: a line of defence getting wider and drawing farther back as time goes on. So far, I thought I was probably outrunning the ripples; they might not even think I'd reached Tours yet. But I didn't dare take the risk. I had to hide in the side roads, and that meant the defence would overtake me. By tonight they'd have warned the Swiss frontier.

Which was fine, because tonight I wouldn't be within two hundred kilometres of Switzerland—and maybe tomorrow some of the ripples would have died down. Maybe.

That reminded me: "We must ring Merlin."

Harvey asked: "What for?"

"Just keep him in touch—and see if he's heard anything. And I'd like him to send a telegram in your name, Mr Maganhard, if you don't mind."

Maganhard asked: "Why? Who to?"

"To the captain of your yacht, or the crew or something. Just saying you're sorry and hope they'll be released soon—something like that. The cops'll see it and maybe they'll be convinced you're in Paris. It might help."

He chuckled his metallic chuckle. "A good idea."

The road got rougher and more winding as we climbed out of the lush farmland of the Loire valley. The verges straggled on to the roads, the trees and hedges looked in need of a haircut. And the road signs were the old Dunlop "Touring Club de France" jobs, battered and rusty from generations of small boys throwing stones.

It had been raining inland and the streams were fat and fast, pocked with small whirlpools and sometimes breaking their banks to leave a row of poplars ankle deep in water like Guardsmen waiting for somebody to order them in out of the rain.

Harvey picked up the maps again and said: "You want to go south of Clermont Ferrand, into the real Auvergne?"

"That's right."

"We won't be moving fast in that country."

"If we get lost, we can always ask a policeman."

He just looked at me.

Maganhard woke up suddenly and said: "Now we know the police *are* looking for us, what will happen if they stop us?"

I shrugged. "Unless it's some character on a bike that we can run away from—we stay stopped."

The girl said coldly: "What happened to the brave gunmen? Are police too much for you?"

"In a way, yes. We agreed before we started that we weren't shooting at police."

"You agreed?" Maganhard asked. "Who authorized you to agree?"

"I thought you didn't like *any* shooting, Mr Maganhard."

His voice had the precise, toneless click of a teletype machine punching out the words. "Through Monsieur Merlin, I am paying your wages. Any agreement should have been reached with him or with me."

58

Harvey and I glanced at each other. He sighed and said: "You've hurt his feelings, now. Stop at the next crossroads and we'll probably get a bus to Châteauroux and a train back to Paris."

I said: "Let's put it another way, Mr Maganhard: do you *want* us to shoot at policemen?"

There was a pause, then: "I want to know why you agreed not to. That is all."

"If you don't see the difference between some character who's been hired to kill you and a gendarme who's been told to arrest you—well, we can skip the moral question. But have you thought what it would do to your chances in the long run?"

"I do not understand."

I took a deep breath. "I imagine this journey's only half the battle for you. When it's over, you don't want to be any worse off than you are now. Right now the cops are looking for you—on a rape charge. They'll look pretty hard, because you're a big man and there's always somebody to scream Influence when a big one gets away. But it's still only a rape charge; we're still sharing their time with a couple of bank robberies, a murder, a prison escape, stolen cars— whatever else has happened today.

"But once we kill a cop, they'll forget everything else. It'll only be us they want. And even if we got away with it, they'd chase us to the hot end of Hell and then get us extradited. There isn't a country in the world would stand up to protect a cop-killer; they've got their own police to worry about. Have I made my point?"

"If what you say is true. It seems most peculiar that the police should react in that way."

Harvey lit a Gitane and said thoughtfully: "It's the way cops think. They don't really mind somebody breaking the law—not personally. They get to expect it. Sure, they work at their jobs, but they go home for dinner at six. They don't think the world's going to end just because some guy gives his wife a face-lift with a meat-axe. Not even if he gets away with it."

He blew smoke at the windscreen. "Cops don't mind people running away like we're doing. They expect that, too

59

—they rather like it. It shows respect. But the guy who kills a cop? He didn't run. He didn't show any respect. That way, he's not just breaking the law, he's trying to destroy it. He's knocking at everything the cops think they stand for: law, order, civilization—and he's knocking at every cop. *That* makes it personal. And he's the man they've got to catch."

Maganhard said quietly: "That is very peculiar."

The car ran on. Now we were on open downland country: fields of green wheat with big three-sided stone farms enclosing yards that opened direct on to the road and spilled hens, geese, and ducks all over it. The geese and ducks just looked affronted and ruffled, like duchesses caught shoplifting; the hens decided the far side of the road looked safer.

That apart, it was a lonely road. People turned to look at you, expecting a neighbour.

Miss Jarman said: "How do you know these things? Are you—I mean, just what *are* you both?"

Harvey said: "I'm a bodyguard, Miss Jarman."

"But—how do you get to be one?"

"Sounds like what guys are supposed to ask prostitutes," he said dryly.

I said: "Just lucky, I guess."

Harvey grinned and said rapidly: "I was in the United States Secret Service, bodyguard detail. They sent me to Paris for when presidents came over to visit. I liked it. I quit. I stayed on, went into private practice."

I caught his eye and his face was quite expressionless. I asked: "When was this?"

"Several years back." So perhaps he hadn't collected his problem before he'd left. Perhaps it was the strain of "private practice".

The girl said: "What about you, Mr Cane?"

"I'm a business agent, sort of. Mostly for British firms exporting to the Continent."

Maganhard said sharply: "I thought you had been in the French Resistance."

"No, Mr Maganhard. Contrary to certain legends in certain places, the French Resistance was French, not British or American. I was in the Special Operations Executive; I

was dropped in to help organize supplies for the Resistance
—that's all. The French did the fighting; I just loaded guns
for them."

Harvey asked: "Where were you?"

"Paris and the Auvergne. But I got around quite a bit,
delivering stuff and organizing the supply lines."

Maganhard said: "Ahh," as if he'd seen just why Merlin
had chosen me. Which was more than I'd seen for myself,
yet.

Harvey asked casually: "Get picked up at all?"

"Once."

"How're the legs?"

"I'm walking."

The girl asked: "What are you talking about?"

"The Gestapo," Harvey explained. "Sometimes—I heard
—when they'd questioned a guy and weren't sure about him
one way or another, they'd kind of tap on his legs with chains
before they let him go. So when he got picked up again,
maybe a year later with different papers, different name, all
the new lot had to do was to look at his legs. They'd know
he'd been questioned before. And in their tiny minds, I guess
two suspicions made one proof."

After a moment the girl said: "Did they do this to you?"

I said: "Yes."

"I'm sorry."

After another moment I said: "It was all a long time
ago."

Harvey said softly: "But not very far away."

As we got south, the clouds broke up and there were bursts
of sunlight, throwing vivid green patches on the hills. The
roads got curlier and narrower and our average speed was
cut right down. Suddenly we were on just a cart-track of
sand and stones wiggling through a pine forest.

I jerked down into second gear and snapped: "God, you've
got us lost. Give me that map."

Harvey shook his head. "Just a bit of *voie ordinaire*. It
gets better later."

"It had better." Then I shook my head. "Sorry."

I was getting too irritable. I'd been driving for nine hours and awake a lot longer, and the D roads weren't as soothing as the main *routes nationales.* By now I was tired and hungry —but most of all, I wanted a drink.

I glanced sideways at Harvey. Well, maybe I could slide off round the corner by myself and gobble a couple of quick ones when I went to phone Merlin.

The road turned into tarmac again and we wove down out of the pines.

Harvey said: "Told you so. When do we lunch?"

"I'll stop in a village soon. Maybe Miss Jarman will go and buy something while I phone Merlin."

"I will if you like. I'd prefer something hot, but I suppose you'll say it's too dangerous going into restaurants."

"I just say it's a risk, Miss Jarman—and all I can do on this job is cut down on as many risks as I can."

She waited a moment, then said: "Before this trip's over, I may get rather tired of watching you avoid risks."

I nodded. "That's likely. But you may get tired of risks, too."

Three-quarters of an hour later we reached a small village just before crossing the N140. It was just a square and a collection of houses and shops of old, solid stone huddled under the shoulder of the hill. I cruised quietly down into it, past the shop that was a combined newsagent and hairdresser, past the *Gendarmerie Nationale* with its tricolour and a notice suggesting that if you wanted any law and order enforced at night you'd better call at the house twenty-five metres up on the right—and into the small, steep-sloped main square.

"There's no point in parking anywhere else," I explained, before anybody asked. "They'd notice a strange car more if it was parked in a side road. But we won't stay longer than we need."

I walked across to the P.T.T. building, set back behind its little railed courtyard from the days when the mail coach used to drive in to unload. I walked straight into the telephone box and asked for Merlin's office number.

Would his line be tapped? It wasn't likely they'd do that to a big Paris lawyer, but by now the police must be wondering how much Merlin knew about Maganhard. They must know the connection.

His secretary said he was occupied; I told her to get him unoccupied, quick. I gave my name as Caneton.

Merlin came on the line, first as a distant voice saying apologetically: ". . . *m'excuse, Inspecteur.*" A crafty lawyer doesn't get overheard by accident: he was letting me know the cops were with him at the time. Then he said: *"Allo? Ah, monsieur: je suis désolé, mais l'arpenteur . . ."* I didn't care how sorry he was about what the surveyor had or hadn't done; I ought to slam down the phone and run.

But that would make the *Inspecteur* doubly suspicious. Now, I had to say something. I might as well make it useful.

"I've turned off to join the Rat-line in the high country," I said, speaking English fast in the hope that anybody overhearing couldn't follow English that fast; I hoped Merlin could. "I think you should send a telegram in our friend's name, to the boat. It'll help mislead everybody."

He gave me another apologetic spiel about the surveyor being a lazy hound but this was, after all, the season for house purchase.

"I'll probably ring this evening, when I know where we're staying the night. Are you being tapped? If you are, say you think the house price will go up."

He assured me that the house price would stay as agreed —for, after all, they knew well Merlin's standing as a lawyer.

I grinned into the phone and said: "Thanks, Henri—and while you're at it, buy me a nice lonely house in a village where nobody's heard of the police or international businessmen, will you?"

He assured me of his best attention at all time. We rang off and I came out sweating.

I walked slowly back across the square, wondering how stupid I'd been. If his phone was tapped, or if they decided for any reason to trace my call, then I'd sunk us. I couldn't out-run the ripples in this sort of hill country. But they'd need a whole department to track down every one of the calls Henri must get every day, so maybe the only danger was tapping. And he'd said not, and he should know.

I argued with myself right into a café. There I ordered a

double *marc,* and bought a couple of packets of Gitanes while the man was pouring it. It took me a minute to polish off the *marc* and half a minute to ask—and get told—how long it would take to drive to Limoges, which was in exactly the opposite direction from our route.

Harvey looked at me curiously as I got back in. I dropped the cigarettes on the seat between us. "One's yours, if you're running out." I started up and drove carefully out of the square. "What's for lunch?"

Miss Jarman said: "Bread, cheese, *paté*, sardines, cherry tart. I got a bottle of red wine if you want it, and a bottle of Perrier."

I said: "I'll take Perrier: I'm driving."

Harvey said: "Same for me—I'm shooting." He looked across at me. "And I didn't even get a quick one in the café."

I gave him a look that was supposed to be surprised. "Me?"

He smiled, perhaps a little bleakly, but perhaps any smile looked bleak on his face. "You. Hell, I don't mind. But I do know how quick you can get a quick one."

WE ate on the move, the girl handing over wedges of bread stuffed with *paté* or cheese. She tried opening the sardines, spilled oil on herself, said: "Damn them to hell," and threw the full tin out of the window. Then, very coolly, she said: "I'm sorry, we seem to be out of sardines."

Maganhard gave a metallic chuckle.

I ate a bit of cherry tart and then lit a cigarette. I felt a lot more cheerful; even if they tried to seal off this area with roadblocks, they wouldn't necessarily catch me. I was almost back into the Auvergne again, and when I was on roads I knew . . . well, the Gestapo had once tried catching me with roadblocks there.

I knew the feeling was due a lot more to the double *marc* than to either the food or my knowledge of the back roads, and I had enough sense to know it wouldn't last more than a couple of hours. But while it lasted, I wanted to cover some ground.

The hillsides became lush, Gothic, overdone; the trees got romantically gnarled and twisted, set among rocks covered with thick moss like the green velvet sofas in old ladies' parlours. The whole thing looked like a set for an opera where they're trying to keep your mind off the singing.

I wasn't fond of this country; it was too thick and damp and it breathed down your neck. I wanted the clean cold uplands, where you can see a man coming at rifle-shot range.

Harvey asked: "Who're we staying the night with?"

"Some friends."

"From the Resistance?"

I nodded.

He asked: "You're sure they're still there? And still friends?"

"Somebody will be. We've got a choice: I knew quite a lot of people down here. One of the Rat-lines went through there—taking escaped prisoners out, bringing supplies in."

We passed through la Courtine, an army town that looked a bit like a barracks itself: open, empty, newly swept, and with a scruffy soldier leaning on every corner. Then dived into the valley of the Dordogne.

Maganhard said: "Mr Cane."

I waited for him to go on, then said: "I'm still here."

"Mr Cane—when we discussed—about policemen, you said you would *skip the moral question*. Why did you not argue it?"

Harvey and I glanced at each other. The old buzzard hadn't said a word in hours—had he been brooding on *this* egg?

I said carefully: "I wasn't sure you'd be interested, Mr Maganhard."

"Why not?"

I shrugged and hoped he could see. "Maybe I made a hasty judgement from circumstances—such as being chased across France by assorted police and crooks. But I judged you wouldn't be interested."

"If we might skip the sarcastic question," he said calmly, "will you tell me why?"

I leant forward and got a look at him in the rear-view mirror. For once, he had an expression on his face. It looked like a smile chalked on armour plate; not appropriate and not permanent—but still there.

I said: "Let's say I try to keep an open mind about people who go in for tax avoidance in Liechtenstein."

"You don't say tax *evasion*, Mr Cane."

"No, Mr Maganhard, I know the difference. Evasion is illegal—and I'm sure what you're doing is legal."

"But not moral?"

"Practical morality, like a lot of things, is mostly a matter of fair exchange. You're running factories in France, Germany, and so on—but you aren't paying to keep those countries running. That's all."

"Any of those countries, having the power that governments have, could decide they wanted more of my money and establish a perfectly *legal* debt that I owed them." His

66

voice had the silky click of stainless-steel cog-wheels. "They may well do so. Would paying that debt make me more moral?"

"I doubt it, Mr Maganhard. I'd say either you're ready to pay for your ride or you're not. Whether you *have* to pay is something different. Perhaps you're mixing up morality and legality."

"I'm sure you can explain the difference."

"I don't suppose so. I'd just say that morality doesn't change when you cross a frontier."

Harvey chuckled.

After a moment, Maganhard said: "You seem to be taking a very strong, and rather strange, attitude, Mr Cane."

I shrugged. "You brought the question up, Mr Maganhard. And I'm not breaking my heart over a bit of tax avoidance. Thousands do it; they'll go on doing it as long as countries like Liechtenstein and some Swiss cantons make tax laws for exactly that reason—to try and suck a bit of blood from other countries. If it ever gets too much, the other countries'll crack down. They'll drive Liechtenstein out of business."

"I meant, Mr Cane, that you must find yourself in a rather equivocal position, attempting to help me as you are. Yet when I talked to Monsieur Merlin on the radio-telephone from my yacht, he told me you had asked to be assured that I was *not* guilty of this—this charge laid against me, and also that I was travelling to save my own investment, not to try to steal somebody else's. You wished to believe *then* that I was a moral man." And all the steel smoothness was back in his voice.

"Morality can also be relative, Mr Maganhard. For instance, I'd say you were more moral than those goons who jumped us in Tours. You don't seem to be trying to kill anybody—but it seems somebody's trying to kill you. I don't have to believe you're particularly moral over taxes to think I'm on the right side in helping you here."

"You also believed Monsieur Merlin over the other charge!" For a moment, the harshness in his voice surprised me. Then I got it: anybody who believed he was such a stiff, upright character as he did, would naturally take the old fate-worse-than-death attitude on rape. He'd believe it was the ultimate crime. Probably that was why he hadn't been able to bring himself even to use the name: he'd just said "this charge".

I wondered if whoever had framed him hadn't had a sense of humour. Among other talents.

I said: "Merlin's a good lawyer—and he said it was a frame. Anyway, I know something about rape charges."

Harvey turned and said cheerfully: "You do? Tell us more."

I said: "For one thing, you don't need witnesses: nobody expects witnesses to a rape charge. All you need to know is that a man was alone in a likely place at a likely time, and have some girl complain he was raping her there and then. If you can get her to sleep with him, you can even get some medical evidence. But either way, it always ends up just her word against his. And even if it fails, or never comes to court, a smear sticks."

Harvey said softly: "And I thought you only knew about machine-guns."

Miss Jarman said: "How *do* you know this, Mr Cane?"

"I did it to somebody once. Oh, it was quite moral, really. It happened in the war. We used it to get rid of a German civil official in Paris—he was being too efficient. It never went to court, of course, and it wouldn't have worked if the German Army hadn't wanted an excuse to get him recalled: *they* found him too efficient, too. So we gave them the excuse."

"What happened to the girl?" she asked.

"We got her out to the country, in case there was an inquiry."

"I didn't mean that," she said coldly.

"I know you didn't. Let's say she was fighting a war and knew it."

Maganhard interrupted impatiently: "I understand all that, Mr Cane. You were telling me why you believed the charge against me was false."

"I was." I fumbled a cigarette out of the pack on the seat beside me; Harvey reached across with his lighter. "Yes—

68

that still leaves a couple of questions. Why should anybody frame you?"

He thought it over. "It makes my movements more difficult. Particularly in France, of course. But it is an extraditable offence that I am accused of, so I might be arrested anywhere. If I were in jail, then something like—like what we are trying to avoid would be more easy. Obviously."

I grinned sourly: he hadn't given anything away. Then I got serious again. "But the girl didn't scream until you'd left France. That sounds like a pretty clear attempt just to scare you off, without risking a trial. Come to that, why weren't you tried in your absence? You can be, under French law."

"Monsieur Merlin stopped an attempt to do that. I believe the prosecution weren't pressing for it."

"It sounds as if they weren't very happy about their own frame—if they thought it mightn't stand up even without you there. Now let's have the basic question: why didn't you fight the charge? If it was a frame, you could get it knocked flat. You'd still have a bit of a smear—but now you've got that *and* you can't come and go freely."

"I thought you'd answered that question yourself, Mr Cane." He sounded slightly amused, if that was the right word for a very small change in tone. "You said that it would eventually come to being my word against the woman's. I don't believe any court in the world is infallible; they might have made a mistake."

"Mr Maganhard, I wasn't talking about going to court; it would never get that far." I sounded puzzled; I *was* puzzled. I hadn't expected to find myself lecturing a man with a home-made million on the facts of legal life.

He said: "I'm not sure I understand." His voice had gone stiff again.

I said: "The disadvantage of a rape frame is the same as its advantage: it all depends on the evidence of one woman. If the woman's really a phoney, then she's been hired. And if she can be bought once, she can be bought twice. So she changes her identification of you—and no case."

"I would regard that as wasted money." The voice was as rigid as cast iron now.

Harvey and I glanced at each other. He smiled briefly and went on leaving the work to me.

"Look, Mr Maganhard," I said carefully. "This would have saved you money. Say you'd given me the job of going to see this woman a month ago. If I thought she'd been bought, I'd have bought her back for a few thousand more. The whole cost—hers and mine—would be about a quarter of what you're paying for this trip. And no risk. Strictly as a businessman, how does that appeal to you?"

"Nobody is strictly a businessman, Mr Cane. One must take the moral question. And the morality of this——"

"Morality? Who's talking about morality?" I found I was shouting, and lowered the volume. "We're talking about a frame-up: where's the morality of that? And if you want to do the moral thing, why didn't you stand up in court and fight it?"

"Forgive me, Mr Cane, but I have been thinking about this far longer than you have." He was calm and very sure. "Since I am innocent, I could gain nothing by going to court. I would merely risk the court making a mistake and finding me guilty. And I will not fight bribes with bribes; I do not see why I should pay for justice that should be mine by right. This *is* a moral question."

For a long time there was nothing but the gentle zoom of the engine and the wind rush along the windows. Then Harvey said: "Well, it's a good way to stay rich: count your money with glue on your fingers."

"Mr Lovell—don't you think there might be a question of right and wrong in how the rich spend their money, as well as how the poor do?"

Harvey looked at me; I lifted an eyebrow back at him, and then fiddled the mirror to catch Maganhard's face. He was leaning forward slightly, and frowning—slightly—at the back of Harvey's neck. But I was beginning to learn that his slightness was only skin deep.

Harvey said: "Mr M.—how the rich spend their money has never been a really pressing problem with me. I'll just say you've got a point of view there."

Maganhard's face twitched briefly into what could have been a smile, scowl, sneer, or almost anything else. But suddenly I thought I could see, under the square solid face, the lean Scots preacher thundering cold hellfire and penny-wise salvation from the stone pulpit.

"He's got a point of view," I growled. "He may lose an empire, but he's got a point of view."

AFTER that nobody said anything much. The sky clouded over again with lumpy grey clouds that didn't look as if they were going to rain, but were just wanting to shut off the sun. The whole afternoon tasted of yesterday's beer.

The *marc* wore off, leaving me feeling dull and sour, and my driving reactions slowed down; I let my driving slow down, too. Beside me, Harvey gave me an occasional new road number or direction to follow; that apart, he was slumped back staring out at the roadside winding past. Maganhard and the girl did nothing but keep some weight on the rear wheels.

Just before five o'clock we went through Condat-en-Féniers and after that we were in the real uplands. Not jagged country, not even really rough, just filed down by a million winds into sweeping slopes and low, bony ridges. The sort of country where most of what you see is sky. The only trees were clumps of pines beside the fort-like farmhouses and at crossroads, but the slopes were a vivid green and flooded with stubby little wild daffodils.

Harvey said: "We're on a *route nationale* now—it's a pretty minor one, but——"

I said: "Don't bother any more. I know this country."

That should have made me feel better. Maybe it just stopped me feeling worse. I started to push the Citroën along a bit faster; the roads were almost empty, and if they weren't straight at least you could see across the bends in that open country. I drove on the accelerator and brake, in bursts up to seventy kilometres an hour on the straights.

We didn't stop. Nobody asked to and I didn't offer. If I stopped now I wouldn't want to start again.

I went north of St Flour, then by-passed Le Puy to the south; twenty minutes later we were crawling up a narrow, winding road between stone walls half sunk into the turf.

The village name-plate, knocked half out of the ground by some cart, said DINADAN. I stopped just beyond it, before the village came into view.

Harvey turned wearily in his seat and asked: "Where are we trying? A farm?"

"No. In the village itself."

He nodded at the roadside. "It's got four telephone lines. It could have a gendarme, too."

I just nodded and got out of the car and stretched. I felt as stiff as a coffin lid and creased as the paper you wrap the fish and chips in. I hoped Dinadan would be what I was looking for; I didn't feel like going any farther up or down the Rat-line.

"I'll be a few minutes," I said. I walked across the road to the uphill side, through a small gate in the stone wall, and into the village cemetery.

Dinadan was an old village, and by now the cemetery was a big place. But it didn't have any of the flavour of the village about it. Where the village was scruffy, ramshackle, narrow and winding, the graves were laid out in neat square rows, clean and well-kept. And there was a lot more variety up here than down in the village.

There were big florid tombs with a sorrowing angel holding down the lid, wrapped up in a three-sided glass house to keep the wind off the flowers, and simple rectangular slabs flat on the ground, and everything in between. But each one was well-kept and legible—and I was there for the reading matter.

It took time and it took memory. When I looked up from one inscription Miss Jarman was at my shoulder. She'd worn better on the ride than I had, but even her soft sealskin was showing creases.

"I wanted a breath of fresh air," she said. "I thought I'd better keep you in sight so that I wouldn't be late. D'you mind?"

I shook my head and walked on down the row. She followed.

After a while she asked: "What are you doing?"

"Finding out what's happened in the village since I was last here."

She gaped at me, then thought about it, then smiled and nodded.

I pointed at one tomb that wouldn't have disgraced a Florentine nobleman. "They finally made old de Gorre *maire* before he died. He'd been trying for it for thirty years, he told me." I nodded at de Gorre and walked on, thinking that they should have planted vines instead of roses around his tomb. He'd have been *maire* years before if anybody had been confident of finding him sober on inauguration day. Well, give the old boy time and the vines would grow naturally.

I pointed at a smaller affair in marble. "He kept the garage; if his son's got the place now, at least we can get our number plates changed. The father was a law-abiding old bastard."

We walked on. Finally, I found the Meliot plots and started checking carefully.

After a moment she said: "Was he a soldier? It just says *pour la France.*"

I looked at the slab she was reading off: Giles Meliot. "Look at the date," I said. It was in April, 1944. "He was with me: we ran into a roadblock up north of here, carrying some guns up to Lyons. He got hit; I didn't." I hadn't seen the slab before; you weren't allowed to go putting patriotic tombs over Resistance corpses during the war. And all they'd put was "For France". Well, by now that was all anybody wanted to know. It was all a long time ago. And I was still running through roadblocks.

Maybe on my slab they'd write: *Pour les 12,000 francs.*

The girl had said something. I said: "What?"

"Did the guns get through?"

"The——? Oh, yes. I got them through. *I* wasn't hurt."

She seemed about to say something else, then didn't. I went on checking up on Meliot tombs.

"Well," I said, "with luck we'll be staying with the Meliots tonight. His parents. It looks as if they're both still around."

I started back to the car, stopping to read the newest-looking tombs as I went. When I got to the wall, Miss

Jarman had vanished. I went down to the car; she wasn't there.

Harvey watched me climb in, but didn't say anything. His face was grey and tired, and the lines were deeper in it. He was almost burned out, but at least he was keeping the last of his energy for something more important than asking what the hell I'd been up to. And at least he'd stayed dry.

The girl hurried down out of the cemetery a few minutes later, and dived into the car. "Sorry I'm late."

I wasn't feeling strong enough to start asking What The Hell myself. I switched on, started up, and we rolled up round the corner of the hill into Dinadan.

It was a small, cramped place of cold slate-coloured stone that looked wintry and always would, in any weather. The houses, narrow enough to look tall, huddled shoulder-to-shoulder for warmth; at bends in the main street you could see behind them the tall skeletons of elms, not yet in leaf, against the grey evening.

Nothing much seemed to have happened to it since the war—certainly nobody had swept the roadside, or filled in the potholes or cleared away any of the stacks of logs and empty oil drums. But Dinadan had more important things to do: first survive, then get rich. Cleaning the place up came a bad third; besides, it would attract the tax inspectors.

Harvey said in a dull voice: "Well, nobody'll think of looking for international finance here."

I turned left at the big fortress of a church, into a side street hardly wider than the Citroën itself. After fifty yards I stopped beside a narrow three-storey house with a first-floor balcony and cracked stone steps leading down from it. Under the steps, there were two lean grey cats feeding off the same saucer as a bunch of chickens. The chickens ignored me; the cats stared as if I'd come to steal their supper.

I stood outside the car for a minute, just lighting a cigarette and giving anyone inside the house a chance to look me over. Then the door at the top of the stairs banged open and a fat bundle of aprons waddled down.

"*C'est Caneton,*" she squawked back over her shoulder, "*c'est Monsieur Caneton.*" Then she stopped dead at the bottom of the steps and the smile fell straight off her face. "*Il n'y pas déjà une autre guerre?*"

"*Non, non, non.*" I waved my hands and dragged a reassuring smile on to my face.

Behind me, Miss Jarman asked: "*What* did she say?"

"She asked if my being here meant another war starting. I suppose I've never been good news to these people."

Madame Meliot waddled forward and hugged me. She was a fat old biddy, but not soft; she nearly bust my ribs. Her brown face was full of lines like a road map, her tough grey hair pulled back into something that might have been a bun. She stood back and smiled and looked me over carefully with pale-grey eyes.

I grinned weakly at her and started explaining: I wasn't *Caneton* any longer, I wasn't with *le Baker Street*, or *l'Intelligence*, I was just me: Lewis Cane. On the other hand, I did happen to be being chased by the police, and we needed a place to spend the night.

She absorbed it all perfectly calmly.

Over my shoulder, Maganhard said quietly: "You can tell her that I'll pay."

"Don't be stupid," I snapped. "She'll do it for me or not at all. If we try and make it a business deal, she'll charge us Ritz prices and then sell us out to the cops in the morning."

Meliot himself came out to the top of the steps: tall, thin, bent, with a long bald head, a big straggling moustache and two days of beard. His collarless shirt and baggy trousers would have cost about five francs, but he could probably have reached into a pocket and pulled out enough cash to buy the Citroën there and then.

She didn't consult him; she never had even when we were using the place as a "safe house" on the Rat-line. The house was her business; the acres of grazing and woodland over the hill were his.

Then she said: "*Pour Caneton, c'est normal,*" and led the way. I winced and followed. For me, perhaps being on the run from trouble *was* a habit.

We sat straight down at the table. The room wasn't big, but it was warm and bright; the furniture wasn't up to the standard of the Good Taste magazines, but it was comfortable and where they'd wanted to spend money, it had got spent. Alongside a tinted photograph of Giles, in a frame so ornate and dull that it must have been solid silver, there was a radio set that looked like the dashboard of a space ship. That made me wince again; I'd been thinking of Dinadan as isolated from newspapers, which it probably still was. But I'd also thought of it in its wartime state, with hardly any radios. On that thing, she could have overheard us on the beach at Quimper.

She confirmed it by nodding her head at Maganhard and saying to me: *"C'est Maganhard, n'est ce pas?"*

I nodded. I didn't feel guilty about not telling her before; it wouldn't have been natural for us to discuss just what I was up to, anyway.

She looked him over critically, then said: *"Il n'est pas un violeur—pas le type."*

I agreed that he wasn't the raping type, and added that the whole thing was a phoney charge brought by business rivals. She nodded; she knew about phoney charges brought by business rivals. Then she said that Maganhard didn't look capable of rape, or, indeed, much else in that line.

Maganhard went as rigid as a post; he'd been following even her accent pretty well.

She chuckled and started out. I yelled after her that if she wasn't careful I'd send him along after midnight and she could find out for herself. She nearly blew the house down laughing.

Maganhard said stiffly: "I cannot stand that sort of conversation, Mr Cane."

"Tough luck, chum, but it comes with the house. You can always sleep out under the trees." I was too tired to want to get complicated. Miss Jarman was wearing a blank, un-understanding expression that the English girls' schools are so good at teaching.

Harvey was sitting slumped, staring at the tablecloth. We could have been talking economics in Chinese for all he cared.

There obviously wasn't much conversation to be got there. I followed Madame Meliot, found that the local garage *had* passed from father to son, and went down to see him.

He remembered me, all right, and I just about remembered him: he'd been a bit young for the war, and unhappy that he was missing it. Now, he was delighted to get started at last.

I asked if he could do me a couple of new number plates, belonging to this part of France, but not to do them too professionally for fear, if we got caught, that they were traced back to him. He had a better idea: why didn't I simply take the plates off his own Citroën ID? They should fit.

I pointed out that if we got pinched, those certainly *would* be traced back to him. He grinned; cops didn't bother him, and, anyway, if he left the car parked out that night, why shouldn't I simply have stolen them? Behind it all was obviously the thought that the great Caneton would never get caught, anyway.

It was a nice compliment, but it was based on a view of me he'd formed when he was twelve and it showed he didn't know much about the *Sûreté Nationale*, either. But in the end, on the promise that he *would* leave the car out all night, I took the plates.

He was bubbling with curiosity, but he was also keen to show me he knew the old Resistance rule of never asking unnecessary questions. I didn't tell him anything; just winked secretly and went my way.

I drove Maganhard's Citroën round the corner of the house out of sight of the main road, changed the plates with a screwdriver, and went back upstairs.

They were halfway through some sort of bird *paté*, a long block of the stuff cut in the middle so as to preserve the tasteful decoration of a dead bird's head sticking out one end, and its tail feathers the other. It looked something like a thrush, which suited me fine: I prefer eating them to being woken by them.

I helped myself to a reasonable slice and told Harvey: "I've changed plates on the car."

He turned slowly to look at me. "You won't get it across the frontier with the old papers."

I nodded with my mouth full. "We weren't going to get

it across anyway. The customs'll have the number by now."

Maganhard stared at me: "What will you do, then?"

"You should have thought of that when you brought your damn boat inside the three-mile limit. Well—if nobody knows we're in Geneva, we may be able to hire a car there. Or, of course, there's always the Swiss railways."

Harvey said thickly: "I prefer a car."

I looked at him and nodded. For his side of the business, trains provided too many witnesses.

Madame Meliot waddled in and scooped up a bottle of red wine from the table and poured me a dose. Maganhard and the girl had glasses of it already; Harvey was on water.

She nodded at him and shrugged.

"*Américain*," I explained, if she'd take that for an explanation.

She did, then turned the label to show me. "*Pinel, ha?*" And she grinned knowingly, and waddled out with the *paté*.

Miss Jarman asked: "Does Pinel have some special significance?"

I nodded. "In a way. The family that makes it: their château used to be a 'safe house' on the same Rat-line. Across the Rhône from here."

I glanced at the closed kitchen door. I hadn't realized Madame even knew about the château—but these things must have got talked about openly after the war. Still, even that wouldn't account for the knowingness of her grin. She must have heard I stayed at the château for a better reason than just that it was "safe". Did they talk about *that* as well?

Maganhard said: "An over-rated wine."

I nodded. True enough—but they knew what they were doing at Pinel. You can't start over-pricing a wine until first you've got somebody to over-rate it.

Madame came back with a vast earthenware pot of *cassoulet*: a mixture of goose, beans, mutton, and God-knows-what that she probably started in September and kept going with additions through to the end of May.

Harvey took a couple of forkfuls, then reached into his pocket, decanted a couple of pills, and swallowed them. Then he stood up, "I need some sleep." He looked at Maganhard: "If you get shot, I'm sorry."

He didn't need sleep nearly so much as he needed a stack of stiff drinks, but in the morning I'd rather have him dozy from barbiturates than weary from spending the night fighting a screaming thirst.

Madame shrugged at me, then led Harvey upstairs.

After dinner Maganhard decided he wanted to pass a message to Liechtenstein, and I remembered I'd promised to call Merlin again. Madame assured us there was a "safe" phone down with the new *maire*; it sounded as if he owed the Meliots money from how sure she was that he was "safe".

Maganhard was quite certain he couldn't give me the message to give to Merlin to give to Liechstenstein. I wasn't keen on phoning any Liechtenstein number direct, but the object of the whole trip was to save Maganhard's business, so I couldn't really argue. Miss Jarman came down with me to the *maire's* house; Maganhard didn't make his own calls, of course.

She asked for her number, then turned to me. "What time shall I say we will be in Liechtenstein?"

"By tomorrow evening—with luck."

"How much luck?"

"A certain amount. If they're watching the frontier, we might have to wait until dark to cross."

She frowned, puzzled. "If they don't catch us tonight, won't they assume they've missed us?"

I shook my head. "Wrong approach to police mentality. If they don't catch us, they'll assume we haven't tried yet. Unfortunately, they'll be right."

Then her number came through and I drifted off to chat with the *maire*.

★ II ★

At half past seven the next morning I was drinking black coffee with Madame Meliot and Miss Jarman.

I wouldn't say life seemed much fun right then, but at least I had that feeling that you know you're going to feel okay sooner or later. I'd sat up for an hour after the telephone calls drinking *marc* with Meliot himself and recalling the Resistance days and asking what had happened to old so-and-so? We hadn't mentioned Giles.

Meliot came in from somewhere outside, clapped me on the shoulder, and then said something I missed to Madame. She turned round and kissed me.

That woke me. I started to say: *"Mais, purquoi——?"*

The girl said: "I think it must be those flowers—the wild daffodils—you left on their son's grave yesterday. He must have seen them."

"I did? Oh—so that's what you were doing when I lost you."

I smiled back at Madame and shrugged meaninglessly. She called me an Englishman and went to get more coffee. Meliot had vanished, too.

I looked at the girl: "Thanks. I suppose I should have thought of it."

"Englishmen never think of flowers. But the gesture wasn't out of character. For a moment I wondered why you'd expect them to put us up, when you'd got their son killed on a job you were doing." She sipped her coffee. "Then, when you said you'd gone on with the guns to Lyons, I understood: you could have thrown his body out at the roadside. Instead, you took it up to Lyons and then brought it all the way back here. It must have been quite a risk. I see why they like you."

Madame came back with the coffee; Meliot came back and poured a shot of *marc* into it. I tried protesting, but it didn't help. They stood around grinning at me while I drank it. Well, there are worse ways to start a day.

Harvey and Maganhard came down, neither of them looking as bright as the desert sun, but at least on their feet. They'd got stuck sharing a room; Madame had made it clear she was entertaining them because they were with me. Therefore, I got the best single room. Logical.

Harvey took a cup of coffee. "You ring Merlin last night?" he asked.

"Yes." I studied him carefully sideways. He looked a little bleared and slow, but his hands on the cup were quite steady.

"What did he say?"

"Said he'd try and get to Geneva overnight on the Simplon-Orient. Then if we stuck on the frontier, without the car, he'll try and think of ways of getting us across. He could be some help."

He frowned into his cup. "He could be dangerous, too—if the cops are really watching him."

I nodded. "Yes—or he could just lead them away from us. We don't *have* to get in touch with him."

Maganhard looked up quickly. "Monsieur Merlin must be with me in Liechtenstein."

I waved my head meaninglessly. I'd take my own decision—and we could always ring him when we were well past Geneva. He'd reach Liechtenstein in a couple of hours by plane to Zürich and then a train or hired car.

Maganhard said: "I am ready to go on." It sounded like an order.

Getting away from the Meliots wasn't difficult. They'd never known me except as a person who had to go when he said so, and with no fuss made. We were rolling by a quarter to eight.

Harvey slipped his gun down to his ankle, then started juggling with the maps. "About seventy kilometres to the Rhône: where do we cross?"

"Le Pouzin, probably."

"It's a big river," he said doubtfully. "They could be watching all the bridges."

"I hope they'll think we'll be crossing north of Lyons. Merlin said he'd sent that telegram to the yacht, so they think we're going from Paris. And Le Pouzin's about ten bridges down from Lyons."

He made a non-committal *mmm* noise.

Maganhard leant forward and asked: "How much do you think the police know, Mr Cane?"

"Well——" I tried to count up. "They know we're in France. They know there's four of us: the crew of that yacht probably talked their heads off. As sailors, the police'd be able to put the screws on by threatening to ban them from France for ever. So they know you and Miss Jarman, but they probably can't describe Harvey or me. Not after just a glimpse on that beach. But apart from the telegram, that's about all."

Miss Jarman said: "What about the man you had a fight with in Tours? Won't they know about him?"

Harvey said: "No. His pals'll have hauled him off to some quack doctor to get him patched up. How would they explain to the cops what they were doing, anyway?"

Maganhard said heavily: "I hope you are right."

"God, I only have to be right the whole time," I snapped. "The cops just need to be right once, that's all."

Harvey smiled his twisted smile. "Your trouble is you're just not enjoying the ride, chum."

I glared at him, but soon my jumpiness passed. A few kilometres out of Dinadan we passed through thick pine woods, fresh logs stacked by the roadside like huge peeled asparagus. Then the road climbed in wriggles towards the final rim of the central plateau before the drop to the Rhône.

The farms died out as the country got steeper. The hill-tops turned into bare grey rock, the slopes into rock slides stitched in place by a few bushes or tough grass.

I swung up in an uphill left-hand curve over the shoulder of a hill, where the road was sunk across a small spur, with rough rock walls speckled with clumps of broom on either side.

Two light-green Renault 4L's blocked the road.

They were carefully arranged, slanted across the road with their back ends almost touching in an arrowhead pointing at us. Whatever I did, I was going to hit them.

I rammed my foot back on the accelerator; it was the only unexpected thing I had left to do. Just before we hit, Harvey snatched down at his ankle and fired two careful shots through the windscreen.

There was a huge clang and jolt, turning into a scream of tearing metal. Then, suddenly, it was quiet.

My face was resting on the steering-wheel, but I didn't seem to have hit it hard. I grabbed for my door handle, had to kick it open, and pitched out on to the road, spilling maps, Mauser, and spare magazine from the open briefcase as I went.

I heard Harvey tumble out of the other side.

Lying flat in a puddle of broken glass, I was covered on three sides by the Citroën, the six-foot rock wall beside the road, and one of the Renaults which had got knocked aside and ended up just behind us. Under the Citroën, I could see Harvey flat against the wall on his side.

He looked across, and said: "Cover above me."

I said: "Yes," and then looked to see what he was talking about.

They'd planned a good ambush, in a place I should have remembered and worried about. The rock walls of the cutting meant we couldn't have swerved, and couldn't jump off the road once we'd hit the Renaults. Then we'd have been trapped in one precise spot, with them waiting up on the banks on either side to blaze away.

But by hitting the Renaults as hard as I could, I'd shifted the whole scene several yards: now they'd have to move before they could shoot.

But we were still trapped inside the cutting—and they were still on the banks above us.

A gun banged over my head and a shot crunched into the Citroën's roof. Harvey fired back. The steepness of the wall meant the people on my side couldn't get at me; Harvey's side couldn't get at him. We would be shooting across, over each other's heads.

Suddenly somebody stuck his head and gun up from the rocks on the bank above Harvey and loosed off two shots in my direction. Broken shale clattered down the rock wall behind me. I ducked, and grabbed for the Mauser, clipped the holster on as a butt, and switched the button to Automatic.

Another shot, from somewhere back up the road, slammed into the battered Renault beside me. And another. As if it were a signal—and it probably was—my first man jumped up from the rocks and started pumping shots past my head.

I jammed the Mauser into my shoulder, clamped my left hand on the magazine, and fired.

It went off in one short *brrap*, trying to rip out of my hands. The man was hit by a sudden wind: his arms flung out sideways, then his head snapped up, and he pitched back out of sight.

Through the ringing in my ears I heard Harvey saying: "I keep telling you the war's over. Keep it single shots."

"I got him." I was trying to work out how many rounds I'd fired; I couldn't. The Mauser fires too fast for individual shots to echo in your brain. I guessed I'd fired ten—half the magazine.

Harvey said: "I count three of them's showed so far."

"Yes. Almost like a war, isn't it?"

"The hell with you." He fired over my head, uphill. By my reckoning, the ranges were a bit long for his short-barrelled gun but he was aiming as carefully as if he'd had a big target pistol.

Then there was a pause. The mixture of three cars—the second Renault was jammed diagonally across the Citroën's nose—gave us a lot of cover. If whoever-it-was had thought to bring a few grenades, they could have blasted us out without showing themselves. But since they'd been showing themselves, it looked as if they'd forgotten the grenades.

A gun fired behind me. I'd thrown myself flat and twisted half round to look up the road before I realized the shot hadn't struck anywhere near me.

Standing there, in the middle of the road, was a man, holding a pistol aimed at the sky. He yelled: *"Arvi!"*

Through under the car, I saw Harvey's arm straighten and the little gun blurred in his hand. He fired three shots. When I looked back up the road, the man was just a heap.

Two more shots came from the hillside above me, one tearing into the Citroën's roof. Harvey fired back over the top of the car, then shouted: "Give me that thing!"

I tossed the Mauser over the Citroën and he grabbed it and fired two short bursts up the hill.

Then he stood clear of the cars, still watching the hill. I climbed slowly on to my feet and walked round beside him, looking nervously over my shoulder. But the hillside was empty.

Harvey said: "Last seen running like hell," and gave me the empty Mauser.

"Glad you find it has its uses."

He didn't say anything, just walked away up the road, thumbing fresh cartridges into the Smith and Wesson. I found the Mauser's spare magazine, clipped it in, and followed.

He was standing, staring down at the man he'd shot. "The stupid bastard," he said softly. "What was he trying to do?—Standing there shouting at me. The damn stupid bastard." He lifted his foot and I thought he was going to kick the dead face—but he just tipped the automatic out of the man's hand.

He looked up at me. "You know him?"

I nodded. It was Bernard—one of the two top gunmen in Europe. One of the men I'd asked for in preference to Harvey himself.

Harvey said: "Yeah, I knew him, too. He must've recognized me—shouted my name. What the hell did he *want*?"

I shrugged. "Maybe to arrange an armistice. Maybe he didn't believe in dog eating dog. We give him Maganhard, we get away safe."

He stared. "You think so?"

"Think up something better."

He looked back at the dead man. "The stupid bastard. Didn't he know it was serious?" Then his voice went soft again, almost puzzled. "I didn't think I'd end up shooting *him*."

I didn't think Bernard had expected it, either—but all I said was: "They sent in the First Team this time."

Harvey nodded and walked back.

That left me and Bernard. I was in a hurry to get away

from this place—anybody who'd heard my Mauser go off wouldn't have written *that* down as a bit of poaching with a shotgun—but not in so much of a hurry to leave bodies in the middle of the road. I dragged him back up the road to where the downhill rock wall ended, then off it, and in among the rocks on the spur.

Then, where Harvey couldn't see me, I gave the pockets a quick once-over. I didn't find anything useful. I climbed down to the cars.

Maganhard was still sitting in the Citroën. The girl was out and, presumably because Harvey had told her to, was picking up the empty Mauser cartridge cases. Harvey himself was studying the Renault jammed across the Citroën's front.

I got into the car and tried the engine. It caught at once, so that at least was okay. I switched off and went round to the front.

Harvey said: "We can bounce it clear." The Renault looked as if it had been through the coffee-grinder. We'd punched in its back end, bounced its front off the rock wall, and then shunted it along ahead of us, sideways. Its rear left wheel was locked solid, wrapped up in torn bodywork like a chocolate in silver paper.

We grabbed it by the rear bumper and bounced. There was a tearing sound and it came away from the Citroën. It was a nice light little car; a few more bounces and it was at the roadside. I'd have liked to have rolled it over and down the hill, but the locked rear wheel wouldn't roll an inch.

I studied the front of the Citroën. We'd lost both our headlights, which didn't surprise me, and the wings around them looked fairly buckled, the left worse than the right. To me it looked as if it was touching the wheel. I looked underneath the car—and then knew what our real trouble was. There was a slow, steady drip into a sticky pink pool between the front wheels.

"We're bleeding," I said. "The main hydraulic reservoir's leaking. We won't get far—and if we want to get anywhere, we'd better start now."

The car had been stabbed in its hydraulic heart; the fluid —the life blood—that powered the steering, brakes, springing, gear-change, was dripping away from the main tank.

"Right." Harvey turned to the girl. "All aboard."

She came up, white-faced, and clutching a double handful of empty shells against her stomach. I opened my briefcase and she poured them in.

Then she said: "I'm sorry—I'm not used to this sort of thing. I didn't know it would be like this."

"Nobody knew," I said. She turned away and got into the back seat.

I put on my driving gloves and twisted the front wing clear of the wheel. The main reservoir was just behind the wheel, so it was the same shock that had punctured it. I thought about topping it up with the can of hydraulic fluid in the boot, but it would just waste time. I climbed in.

The hydraulic brake warning light came on—and stayed on. I shoved the lever into first gear, took a deep breath, and we crept forward. We weren't dead yet—but we were dying.

Maganhard asked: "Can we get the car repaired quickly?" He sounded quite calm about it.

I said: "No. We can't get it repaired at all. We daren't take it near a garage, not even through a village: we're full of bullet-holes, and the trouble with a bullet-hole is that it looks like exactly what it is."

We had two holes through the windscreen on Harvey's side, from his own shots just before we crashed, one through the boot lid, two through the roof, and another through Maganhard's door.

"What do we do next then?"

"Get as far away as we can without meeting anybody, dump the car, find a phone, ring somebody up, and say 'Help'."

I thought the next question would be "Ring who?", and I hadn't worked that out yet. But all he said was: "We'll be late, then."

There wasn't any answer to that. I glanced at Harvey. He was just staring bleakly out ahead, his eyes searching. He hadn't forgotten there was still a gunman on the loose out there, though I didn't think we'd see him again.

I turned off up a narrow, winding road up over the hill.

Already the steering was getting heavy as its power faded. Soon I'd have no gear-change left; then the springing would sag right down; finally, the power brakes would go, leaving just the mechanical foot-brake.

The car would keep going, because the engine would keep turning—but it wouldn't be comfortable, and once I'd stopped I wouldn't get started again, not without a gear-change. I left the lever in second, as the gear I most wanted.

Harvey said suddenly: "If we end up in the backwoods somewhere, how do we find a phone?"

"I think I can end us up quite near one."

The second hydraulic warning light came on: amount of fluid dangerously low. The steering was really dragging at my hands, on those bends, and the springing was letting through jolts. The car was dying.

The road straightened and flattened slightly. If it was the one I remembered, it led us up on to the top of a ridge, without a village for fifteen kilometres. It wasn't getting us any closer to the Rhône, but that might be an advantage if the police started setting up roadblocks. I wanted to be away from our obvious line of escape.

We crawled over on to the top of the ridge and I speeded up. The steering was entirely mechanical now, and we were running on square wheels. I hadn't had to use the brakes uphill, so there should be one last stopping effort left in them.

I went fast past a couple of farmhouses and a parked cart, then eased up and let the engine slow her down. We'd done about twelve kilometres since the ambush. To our left, the ridge sloped down to open, rolling country; on the right it was a steeper downslope of pine forests. At the bottom there was a minor main road with a fair selection of villages.

I covered about another six kilometres before I recognized the track through the woods. I slowed on the mechanical foot-brake, but not enough. At the last moment I jabbed the pressure brake. The car stood on its nose and made the turn, the engine jerking unhappily at far too low revs. We started down the track.

If we'd had square wheels before, now they were triangular. The car floor banged on the ground, and engine noise came up under my feet, so we'd crumpled the exhaust pipe. The slope got steeper. I pumped the brake: we slowed, but the slope got worse. I jammed the mechanical brake full down. The back wheels locked and we slid, slamming on to the ground. The exhaust pipe tore out with a clang.

I grabbed for the ignition and switched the engine off; the car added a shudder. I picked a clump of young trees and wrenched the wheel. We left the track, hit the ground again with an enormous bang, and ran gently to a stop in the trees.

"And that," I said, "is the end of the line."

I knocked open my door. We had fir trees over us, all round us, and the ones we'd knocked down underneath us. With any luck, the Citroën wouldn't be found for a few days.

I said to Harvey: "You better clean out the car," and went round to fight open the buckled bonnet. When I found a screwdriver I got off the Dinadan number plates, and took both them and the old ones with me.

By then the luggage had been hauled out on to the track and Harvey was carefully wiping the car clean of fingerprints.

Maganhard said: "That was my car. I doubt the insurance will pay for it."

I stared at him, then shook my head slowly. "No, if they can't find an escape clause in some of the things we've been doing, they're losing their touch." I walked back up the track to find and hide the exhaust pipe.

When I got back Harvey was propping up a couple of flattened trees to cover the entry wound we'd made in the plantation. I kicked our skid-marks around and hoped it would rain soon. Then we were ready to go.

WE walked down the track. The luggage was two soft leather
Italian grips with long handles like overgrown handbags,
my briefcase, and Harvey's Air France case. It didn't take
much effort, but it was far too much to carry in public if we
wanted to look like tourists out for a stroll. We'd have to
hide it for a time.

After half an hour we reached the stream at the bottom of
the slope. I picked a muddy patch, shovelled a hole with one
number plate, then planted all four in, and kicked the mud
back on top.

Maganhard said: "They will trace the car by the engine
number."

"Yes, but it'll take them a few hours longer."

The trees ended at the stream, but a few hundred yards
along to our left, they started again on the far side. We
walked along there, crossed, and went up through more
woods towards the road. By my reckoning that put us about
a quarter of a mile from the nearest village.

Harvey, who'd dropped naturally into place just behind
Maganhard's right shoulder, turned round to me and said:
"Well—what's the plan?"

"I don't think we'd all better go into the village; four of
us'll look suspicious—and they may have got the word about
the ambush by now." It was half past nine, over an hour
since the shooting had started.

Harvey said: "Okay. That means either just you or you
and her. I stay with him." His voice was quite definite.

I nodded, and turned to the girl. "Miss Jarman—if you'd
like to come with me, I'd like you to. A man and a woman
look more innocent than a single man on his own."

"Whatever you say." Not exactly a rush of enthusiasm,
but not everybody feels all that good an hour after being
shot at for the first time. It can be quite a shock realizing
that people are really trying to kill you, personally.

Harvey said: "About who you ring—I have an opinion."

"Go on."

"You don't ring Dinadan."

I hadn't been going to; when you're on the Rat-line you never change your mind and go back to the same place again. But I wanted to hear Harvey's reasons as well. I said: "You tell me why."

"The mob who planted that ambush knew exactly where we were—*exactly*. They made it as far away from the village as they could, but they were still on the only road we could have taken, if we were going for the Rhône. They knew we were in Dinadan—and they hadn't followed us from Tours."

I nodded slowly. "They knew all right. I think your ideas about Dinadan are wrong, but I won't argue it now. I wasn't going back, anyhow."

Harvey looked at me with cold carefulness. Then he said: "Okay, we're in a hurry. Anybody else from your Resistance days round here?"

"There's a man up in Lyons——"

"Too damn far," he said briskly. "What about this wine château you were talking about last night—the Pinel people? That's a Côtes du Rhône wine; their place should be closer."

I shook my head. "I'm not keen on it."

"Don't you trust them?"

"I trust them all right——"

"Then ring 'em. They'll have delivery trucks and jeeps and things—they can pick us up easy."

"There's a personal problem for me there."

He slanted his eyebrows. "Right here and now," he said quietly, "we have exactly four personal problems. And yours is a murder charge—same as mine. So if you trust these people——"

"All right." It was perfectly reasonable. I couldn't argue. "All right. I'll ring them."

"That's fine." He nodded. "And I have one more idea: don't walk—run."

Miss Jarman and I reached the village in about ten minutes. The thirty-odd kilometres from Dinadan had made a big difference: now we were definitely in the south of France, and almost in summer. The farmyards were beginning to look dry and dusty, with roses blooming along the walls. The village itself was built of warm yellow southern stone, roofed with curly red tiles.

There were three little rusty green tables planted outside a café in the square; we sat down and I ordered coffee and a Pastis.

When the waiter had gone, Miss Jarman said: "Are you really liable to be charged with murder?"

"We killed a couple of people—intentionally. That's murder, all right."

"But they were trying to kill us. Isn't that self-defence?"

"Self-defence is an excuse for killing, if you stand up in court and prove it. But, like somebody else you know well, we aren't going to stick around and fight it. So it'll stay on the books as murder."

"Rape and murder aren't quite the same thing."

"No, especially when Maganhard didn't rape anybody and—technically—we did murder somebody. But the big difference is that they don't know who we are; they do know him."

"Will they find out about you?"

I shrugged. "In the end, maybe. But long as they can't prove anything, we should be all right. There's not going to be a public scandal about a couple of Paris gunmen getting killed. The cops won't have much pressure on them to solve it."

The waiter brought her coffee and my Pastis and I asked about the times of buses to Vals-les-Bains, which was roughly in the opposite direction to where we wanted to go. As I'd hoped, there wouldn't be one for hours. I asked if I could make a phone call.

It took a little time to get through, then a man's voice, cool and dry and old, answered: "Clos Pinel."

"Est il possible de parler à Madame la Comtesse?"

"Qui est à l'appareil?"

I hesitated, wondering what name I should give these days. Then something about the voice sank in. *"C'est vous, Maurice?"* I demanded. I'd somehow thought the old boy must have died or been pensioned off or something by now. I added: *"Ici Caneton."*

This time he hesitated. When he spoke again, his voice was a little warmer. *"Monsieur Caneton? Un moment . . ."*

After a moment, a woman's voice said: "Is that really you, Louis?"

"Ginette? Yes, I'm afraid it's me."

"My dear Louis, when you decide to stay away, you bury yourself. Are you coming to see me now?" Her English was nearly perfect; only her accent showed she hadn't spoken it in England for a long time. But I wasn't listening to the accent, only the husky gentle voice itself.

"Ginette—I'm afraid I'm in trouble. There's four of us. I hate asking—but can you help? Pick us up and move us along a bit? You don't have to know what it's about."

"So I don't have to know?" She sounded both amused and reproachful. "What a thing to say, Louis. Where are you?"

I told her the name of the village.

Her voice got brisk. "A grey Citroën van with the name of the Château will meet you in one hour and a half. It will bring you here."

"Hell, you don't need to involve the Château, Ginette. Just get us across the Rhône and we'll——"

"This is still a safe house, Louis. For you."

I gave in. It's not only bad manners to argue with the person making the arrangements—it's also stupid. Particularly when they know the game as well as you ever did.

"We'll be just through the village, on the south road," I said.

She rang off. I walked back to the table. "We're okay." I looked at my watch. "We'll be picked up at half past eleven."

Miss Jarman nodded, then asked. "Where is this château?"

"Just across the Rhône from here."

"Who are the people there?"

"Belonged to a man called the Comte de Maris. I knew him in the Resistance. But I read he was drowned three years ago. Yachting accident."

94

"Leaving the Comtesse? Was she the personal problem you mentioned?"

I blew smoke into my Pastis. "Why would you think that?"

"I wouldn't, necessarily, but I'd certainly think it first." She was smiling cheerfully.

I scowled at her. "So let's leave it at that."

But not her. "I suppose she was also in the Resistance? Was she the Comtesse then?"

"No," I growled.

"So she married him and not you. Well, so would anybody —if he had a title and a vineyard."

I winced. It was an idea I didn't like thinking about.

She added thoughtfully: "But I don't suppose that was it. I'd think you must have been pretty unlovable when you were younger—and you must have been rather young, then. Was that why they called you *Caneton*—duckling? Or was it just a pun on your name?"

There was a sudden squeal of tyres and a police jeep rushed into the square from the north road. And stopped.

I said quickly: "Sit still and look interested. It'd be natural." She widened her eyes at me, then twisted to watch the jeep. It was a battered blue affair with flapping canvas and perspex doors. A sergeant zoomed out of it and rushed into the café. Three others jumped out of the back; one hurried off to the bottom of the square. The others stared busily around and then lit up cigarettes.

I said quietly: "I think we can assume that somebody's found the wrecked cars, and at least one body. They wouldn't be running like this for a crashed car."

Her eyes were a hard, wide china-blue. "Have you got your gun? What do we do?"

"No, I don't have it—thank God. It's a bit big for these social occasions. We just sit and wait."

"For how long?"

"Until it won't look as if we're running away."

The sergeant and the proprietor came out of the café, both talking fast and neither listening. I leant over and called: *"Qu'est-ce qui se passe?"*

The sergeant gave us a fast glance that probably didn't

even register what sexes we were, said a last word to the proprietor, and strode back to the jeep, yelling for his men.

The proprietor came over and started explaining about how the bandits in the hills had had a battle this morning. A car shot up, at least one man killed. He stretched the "at least" to suggest a platoon of undiscovered corpses.

I made appreciative noises and said that odd things happened outside Paris. He swept Paris aside with one gesture; did I know that of the great crimes of the last decade not one had happened in Paris? They were getting feeble, there. Take the *affaire* of the headless girl . . .

The cop galloped up from the bottom of the square, got in the jeep, and they drove about thirty yards into the street leading south—the one we'd come up. Once there, they all jumped out again and started spreading spiked metal balls across the road to cripple any car trying to rush them. Then they brought out a couple of sub-machine guns, leaned against the jeep, and lit up again.

I ordered another coffee and a Pastis. When the proprietor had gone, Miss Jarman said: "What do we do now?"

"Go on waiting."

"But they're blocking the road. We're cut off from Mr Maganhard——"

"I know. I'll have to go round the back of the village and bring them up on to the north road. We'll have to stop the Pinel van there. It shouldn't be too bad; the cops aren't being very serious."

"They aren't?" She looked at me incredulously.

"They're standing where the taxpayers can see them, not where they'll do any good. Anybody coming down that road could see them at twice the range of their guns. But they still think they're looking for local bandits who wouldn't try to escape from the area, anyway. This blockade's just for show. The trouble starts when anybody says the word 'Maganhard'."

Two shots sounded, distant, but not too distant, and clearly the flat short snap of a pistol.

Miss Jarman raised her eyebrows at me. "Or, of course, when your friend Harvey starts shooting."

✳ 13 ✳

I swung round to look at the blockade. The cops were firmly behind the jeep by now, peering round it up the road to the south. There was nothing to see. I heard the proprietor come pounding out behind me.

Then the sergeant came running back, yelling for the telephone. He looked more surprised than worried.

The girl asked: "What will they do now?"

"God knows. But probably get some more men in. We may have to move." I started working up a worried expression. It wasn't difficult.

When the proprietor and sergeant came out again I jumped up and started demanding police protection. I hadn't come down here to get involved with bandits. The village was obviously about to be besieged. Where was safe?

The sergeant sneered and told me I was safe where I was. I pointed out that only thirty yards away his own men were taking cover—was I expected to sit in the open? Were there any bandits down *that* way? I pointed north.

He said No, and if I wanted to go that way, he'd be glad to be rid of me. He ran back to the jeep.

I paid up quickly, took Miss Jarman's arm, and scuttled out of the square northwards. A last look over my shoulder showed a couple of cops, one with a sub-machine-gun, running back from the jeep and turning up a small alley past the café towards the stream, to start an out-flanking movement.

I hurried us on.

When we were clear of the village, I found a stone wall leading across the fields towards the stream. I told the girl to stay there. "The van shouldn't be along for about half an hour. But if it comes, stop it. I don't want it going into the village."

Then I took off, running in a crouch, down behind the wall.

A few minutes of that convinced me that my running-crouched days were long past. I straightened up behind a tree, breathing fast and shallow, then went on more slowly. I had nearly a quarter of a mile in all to go to the stream, and I had to go that far to make sure I was clear of the farmland—and also to give me a sense of direction.

I splashed across and into the trees, then turned and trotted south on the far bank. Through gaps in the trees I kept an eye on the church spire just over the slope. I knew I was safe until I got level with it; after that, there would be the two cops to worry about.

When the spire was square on my left, I slowed down. Across the stream there were wide, lush green fields, separated by fat stone walls. The woods where Harvey and Maganhard were parked started about a quarter of a mile farther on. I didn't think the cops would have crossed the stream but I thought they'd have come as far as it; it was an obvious natural boundary to any search area.

But they might not be searching—just sitting, watching. Waiting for reinforcements. I slowed down even more, and started edging away from the stream, deeper into the trees.

Something splashed in the water. I froze against a tree, then raised one eyebrow round it.

One of the cops was lifting a wet foot and shaking it angrily. Then he pulled himself ashore on my side, sat down, and emptied his boot. After that he picked up his sub-machine-gun and started peering carefully at the soggy bank, looking for tracks.

He was about thirty yards from me, and there wasn't enough undergrowth for me to move without being seen.

He took his time. He walked several yards along the bank, still looking at the ground, then looking for an easier place to cross back. Finally he crossed, climbed up into the field, and walked slowly away on a diagonal track towards the woods and the road. I took a deep breath and started running.

A few minutes later I was level with the woods on the opposite bank and looking for the place where we'd first crossed, coming down from the car. Something glinted among the trees ahead. I moved cautiously, from tree to tree.

Gradually it grew into a small light-green car, a Renault 4L, half buried in the low branches of a young fir.

Then I remembered the proprietor talking about *one* car being shot up . . . I should have listened harder. The third man, the one who'd run away, had got one of the cars started and had trailed us. It wouldn't have been difficult—he didn't need to keep us in sight. We'd left a blood-trail of hydraulic fluid for anybody who knew to look for it.

And those first shots had been when he'd caught up with Harvey and Maganhard . . .

I yanked open one of the buckled doors, in the desperate hope that there might be a spare gun lying around. There wasn't, of course.

I ran down to the stream, crossed, and started up towards the road. The stream was closer to the road here; I reckoned I had only about two hundred yards to go. I knew just where I'd left Harvey and Maganhard—but they'd have moved when the shooting started. Where to? Were they still even alive? There'd been only two shots, and it's just about impossible to kill two people for certain with just two pistol shots. So there must have been one shot from the new friend and one, in reply, from Harvey. Unless the first shot *had* killed Harvey, and the second had been a careful, aimed execution of Maganhard . . .

I stopped and sank down to a crouch beside a tree. That sort of thinking was tying my brain in knots. All I really knew was that I was walking into a gunfight without a gun. *Why the hell hadn't I carried the Mauser?* Because it was too big. So why hadn't I picked up Bernard's gun when I had the chance?—I could have carried that. No answer. I moved off again, bent double.

I had about a hundred yards to go. There still wasn't enough undergrowth to give any real cover for movement, but at least the ground was damp enough not to make any noise underfoot. I crept from tree to tree.

Fifty yards. Now I could see a gleam of sky ahead through the trees, where they ended at the road. I stared into each low patch of grass or bramble, looking for the outline of a lying figure, the movement of a hand, the glint of a gun-barrel. I saw dozens, but none of them were there.

Maybe I should call to Harvey. And maybe I should keep my head shut unless I wanted it blown off.

Then I saw something, right ahead. A shape, a heap, in the open and not moving . . . It was the luggage. I started breathing again. But now was the time to speak or forever hold my peace. I slid down among the roots of the tree and said quietly: "Harvey—it's Cane."

Something moved in the brambles over to my right. I jerked forward. A gun banged and chips of wood spattered around me. I threw myself into the clump of bushes in front. Too late, I saw somebody kneel up among them.

Gunfire singed my face and battered in my ears. I lay flat, trying to work out if I were dead.

Harvey said: "Davey Crockett, I presume? Welcome to the Alamo. I was hoping you'd come along and tempt him out of cover."

"Any time." I started unwrapping myself from the bushes. A few yards over to my right, a man was lying half out of the bramble patch. Harvey walked across to him. He walked stiffly, and then I saw a stained rip in his jacket over his left ribs. I yanked myself free and went after him.

"Are you hurt bad?"

"Not serious." His face was set hard as he tried to lift the man with his foot. He let him fall back, convinced he was dead.

"I'd been stuck in cover about twenty minutes waiting for him to make a move. What's the news?"

"Let me have a look." I started tearing open the blood-stained hole in his shirt. "The news is we're being picked up, but the cops have got a roadblock in the village. They heard the shooting and they're out in the fields." I nodded over my shoulder. "It's just a gash—but you'll have to run with it. Can you?"

He nodded.

I said: "Then go round the village and up to the road."

Maganhard came up behind us, carrying my Mauser as delicately as he would a dead rat. I took it off him.

Harvey said to him: "Liechtenstein's now that way." He pointed to the stream. "Get the luggage and run."

Maganhard said: "I do not mind about the luggage——"

"*I* mind," I said. "It's evidence of who was here."

Maganhard went to fetch it. Harvey called after him: "Remember—the business you save may be your own." Then he looked at the dead man. "Though he's a good piece of evidence himself. They won't think he committed suicide."

A voice from the field shouted: "*Ai! Allons-y!*"

I said: "I may be able to fool them a bit. Stay across the stream and away from the bank: they'll look for tracks there. And *don't* come back for me, whatever you hear."

He crooked an eyebrow at me: "You aren't going to be the boy on the burning deck, are you?"

Maganhard went trundling past, carrying the two cases. I said: "I'll be along."

He turned away, then back. "It's the first time I've ever been hit," he said thoughtfully. "He came up behind me; got me by surprise."

"I'd assumed *that*, for God's sake."

He didn't seem to hear me. "But it's not an excuse really. People shouldn't get up behind me and take me by surprise. My job." Then he loped off down the track, his left elbow pressed tight into his ribs, his Air France suitcase in his hand.

I took a deep breath that was only partly because of the running and jumping I'd been doing recently, found the Mauser holster, and clipped it on as a shoulder-piece. Then I walked over to the dead man.

He was a smallish man with long dark hair, wearing a shabby grey double-breasted suit. His gun was a U.S. Army Colt ·45 automatic. I put it in a pocket, picked him up, and staggered through the wood towards the fields.

Near the last of the trees I put him carefully down again, got out his gun, broke out the magazine, and counted the rounds. There were too many for what I planned; I left him just three. Then I sneaked forward to the edge of the field.

One of the cops was standing in plain view about a hundred yards away, up to the middle of his thighs in long grass, and staring hard at the trees. I couldn't see the other. I pulled back and went on hands and knees to the road.

I needed to account for the four earlier shots—and a dead man. I tucked the Mauser into my shoulder and fired two

101

careful shots at the nearest house in the village, a quarter of a mile off. I saw a cloud of dust fall off the wall. Now the cops down there knew they'd been fired at; maybe they'd believe some of the earlier shots had been aimed at them too.

I crept back to the dead man. The cop was still in the middle of the field, staying out of what he thought was accurate pistol range. With the Mauser and its shoulder-piece, I could have plucked his eyebrows at that range. Well, that was about what I wanted to do. But I would have preferred to know where his partner was.

I propped myself carefully behind a tree, and shouted at him. I told him to come on if he felt brave enough. Gendarmes had killed my father and brother. Now let him try and kill me. I was going to take one with me when I went.

I tried to make it sound crazy; an impression of craziness might help fog up some awkward details. He had half ducked when I started shouting, but stayed in view. I put a shot close enough to his head for him to know I meant him. He threw himself flat.

His partner knelt up suddenly from the grass near him and loosed off his sub-machine-gun in my direction. Sprigs of fir and cones spattered down on my head. That was good enough for me. I let out a long dying scream, ending in a nasty little choked gurgle.

Then I threw the empty Mauser cartridge case into the field, patted the dead man on the shoulder, said: "That'll teach you to shoot at cops," grabbed my briefcase, and ran.

I caught up with them just where they were about to recross the stream and get to the road. By there, my run had turned into a gentle trot.

Harvey gave me a bleak little smile and said: "I like the idea, but d'you think it'll fool them for long?" He must have heard all my little performance.

"Long enough, maybe."

"Sooner or later they'll find the guy got hit by a thirty-eight, not one of their machine-guns."

"They won't rush a post-mortem on him if they think they already know what happened."

We splashed across the stream and up into the cover of

the wall leading to the road. I looked at my watch and made it just over half an hour since I'd left Miss Jarman. My feet were beginning to remind me that I'd got them wet four times since then. We stumbled on.

Parked in the gateway at the top of the field was a grey Citroën van with corrugated sides and CLOS PINEL painted across its rear doors. Miss Jarman and somebody else were kneeling by the front wheels, pretending to be interested in the tyres.

As we staggered up, blowing like a herd of tired horses, the other person stood up and came quickly to the back of the van. It was Ginette, in a neat grey skirt and a smudged old suède jacket.

And older than when I'd last seen her, twelve years ago—but not twelve years older. Perhaps a gentle weariness in her dark eyes, a slowness and steadiness in her expression. But the same dark-chestnut hair, the soft pale skin that never seemed to be touched by the sun, the same sad amused smile I'd remembered far too well.

She touched my arm. "Hellow, Louis. You haven't changed a bit."

My legs were soaked to the knees, my jacket and shirt were covered in mould and pine-needles, half my hair was dangling in my face, and half the forest was in my hair. And I had the big Mauser in my hand.

I nodded. "Maybe I should have." We started climbing into the back of the van.

14

WHEN the doors opened again, we were on the gravel drive-way just in front of the Château.

It was the sort of château that looks like one—to an Englishman. Probably that was why one of the earlier Comtes had built it that way: he wanted something that would make a good picture on his wine labels.

It didn't belong in this part of the country; he'd pinched the idea from up on the Loire. It was a solid piece of fake Gothic, with tall windows and a round tower at each side, with peaked witch's-hat roofs of blue slate that jarred with the warm pink southern stone of the house itself. But that wouldn't show on the neat engraving on the labels, of course.

By now the others had climbed out. I turned to Ginette. "I don't know if you want any introductions . . ."

She was looking curiously at Maganhard. "I think I'd better know," she said.

I said: "Mr Maganhard—Ginette, Comtesse de Maris." Her eyebrows lifted just a fraction at his name. He took her hand, came to attention, and bowed slightly.

I introduced Miss Jarman and Harvey. He wasn't looking his best: the lines on his face weren't any deeper, but the whole face had frozen.

Ginette said: "I believe you are wounded. If you will go inside, Maurice will bandage you." I saw the grey-haired, white-jacketed character hovering in the background, up on the terrace in front of the windows. I went up and shook his hand, and the old brown crab-apple face crinkled into a vast grin. We asked each other how things marched, and said they marched as well as one could hope. Then he said it was quite like old times, grinned again, and led Harvey off inside.

The others came up on to the terrace. Maganhard said: "How long are we staying here, Mr Cane? I believe we have gone less than one hundred kilometres today."

Ginette said: "We needn't discuss that just now. Giles, will you give Mr Maganhard a drink?" She swung round on the girl. "My dear, let me show you your room." She collected Miss Jarman, who was looking a bit pale, and led the way.

Nothing inside the Château seemed to have changed much—but no reason why it should when you've got a big house filled with furniture that's taken a century to collect. The front room on the right as you went in was still a sort of office/drawing-room, and the booze was still tucked away in a solid dark Louis Treize cupboard facing the window.

I peered in at the bottles. "What'll you have?"

Maganhard said: "Sherry, if you please."

"Sorry, the French don't drink the stuff."

"A weak whisky and soda, then."

I hauled out a bottle of Scotch and mixed him one. I poured myself three fingers of it, neat.

Maganhard sipped. "What do you plan now, Mr Cane?"

"I want to cross into Geneva early tomorrow morning—just before dawn."

"Dawn? Why not before?"

I found a slightly crumpled packet of Gitanes and lit one. "We've got to cross illegally—we daren't show our passports now. So we've got to wait until night. If we get there just after dark, we'll be stuck in Geneva overnight; it'll be too late to hire a car and I don't like overnight trains. The Swiss don't use them much—we'd be too conspicuous.

"But if we cross just before dawn, we won't have to hang around looking obvious. The streets'll start filling up, we can get moving quickly."

He frowned into his glass. "I believe Monsieur Merlin said he would be in Geneva. If we rang him there now, he could have a car waiting for us. So we could cross immediately after dark."

I shook my head wearily; he wasn't going to like what I was going to say. Hell, he probably wasn't going to understand it. "Things have changed since I spoke to Merlin yesterday. Somebody's been tracing us; they could have done it by tapping Merlin's phone. If so, why shouldn't they be doing the same thing in Geneva?"

"You said the police would not dare do that to an important lawyer."

"That doesn't apply to the Other Side—and it's them been doing the tracing."

He frowned. "Is it so easy to intercept a telephone?"

"No—in a city it's damn difficult; that's why I wasn't worried about it yesterday. But after this morning, we know a bit more about these people: if they know enough to hire a man like Bernard, then they could know anything."

"Mr Lovell thought it was the people in Dinadan who had betrayed us."

"Yes, but he hadn't thought that through. The Meliots wouldn't have known who to betray us to, except the police. Nobody could have got at them in advance because nobody knew we were going there."

He took a sip of whisky to help him swallow this. Then he said: "I must have Monsieur Merlin with me in Lichtenstein."

"All right—but we won't ring him until we're across the frontier. From here, nobody rings anybody. I'm putting a complete ban on that phone." I finished my Scotch with a gulp.

Then I said carefully: "Of course, there was another phone call made last night."

I felt him staring at me. "My secretary rang my associate in Liechtenstein," he said stiffly.

"She says."

After a moment he said: "You mean that she may have rung somebody else? That is impossible."

"I didn't listen, so I wouldn't know. But if I wanted to get at you, the one person I'd like on my side is your private secretary." And this time I met his stare.

The door opened and Maurice, with his Louis Treize expression firmly in place, announced: *"Messieurs sont servi."*

There were only three of us: Ginette, Maganhard, and

myself. Harvey didn't apparently feel like food, and Miss Jarman had gone straight off to sleep.

Ginette gave me a slight frown and asked: "What have you been doing to that child, Louis?"

I shrugged. "Maybe killing people near her."

"This morning?"

I nodded. "We got jumped, up near Dinadan." I took a deep breath. "One of them was Bernard." She'd known him, in the war.

But she just went on stirring her *soupe au pistou*. "I had heard he and Alain had gone to—to that sort of work. After that, I suppose it does not matter who kills them."

I started to say that it had been Harvey, not me, then decided she must have guessed. She'd thought a lot of me at one time—but never that I could beat Bernard.

But it hadn't been quite the gay chatter you can switch round to the spring fashions, the latest Mexican divorces, and who-elected-*him*-anyway? We finished the soup and started an *omelette aux fines herbes* in the general atmosphere of a funeral feast at a Home for Incurables.

By the time Maurice brought in grilled trout I either had to say something cheerful or ask for half an hour alone with the gas oven.

I said: "Thank God for fish. Now I won't have to drink your Pinel."

Ginette leant back and looked at me reproachfully. "You used to say that trout were the only fish that weren't an excuse for a rich sauce. That was why I ordered them."

"Oh, I still say it. Anybody who cooks trout in a fancy way is a grave robber, a violater of children, and cheats at cards, too. But here, they're doubly welcome. They mean I don't have to drink your dreadful wine."

She made a graceful gesture of despair and looked at Maganhard. He was carefully staying out of the conversation, doing a surgical job on his trout—and probably remembering he'd called Pinel an "over-rated wine" last night.

She said: "Isn't it fascinating to hear the English giving opinions on things they know nothing about? They *sound* so convincing."

Maganhard quickly shoved a piece of trout into his mouth.

I said: "The British are essentially a humble people. They long ago realized it would be a terrible pride to try and *be* right. So they concentrated on *sounding* right. And there you have the basis of the English upper classes, the public schools, the late Empire."

Maurice leant over my shoulder and poured me a new glass of white wine, smiling gravely to himself. He knew a lot more English than he tried to speak.

"And what do the English think of the French reputation for logic and diplomacy?" Ginette asked.

I waved a fork. "An insufferable pride. Anyway, the British have never believed it."

She sighed. "I know. They still think we are a wild, emotional people who crash cars and stamp on grapes. But, *mon Louis*"—she pointed her knife at me in a most un-Comtesse-like way—"but now you have competition from the Americans. They also can sound very right."

"Quite true." I tasted the new wine: a cold, sharp white Burgundy. "But they do it by setting up million-dollar research programmes. It's easy to sound right when you do that: our way's far cheaper. Still, we've had to give up sounding right about nuclear physics, I believe—but we've doubled our opinions on wine. Millions of dollars will never prove us wrong there. You should go to London, Ginette: you've no idea how right we can sound about wine these days."

I glanced at Maganhard. He was smiling a bleak smile into his trout.

Ginette banged her knife down. "Ah—we knew it: an English plot. When things are going badly, you pick on *la France*. It is an old story to us. So now the English will tell us how to grow wine: that is very interesting. Go on, Louis —tell me."

"My dear Ginette—if I were honest, I would tell you to stop making wine at all and grow cabbages on that hill——" I nodded at the back of the house and the vineyards beyond it. "However, a hundred years ago the de Marises realized they could never improve Pinel and concentrated instead on making it famous. So now you sell the most expensive cabbage soup on the market. Which means you can afford far better wines for your guests."

She smiled quietly at me and tinkled a bell by her plate. Maurice appeared, whipped away our plates, and put a cheese-board on the table—with a bottle of Pinel. I made a face.

She twisted it to show me the label. "What do you think of our new design, Giles?"

The picture of the Château was gone. Instead, it was a simple affair of copperplate script on a white label that was shallower but longer than usual. The paper had a thick but almost transparent look, like a good watermark paper.

She said blandly: "You don't recognize it?"

I shook my head doubtfully. It looked familiar, somehow . . .

She grinned. "The old English five-pound note. The exact size and amount of lettering. I never understood why you stopped making that beautiful money."

I said grimly: "They said it was too easy to forge. Now, I see why." I turned to Maganhard. "Ginette's work in the Resistance was forging: she used to make passes and ration cards for us. Nice to see somebody's wartime training being useful in peace, isn't it?"

He twitched a small smile at me. "I believe that is the principle on which you are working for me, Mr Cane." He half stood up. "If you will excuse me, Comtesse, I would like to go and rest. I have things to think about."

Ginette nodded gracefully. "Maurice will take you——"
I said: "Hold on."

Maganhard stayed where he was, bent awkwardly, half out of his chair.

I said: "I think the time's come for me to know a bit more about just why you're going to Liechtenstein."

"I do not see that that is necessary." But he sat down again.

"Let me get one thing clear, then: after this morning's affair, we all ought to be dead. Bernard was rated a better gunman than Harvey Lovell—and I expect the ones with him were rated far better than me. Luckily things didn't go by the form book—but it means whoever-it-is has got very damn serious about trying to kill you. That's one point.

"The other is that *they* know what you're trying to do—but I don't. And both together gives them just too much of a margin. We've already been outguessed twice. The next time . . ." I shrugged.

He just went on giving me his steel-statue look. Then he asked: "What do you wish to know?"

"The whole damn story."

15

HE frowned and glanced at Ginette. I said: "I'll go bail for her; we're both security-minded."

He frowned again, then probably remembered that if she *wasn't* security-minded, he was sunk, anyway.

Ginette smiled distantly and pushed the cheese-board towards him. He shook his head briefly, then turned to me. "What do you know about Caspar *Aktiengesellschaft*, Mr Cane?"

"Just that it's a holding and marketing company, registered in Liechtenstein, that owns majorities in a lot of electronics firms in this end of Europe. And that you're something to do with it."

"Quite right—as far as it goes. I own thirty-three per cent of the corporation."

"One-third."

"*No*, Mr Cane." He allowed himself a two per cent smile —practically laughing out loud, for him. "Do you know the other advantage of Liechtenstein registration—apart from the tax advantages?"

I shrugged. "Secrecy of ownership, I suppose."

He nodded decorously. "Quite right. Nobody need know who owns a company. Let me explain: I own thirty-three per cent. The shares are divided thirty-three, thirty-three— and thirty-four."

By now he was begining to enjoy showing how ignorant I was.

I said: "So the thirty-four can out-vote you, or the third man, but not both. So who are they?"

"The other thirty-three per cent is held by a Liechtenstein resident, Herr Flez. He handles the day-to-day affairs of the company and conforms to the recent law that a Liechtenstein resident must be on the board of such companies." From the tone of his voice, I got the idea that Flez's worth was mainly that he conformed with the law.

When he stopped there, I said: "So—who owns the thirty-four per cent?"

"The problem, Mr Cane," he said, "is that we are not sure."

I took a sip of the Pinel which I found had been poured for me. It wasn't bad, but it wasn't much else.

I shook my head. "Sorry—I don't follow. As major shareholders, *you* can look at Caspar's books and see who owns shares." Then a new thought struck. "Or are we talking about *bearer* shares?"

He dipped his head gravely. "That is quite right."

"Jesus. I thought they'd gone out with chorus girls drinking champagne out of slippers. You really can count your troubles now, can't you?"

He got a little stiffer. "It was a question of secrecy. Any company must have managers handling certain parts of its affairs. And they have wives and friends to whom they might talk. With bearer shares——"

"I know all that." Bearer shares. Pieces of paper—share certificates—certifying ownership of so many shares in a certain company. But without an owner's name on the certificate, or in the company's books. Pieces of paper which belonged to anybody who happened to have them—unless somebody else could prove differently. No records of ownership, no stamp duty paid when they changed hands. So probably nothing to prove they'd changed just by somebody sticking his hand into somebody else's pocket.

I nodded. "All right—who *should* this thirty-four per cent belong to?"

He sighed gently. "The man who most wished to be secret. Max Heiliger."

I'd heard of him. I glanced at Ginette—and so had she. One of those misty, legendary background figures whose nephews get into the gossip columns—mainly because they're his nephews. But nothing about Heiliger himself— even if you could find out something. You might also find out he owned the paper you worked for.

Then suddenly I remembered something he *hadn't* managed to keep out of the papers.

"He's dead," I said. "Killed in a private plane crash up the Alps a week or so ago."

The smile was small and bleak. "That is the trouble, Mr Cane. A few days after Max was killed, a man appeared in Liechtenstein with Max's share certificate demanding an important change in Caspar's affairs. You understand that with his thirty-four per cent he can out-vote Herr Flez's thirty-three—unless I am there."

With bearer shares there can't be any voting by proxy. The only proof that you *are* a shareholder is if you're there waving your share certificate.

Maganhard went on: "Under the company's rules, any shareholder may call a meeting in Liechtenstein by giving not less than seven clear days' notice, midnight to midnight."

"When does that notice expire?"

"He called it for the soonest possible time. The meeting must begin at midnight tomorrow plus one minute. We have a little more than thirty-six hours."

I nodded. "Should be time enough. But even if it isn't—can't you call a meeting for seven days later and reverse his decision?"

"His proposal, Mr Cane, is to sell all of Caspar's holdings. *That* could never be retrieved."

I sipped at my glass. "Wants to cash the company in and run for the hills, does he? He doesn't exactly sound like a legal heir. Who is he?"

"According to Herr Flez, he called himself Galleron, a Belgian, from Brussels. I have never heard of him."

I glanced at Ginette; she shook her head. She hadn't heard of him, either.

Maganhard said coldly: "And even if a court decided that he was *not* entitled to this certificate, *that* would not bring back Caspar's holdings either."

I asked: "How much would Caspar's holdings be worth, now?"

He lifted his shoulders. "The companies we control are valued very low—because, of course, all the profit is directed to Caspar. But we would be selling not just our shares, but *control* of these companies. That might make the prices ten times what they are now. One might guess—at thirty million pounds."

After a time I wagged my head to show that I understood. I didn't, of course. You can't understand a sum like thirty million. Perhaps Maganhard and Heiliger and Flez hadn't really understood it, either. When you start playing around with that sort of money in dark corners, you shouldn't be surprised at the people you meet in dark corners.

"I see," I said. "Thirty-four per cent of that would keep a man in beer and cigarettes until his pension came due."

He stood up. "Do you now understand enough to get me to Liechtenstein safely?"

"At least I've got a better idea of the odds against it."

He bowed to Ginette, frowned at me, and went away.

Ginette shoved back from the table and swung to face me. "Well, Louis?"

"Well, Ginette?"

"What do you believe of this—fairy-tale?"

"Maganhard's story? I'll give you odds it's true. If he had any imagination, he'd have seen this sort of trouble coming."

"But this Belgian—Galleron—can he do this thing?"

"With bearer shares you can do damn nearly anything. They shift the burden of proof: you don't have to prove you own them—somebody's got to prove you don't. Jesus, the trouble these people go to just to make trouble for themselves."

She cocked her head at me, puzzled.

I said: "People like Heiliger—and Maganhard. They spend their lives wrapping up their money in bearer shares, Liechtenstein registrations, numbered Swiss bank accounts —all so that the tax man can't find it. Then they drop dead —and *nobody* can find it. Nobody inherits anything off these characters; the banks hang on to most of it. How d'you think Swiss banks get so rich? Some of them have still got Gestapo funds they've refused to reveal. You think they're keeping it for the Gestapo? The hell. They're just keeping it."

"I did not realize you knew so much about High Finance, Louis. You must be a millionaire by now—no?" She smiled at me. "I would like a cognac, please—and not a lecture on how the English would make it."

I gave her a look and went across to a tray of fat, dusty bottles that Maurice had left on the long sideboard. I found a 1914 Croizet and tried to pour but there was only a dribble left.

"Sorry," I said. I was, too; I would have liked a drop for myself. I don't much like the sweet modern brandies, but I've no prejudices against a 1914.

She frowned. "That bottle was opened only a week ago. I have taken perhaps a glass a day."

"Maybe Maurice has got the taste."

She tinkled the little bell. After a while, Maurice padded in. I walked away over into the patch of brilliant sunlight slanting through the french windows, and stared down into the valley, not listening.

The garden below the gravel terrace was a steep slope of coarse, close-cut grass ending in a mass of laurels and monkey-puzzle trees that hid the road. And up beyond it, the hazy blue hills on the far side of the Rhône, very calm and gentle. From here you couldn't see the dead men and crashed cars and the police running round biting each other's tails and sweating into telephones.

Ginette said: "All is solved, Louis. Maurice gave your friend Mr Lovell a glass—and he took several glasses."

I stood in the sunlight feeling as cold as a corpse's toes. She was smiling cheerfully.

"It only needed that," I said. "Only that."

16

HE looked like a man sitting out on the terrace in the sun, taking occasional small sips at a glass of whisky, chatting with Miss Jarman. And why should he look anything else? There was no reason why I should have expected to find him in a dark back room with the bottle tilted to his face. He didn't have to be a fast drinker. All he had to be was continuous. He'd go on sipping until he dissolved.

But that's the only difference.

His face had loosened up, and his wound didn't seem to be troubling him. He'd changed into a black wool shirt that hid the bandages. The girl, parked on another white-painted metal garden chair, was wearing a flame-coloured silk blouse, a skirt of expensive oatmeal tweed.

Harvey stood up as we came across. A smooth, balanced movement.

I said: "Turned out wet again, hasn't it?"

"It's been a long trip, so far." He smiled crookedly, and offered Ginette his chair. She shook her head politely and leant against a tall flowerpot in the shape of a Grecian urn.

I said: *So far* is right. We aren't there yet. We're starting at midnight."

He slanted his eyebrows. "Not spending the night?"

"I want to cross at Geneva at first light. Will you be ready?"

Miss Jarman was looking at me with a curious frown. "Do you think he should rest, with his wound? I think so."

Harvey said gently: "I don't think he meant that."

She frowned again. "Well, what did you mean, Mr Cane?"

"Tell us what you mean, Cane," Harvey said, still wearing his twisted smile.

"I mean the man's an alcoholic!" I snapped. "By midnight he'll be a puddle singing Sweet Nellie Dean!"

The Psychological Approach, of course.

The girl came out of her chair like a loosed spring. "Who

told you that?" she demanded. "Why shouldn't he have a drink? He got hurt!"

It surprised me. I hadn't quite expected her as Harvey's defence counsel. I calmed down a bit. "All right. So he got himself shot. But he's still a three-shifts-a-day boozer."

She turned to him. "Is that true, Harvey?"

He shrugged and smiled. "I just wouldn't know. I ain't been psychoanalysed except by Professor Cane here."

She swung back to me. "What makes *you* so sure, then?"

I shook my head wearily. "Just hang on and make your own analysis. By midnight he'll be as much use as a kid with a cap pistol."

He seemed to shudder—and the little revolver was pointing at my stomach. The glass in his left hand was quite steady. Half a bottle of 1914 brandy and a layer of Scotch on top must have slowed him up a little—but at least he hadn't reached the stage when your resistance to alcohol cracks and you can hit the stratosphere on just two glasses.

I let out a long breath and stared down at the gun. "You must try that sometime when I'm *expecting* to have guns pulled on me by my friends."

He chuckled. "Like midnight?"

He slid the gun back into his belt-holster and pulled his shirt down over it.

Then he seemed to notice the silence.

For some time nobody said anything. Then Ginette brought her hand from behind her back and flipped a small gardening hand-fork into a flowerbed. It hit spikes first with a small crisp *thud*. Harvey's eyes opened a little wider.

She said calmly: "I was playing these sort of games before you were, Mr Lovell—and when they mattered a great deal more."

Harvey looked carefully round at each of us. Miss Jarman was watching him with a slight, perplexed frown. Then he drained his glass quickly and nodded. "I get it. Maybe the Professor was being a bit more subtle than I figured. So—what d'you do now, Professor? Sit on my hands the rest of the day?"

"You could take a couple of pills and get to bed."

"You don't want to stick around and play watchdog?"

117

I shook my head. Miss Jarman said: "Harvey—is it *true*?"

He banged the glass down on the metal table. "If the Professor says so." Then he walked in through the french windows, and his face was a mask again.

There was another silence. Then Ginette unpropped herself from the flowerpot-urn and held out her hand.

"A cigarette, please, Louis."

I dealt her one and lit one myself. She started to walk slowly down on to the sloping lawn. Miss Jarman hung back, staring at the french windows where Harvey had gone.

"Shouldn't somebody go and—and keep an eye on him?" she asked doubtfully.

I shrugged. "I'm not stopping you. But that's what he wants: somebody to sit and criticize him, somebody he can blame for something, somebody he can pull a gun on. Somebody to play the enemy. He doesn't want to remember that he's all alone with the enemy."

"Professor Cane," she said flatly. "Your Problems Solved While You Wait."

"Not solved; just diagnosed. Like the doctor who told the man with rheumatics to get himself turned into a mouse because mice don't have rheumatics, I don't bother with details."

I could hear the next question whistling down at me like a bomb. I'd just got the direction wrong: it was Ginette who asked it.

"How do you cure him, Louis?"

I took a deep drag on the cigarette. "You smash his life," I said slowly. "You destroy it—his past, his work, everything you can get your hands on. They have a fancier name for it than that, of course—but that's what they do."

"Why do you need to do that?" Ginette sounded a bit too calm, like a prompter at the edge of the stage. Maybe that's what she was.

"Like you burn a house where you've had the plague in. There's a germ in there somewhere. So you burn everything: furniture, carpets, beds—the lot. It's the same with an alcoholic: something in his life made him a drinker. So, you smash up the life. Maybe, at the end of that, he won't be one any more."

Miss Jarman said coldly: "I don't believe it."

I shrugged and took another drag on the cigarette and pitched it into the laurels.

She said: "They must know something better than that by now."

"The miracles of modern medicine, eh? A few years ago, most doctors would have looked on him as a moral failure and told him to snap out of it—and then reckoned they'd done a good day's work. By now they've got this far. They don't yet know what causes it, in most cases. They just know enough to burn the house down. Progress."

Ginette said: "And they call that a cure?"

"No. I'll grant them that—they don't call it a cure. That'd be putting him back to taking a beer at lunch-time, a martini at six o'clock—and able to leave it at that. They can't do that. They just unhook him from the stuff; stop him drinking for ever. But at least they don't call it a cure."

Miss Jarman said softly: "Is that all they can do?" Then she turned on Ginette. "Is that true?"

"My dear child," Ginette said gravely, "if I could tell when Louis was telling the truth I might have married him fifteen years ago."

I gave her a sharp look, then said to the girl: "But just remember what life you'd be smashing, for Harvey. He's a bodyguard. If he keeps that up, he isn't likely to die in bed, anyway, sober *or* drunk."

She pounced. "Is that his trouble?"

"I don't know. As I said—most times nobody knows the trouble, not unless a man's had deep pyschoanalysis. And personally, I'd say that was just another way of burning the house down. But if you want to guess at causes, Harvey's killed a number of men in his time—and he knows he's going to kill more. Not everybody finds that easy to live with. Anyway," and I resumed my normal level of tact, "why should you care?"

Her chin came up. "I like him."

"You didn't yesterday. You thought we were a couple of Hollywood gangsters."

"I've changed my mind about *him*." Then her eyes became worried. "No, I'm sorry. I was wrong about both of you. But you know him—can't you help him?"

I shook my head. "I'm part of his old life. Two days ago I didn't know him from Abou Ben Adhem, but I'm still part of it. He connects me with guns; if they have to go, so do I."

She stood for a moment, arms folded and hugging herself tightly, staying very still and staring sightlessly down the long lawn. Then she suddenly unfolded. "I'm going back to —to talk to him." She turned.

I said quickly: "He knows all this himself. He stayed dry for three days up to now, because he knows he can't mix guns and booze. So he's not fooling himself; he knows the way out. All he needs is a good reason to take it. Just stopping killing may not be enough."

"What do you mean?"

"Just why a man becomes an alcoholic doesn't always matter much. Alcohol becomes a cause on its own. So he needs a reason to stop—not just no reason to go on."

Her eyes searched my face. Then she nodded slowly, and walked away and into the Château.

17

GINETTE watched her go. "Were you trying to tell her to become his reason, Louis?"

I shrugged. "Just telling her you don't dry a man out with a couple of church pamphlets and a cup of cocoa."

"And is it really true, there is no cure?"

"One in a hundred, they say. That many they can send back to normal drinking. But they don't know how or why. Should I have told her that?"

She shook her head thoughtfully. "No. I do not think she believed you, anyway. She is young enough to believe in miracles. Perhaps even young enough to perform them." She looked at me. "And is he one in a hundred, Louis?"

"He's one in several million already. How many people become bodyguards—and as good as he is? He's rated the third best in Paris." Then I remembered. "Second best, I suppose now, with Bernard dead."

She gave me a hard look. "If he remembers that himself, it may not help him."

I just nodded. She was right—and it wasn't something Harvey was likely to forget.

She started walking around the edge of the coarse lawn. I dropped into step beside her.

"And where do they rate you nowadays, Louis?"

"I'm not a gunman," I said coldly.

"Ah—of course. You are a general now. Not just the man who carries the gun. You tell them where to have the gun-fights. Perhaps you think it is not the same battle?—that in the end it will not eat you, too?

"You see," she said, "by now I know how gunmen think. That they can never be beaten. Like the fighter pilots. Like the knights in armour, always looking for the next dragon. Always—until the last dragon. And always there is a last. Both Lambert—and you."

"I'm still not a gunman, Ginette."

"Neither was Lambert. Did you know how Lambert died?"

"I read in the papers. A sailing accident down near Spain."

"Did you believe that, Louis?"

I shrugged. It had seemed odd, but I hadn't had anything else to believe.

She went on: "We kept a boat down near Montpellier— where you and Lambert used to collect the guns they landed from Gibraltar and North Africa, in the *feluccas*. And perhaps once a year, he would go out with some old friends, to do a little smuggling. Some tobacco from Tangier, perhaps, or coffee or motor parts for Spain. Not for much profit; just so that he did not grow old too quietly. But one time, the Spanish coastguard was more awake. They machine-gunned the boat. It was most unsporting—but possibly nobody told them he was doing it for the sport?"

I just waved my head meaninglessly.

She said quietly: "In the newspapers, he was caught in a storm. He was a Comte, of course, and a Resistance hero—so they found a storm for him. It was very kind. But even for him, there was the last dragon."

After a while, I said: "I'm not doing this for the sport."

"Perhaps—but why are you doing it?"

"Because I was hired to do it. It's my job."

"What *are* you now? You never became a lawyer?"

"No, not in the end. After the war, and then my time with the Paris embassy——"

"You were in the British Secret Service there," she said, gently reproving. "We all knew."

"I *know* you all knew, damn it. That's why I quit eventually."

"But, Louis, we thought it was so kind of London to send a spy whom we all knew and liked." A bland smile. "I'm sorry—please go on."

"Not much further to go. I had a lot of contacts over here. I knew quite a lot of European law, and as I was pretending to be one of the Commercial Attaché's people I was already getting asked about business problems. So I set up as a sort

122

of business agent: putting people in touch with people, advising them, doing some legal work."

"And also some illegal work?"

"No." I lit a cigarette, then remembered to offer her one. She shook her head. "No—it doesn't have to be. There's still a lot of help and advice a lawyer can't, or won't, give— and it doesn't have to be illegal. Hell, it's even legal to kill a man who's trying to kill you, anywhere in Europe. But you try and get a lawyer to do it for you."

"So then one calls on Monsieur Cane and Monsieur Lovell?"

"If you can't get anybody better."

She smiled her half-sad smile. "I'm sure Monsieur Maganhard would take only the best to fight his fights."

I stopped dead and said very deliberately: "Ginette— Harvey and I were hired to keep Maganhard alive. Bernard was hired to kill him. There's a difference; there's a damn *big* difference."

"Even with a man like Maganhard?"

I shook my head angrily. "You don't like Maganhard. All right—I don't much like him myself. But in this, he's in the *right*. He's not trying to kill anybody—but somebody's trying to kill him. And if Harvey and I hadn't been along, he'd have been dead by now. That's quite a decision to take."

"You did not have that decision."

"I don't know," I said slowly. "Maybe I did have it. Maybe if I believed that Harvey and I could get him through alive, then I had to believe that if we didn't go, he wouldn't get through alive. Once you've become a man like me, you can't just step aside. That's a decision in itself."

"Yes," she said quietly, not looking at me but staring out across the valley. "Yes—you believed that you, only you, could fight this dragon. And the next also. And the next. So you will never step aside. And so there will one day be the last one."

I said harshly: "I'm a professional. When Lambert took that boat out, he was an amateur; he'd been growing grapes for fifteen years. If I'd been in that boat, it either wouldn't have sailed—or it wouldn't have got sunk."

"Oh yes," she nodded dreamily. "Yes, he was an amateur

123

by then. Almost enough of an amateur to step aside, not to go."

Then she looked at me and smiled her sad half-smile and said: "I killed Lambert."

I said: "You're crazy."

"No. I could have stopped him going. But I believed I was doing a woman's job—not interfering. And I also believed that it would never happen to him, not this time. Perhaps next time—but perhaps I believed there would never be a next time. You see?—I can also think like a gunman. I could have stopped him—but I let him go, so I killed him."

I moved my face stiffly in a lot of pointless expressions.

She said slowly: "So I was wrong. And so perhaps I was wrong in another way . . . I married Lambert because I believed, with him, the war would be over. With you—when you stopped being Caneton you went immediately into the Secret Service. Your war was not over."

I nodded vaguely. Maybe so.

"I did not know then that it was *my* work to see that the war was over. So I should have gone with you, instead, and stopped you fighting your war." She looked at me steadily. "I wanted to, Louis, I wanted to."

My face felt as stiff as a stone post. It isn't every day the only woman who ever mattered to you tells you she was wrong in marrying someone else—and is maybe telling you it isn't too late yet. If you're lucky, it happens just one day in a lifetime. And on the day you're booked to haul a rich tax-dodger to Liechtenstein.

I shook my head. "You were right first time, Ginette. With me—I'd have been off playing games with people like Maganhard or——"

"Pardon me, but you would bloody well not."

I looked at her quickly; she seemed very calm, very certain. Maybe a bit too much so.

"It was fifteen years ago," I said.

"You believe you have changed so much in that time?"

I scowled. "All right, maybe I haven't changed enough: I'm still Caneton. But it's too late to change that now. I'm

124

too old to go back and start learning to be a lawyer and how to do legal things like getting film stars out of drunk-driving charges."

"You would not have to go back. There is work here: Clos Pinel needs a manager."

Just like that.

The garden was quiet around us, as quiet as it ever gets in the south, with just the dull chirping of cicadas that you can't believe even cicadas listen to. The sun was a flare of white light drifting towards the blue hills, and leaving just a hint of the faint burnt smell of summer. And all I had to say was Yes.

But there were other hills: the green, misty damp slopes of Switzerland. And I'd said Yes to them three days ago.

I said: "I've got a job, Ginette. One that I'm good at."

"I am not offering you charity, Louis. You would work very damn hard in this business."

"Would I have to learn to love Pinel?"

"It would not be much more illegal than your work now."

I shook my head slowly. "I've still got a job."

"You would be good at it," she said rapidly. "We want your contacts, your experience of business and the law. We export everywhere now, to London, to——"

"Ginette!" Her voice had had a hard brittle edge that in anyone else I'd have called fear.

She held herself very still, her head up, her eyes tight shut.

I took a step and put my arms round her and her body reached against me, hard and trembling. Her face lifted to mine.

A pistol cracked in the Château.

18

I WAS saying: "Nobody fires just one shot to kill a man; always two. And if he'd killed Harvey, there'd be Maganhard, or Harvey if he'd killed Maganhard. Tell me I'm right—quick."

She was crouched, too, down beside the laurels at the edge of the lawn. Old reactions die hard.

"It's your drunken friend Harvey shooting up the bottles in the Wild West saloon."

I'd guessed that, too, but it didn't make me feel any better. Why should he stop at bottles? And I still wasn't carrying the Mauser.

I stood up reluctantly and walked across the gravel towards the front door. It felt as wide as the desert.

Inside the front hall three people were standing as stiff as a waxworks tableau. Harvey was leaning against the wall on my right, with the gun pointing vaguely down towards his own feet but not looking any less dangerous because of that. Maurice was backed up against the opposite wall, staring at Harvey with a look about as friendly as a hungry vulture. Miss Jarman was just standing. The phone was off its hook and lying on the floor.

The gun twitched my way as I came in. I said: "Put that damn thing away. What's happened here?"

Harvey said: "I just kind of don't like men attacking women—you know?" His voice was carefully languid, but a bit thick, as if he was having to pick each word one at a time. Probably he was, by now.

"Well, it's over now. Get back to your bottle." I turned to Maurice. "*Pourquoi*——"

Harvey said carefully: "I heard her yell so I came out and there was this guy fighting with her."

Miss Jarman said: "I was just trying to use the telephone, when——"

"*Who to?*"

126

She stared innocently at me, eyes wide. "To . . . a friend.
I thought——"

I took a couple of quick steps and picked up the phone.
"*Qui est*——" But the line was dead by now. I slammed it
back.

"I put a security blackout on the use of this phone," I
said. "Maurice was just interpreting that for me. Call it a
misunderstanding. All right—*who* were you ringing?"

"A friend." Her chin was up and she had the girls'
boarding-school expression on her face. *She* wasn't telling
who put frogs in the Latin mistress's bed.

"All right," I said again. "But if you're selling us out,
remember the methods they've used so far: you stand as
good a chance of stopping a bullet as anybody. Maybe
better, if they don't get me with the first shot."

Harvey had straightened up off the wall. "And kind of
what the hell are you talking about?"

I swung round. I'd had just about enough of him and his
thirst and his tendency to pull his gun on the wrong people.
Maybe he wouldn't get his gun up level before I'd broken
his wrist for him . . .

Ginette said: "Give Louis the gun or I will kill you."

We both looked. She was standing in the shadows at the
back of the hall, leaning stiffly against the wall, with the
Mauser held in both hands out in front of her.

"It is on automatic, Mr Lovell," she added.

"You wouldn't fire that thing in here," he said slowly.
He studied her carefully: the way she was holding it meant
she knew what she was holding—and he could see that.

She said contemptuously: "Bet your life on it, then."

He took a long breath. A gunman believes he can never
be beaten—but he knows damn well when he has been.
She had the Mauser aimed low, to allow for the kick.
Whatever he did now, he'd get filleted like a fish if she
pulled that trigger.

He tossed me his gun.

Ginette said: "Thank you. Please remember I have the
exclusive shooting rights in my own home. Where did that
bullet go, Maurice?"

He indicated a hole in the wall near the telephone.

Ginette came up to us and offered me the Mauser. I shook my head. "It's over now. I'll get him to bed." I stuck his gun in my pocket.

Harvey was watching me with a faraway look and a twist of cynical amusement at the edge of his mouth. "I could take you even without a gun," he offered.

I shrugged. "Maybe. We've both been through unarmed-combat school. It wouldn't prove anything."

He nodded and started towards the stairs. I said to Miss Jarman: "Get whatever bottle he was using."

"Don't you think he's had enough?" She was still back in the fifth-form dormitory.

I shook my head wearily. "It doesn't matter what you or I think. Just get the bottle."

I followed Harvey upstairs. At the top we met Maganhard; Harvey pushed straight past without seeming to notice him. Maganhard gave him a steely look that turned immediately into a suspicious glare. He turned to me and seemed about to say something—but I pushed past as well.

In his bedroom, Harvey yanked the silk cover straight off the bed and dropped face down on to it, all in one movement. After a moment or two he rolled on his back. It took an effort.

"Maybe I'm tired." He sounded faintly surprised.

Behind me, Miss Jarman came in with a bottle of Queen Anne whisky and a glass. I took the bottle; from the weight, he'd been working on it hard.

She asked: "What are you going to do?"

"Get him ready for tomorrow." I poured a small dose into a glass.

"With that?"

"It's what he usually gets ready for tomorrow on." I gave him the glass. She stared at him, then me. "You don't really care, do you?"

"Who were you ringing?"

She glared. "Perhaps one day you'll know." She slammed the door as she went out.

Harvey raised his glass to me, and sipped. "You honestly think she's selling us out?"

"Somebody is."

"I kind of hope not," he said thoughtfully. "She's a nice kid."

"It's mutual. She wants to cure you."

"I noticed." He sipped again. "And you don't care?" He watched me with his little cynical smile.

"Not my business. After tomorrow, you and I daren't meet. You know that."

"I know." He emptied the glass.

I stretched out my hand for it. "More?"

He shrugged his shoulders on the pillow. "I guess so."

I walked back to the bottle on the dressing-table. He said: "If I'm a good boy, do I get my gun back?"

"Sorry; I'd forgotten." I'd been hoping he'd remind me. I took out the little revolver, swung the cylinder, and poked out the empty cartridge. "Got any more rounds?"

"Coat pocket."

His jacket was hung on a chair. I got my back to him and groped in both side pockets. I got a fresh cartridge with one hand, and a bottle I hoped was his sleeping pills with the other. I slid the round into the gun, closed it up, and tossed it on to the foot of the bed.

By the time he'd reached for it, checked it over just as I knew he would, as any gunman would after somebody else had handled his gun, there were three tablets at the bottom of his glass. I didn't know just what they were, or what dose they should have been; I *did* know that mixing two depressants like alcohol and barbiturates isn't a good idea. But it was less risk than he'd meet tomorrow if he finished off that bottle tonight.

I poured whisky on top and gave it a moment to dissolve them by going to find a glass of my own over by the washbasin. A bit of cloudiness wouldn't show through the cut glass tumbler, and by now his sense of taste would be shot.

I poured my own drink and gave him his.

"You're an understanding sort of bastard," he said slowly. "Or maybe you're just a bastard. Understanding somebody is a pretty lousy thing to do to him." He turned his head wearily and looked up at me. "Well, you're the Professor, and hear I am on the couch. D'you want me to tell you my dreams?"

I sat down on the chair with his jacket slung over the back. "Could I stand them?"

"Maybe. They ain't fun, but you get used to them."

"D'you get used to how you feel in the mornings?"

"No. But you can't remember how bad it was, ever. Still, if you thought tomorrow was as important as today, you wouldn't be a—a drinker, would you?"

"You're over-simplifying," I said. "You want to think you're basically different in outlook from everybody else. You aren't. You just drink more, that's all."

By now the pill bottle was back in his jacket pocket.

He smiled. "That's good head-shrinking, Professor. But you want to know the worst thing? You don't taste it any more. That's all. You just don't taste it." He sipped and held the glass up to the light and stared through it. "You just remember going into some place in Paris where they know how to mix a real martini. Get in there around noon, before the rush starts, so they'll have time to do it right. They like that: they like a guy who really cares about a good drink—so for him, they get it right. Mix it careful and slow, and then you drink it the same way. They like that, too. They don't have to think you're going to buy another one. Just once in a time they like to meet a guy who'll make them do some real work and appreciate it when they've done it. Pretty sad people, barmen."

He took a gulp at his drink and went back to watching the ceiling. His voice was slow and quiet and he wasn't talking to me and perhaps not even to himself. Just to a door that had closed on him a long time ago.

"Just cold enough to make the glass misty," he said softly. "Not freezing; you can make anything taste as if it might be good by making it freezing. That's the secret of how to run America, if you want to know it, Cane. And no damn olives or onions in it, either. Just a kind of smell like summer." He moved his head on the pillow. "I haven't had a martini in an elephant's age. You don't taste it. Now—now all you think of is the next one. Christ, but I'm tired."

He stretched an arm to put the tumbler on the bedside table, missed, and it thumped on the carpet, spilling a few drops.

I stood up. His eyes were closed. I put down my own glass and moved softly towards the door. I had my hand on the knob when he said: "I'm sorry, Cane. Thought I could last it out."

"You lasted. It was the job that stretched."

After a few moments he said: "Maybe . . . And maybe if I hadn't got hit . . . Probably not, though." Then he turned his head and looked at me. "You said something back there: that I wasn't basically different from anybody else. I kill people, Professor."

"You could give it up."

He smiled very slowly and wearily. "But not until after tomorrow—is that right?"

After a few more moments, I went out. I felt as noble and helpful as the spilled dregs on the carpet.

Maganhard and Ginette were standing at the top of the stairs looking as if they'd been trying to find something polite to say to each other but not getting far. Maganhard swung round as I came along and forgot about politeness.

"You didn't tell me Mr Lovell was a drinker."

"I didn't know myself until after we'd started." I leant against the banisters and reached for a cigarette.

"Then I will speak to Merlin about this. I could have been killed just because——"

"Shut up, Maganhard," I said wearily. "We've lived through yesterday and today, and if you don't think that's an achievement, then you didn't know what was going on. We couldn't have done more with anybody else. Now go to bed."

"I have not had my dinner yet," he said huffily. He had Austrian blood in him, all right.

Ginette said soothingly: "Maurice will serve you very soon, Herr Maganhard. He will give you a drink now, if you wish."

He gave me a stare that he'd been keeping at the back of the freezer compartment, then marched downstairs, his back very straight.

I stayed leaning on the banisters, found my matches, and

lit the cigarette. "I'd forgotten dinner. I thought today had gone on long enough already."

"Is that the way the Agency Cane usually treats its clients?"

"Pretty usual. I told you I didn't have to like them."

"I think you had better take the work here—quickly."

I looked at her, but she didn't meet it. She just propped herself against the banisters beside me; the movement brought her hands up in front of her, and she seemed to notice that she still had the Mauser.

She looked it over. "Do you remember, Louis, what these once meant to us? Liberation . . . freedom . . .words like that?"

"I remember."

"Perhaps things have changed since then." She sighted the gun casually down the stairway, her thumb sweeping instinctively over the safety catch and the single/automatic button. She knew about Mausers.

"Pistols haven't changed."

"You believe the Resistance was always just pistols—not the words?"

"Nothing is ever just pistols; men don't die by guns alone. Guns always need words behind them, telling them they're doing the right thing."

She glanced quickly at me. Maybe I'd sounded a little sour; maybe I *was* a little sour, thinking of riding north at midnight and the state Harvey would be in then. And perhaps wishing it wasn't all just to save a man like Maganhard from a few deaths, a few taxes.

Or maybe I was just feeling old and tired.

"In the war," she said thoughtfully, "we never asked if we were right. The answer was too easy. But—perhaps sometimes we were wrong. We helped make men like Bernard and Alain." She lowered the gun. "You believe because your Maganhard is right, you must be right?"

I said cautiously: "Something like that."

But she just nodded to herself. After a while she said: "But perhaps your next Maganhard will be wrong—and you will not have stepped aside."

It wasn't a new idea; it was an old familiar ghost at the

back of my mind, that I remembered only when I was feeling tired and low. On the nights when you dream of the faces of men you knew and who are dead.

I'd been right about Maganhard. I'd trusted Merlin and Maganhard himself and my own judgement—and I'd been right. But one day, I could be wrong. One day I'd have a client as crooked as a mountain road and the men jumping up in ambush would be plain-clothes cops . . .

A lawyer can say his client deceived him. But I'd be standing there with the Mauser warm in my hand.

I shook my head wearily. "Maybe, Ginette. But not this time. And next time is next time."

"There is going to be a next time?" She was watching me with her steady sad eyes, with the glint of lamplight on her chestnut hair, like the sheen of old, polished wood.

"Ginette—it's fifteen years. You aren't in love with me."

"I do not know," she said simply. "All I can do is remember, and wait—and perhaps make sure you do not get killed."

"I'm not going to get——" I knew it was the wrong thing as soon as I'd said it.

But she said: "No—tell me it won't happen. That it can't, not to you, not to Caneton." And her fight was over. If I was going on, then she wanted to believe it could never happen to me; that if there had to be dragons, there would never be a last one. She wanted to think like a gunman—again. And forget that she had believed it before—and been wrong.

I winced. I should never have come back. Fifteen years I'd stayed away from this quiet house where she had tried, so hard, to find an end to war. And when I'd come back, it had only been because I was still at war.

"You can't be sure," I said slowly. "In the end, it depends on me."

"I know." She nodded and smiled gently. "I remember."

There were footsteps on the stairs. Maurice was walking carefully up, carrying a loaded tray, including a bottle in a wicker cradle.

I said: "Harvey won't want anything. He's probably asleep already."

She straightened up from the banisters, moving with the lazy grace of a cat. "I told Maurice you and I would have dinner in my room."

I stared at her, then opened my mouth. She shook her head. "The argument is over, Louis. You are going on; I understand. That is all."

There were a thousand reasons why not—but suddenly I couldn't remember any of them. Only that I'd been away so long.

"I'll come back," I said thickly.

She smiled her half-sad smile. "Don't promise anything, Louis. I am not asking for promises."

She walked down the corridor after Maurice. After a moment I followed.

19

We headed north on the N92. We were in the same Citroën delivery van, with Ginette and I sharing the driving. And a stack of crated bottles across the back of the van to block anybody's view of the other three passengers if the rear doors were opened.

We'd practically had to pour Harvey aboard. He'd been in a deep, drugged sleep, and by now was probably in it again; we'd dumped a couple of old mattresses and a few blankets in there. But I'd guessed Maganhard wasn't asleep even before he stuck his little iron voice out of the window behind my neck.

"How are we entering Switzerland, Mr Cane?"

"We are going up to near a place called Gex, just a few miles north-west of Geneva. We'll drop off there and just walk across near the airport."

He tasted this and—as I'd expected—didn't much like it. "I understand we must arrive in a big town where we can hire a car, but why not go to Evian and cross the lake by boat to Lausanne?"

"Because that's exactly the sort of tricky thing they'd expect us to do. The Geneva frontier's what we want: it's almost impossible to guard. There's about twenty different roads going across, and most of the frontier's farmland. We'll just walk through."

"It must have been guarded in the war," he objected.

"Sure, but even then you'd be surprised at the number who got across. The Swiss kept a big internment camp up there, all ready for them."

"Mr Cane," he said coldly, "if we arrive in a Swiss jail, it will not be any better than being in a French jail."

"Probably a lot cleaner. But I'm hoping the Swiss police won't be looking for us: they can't do anything until the French ask for it—and the French may not want to admit they might have missed us. Not just yet."

I had a private hope that we might break the line of evidence here—out-run the ripples again. If we could cross the border unseen and leave the Gendarmerie believing we were still in France, we'd have done it. A lot depended on whether or not they'd identified the wrecked Citroën DS as Maganhard's. I was pretty sure they must have found it by now: the extra shooting and the wrecked Renault would have started them combing the area more thoroughly than I'd first expected.

In one way, I hoped they *had* identified it. It would switch suspicion away from the northern route from Paris, but it might also convince them that we were stuck somewhere, hiding out, without transport. I wasn't worried about them thinking of the old Rat-line or Clos Pinel: they wouldn't think of them unless they knew I was involved—and I still believed they didn't know about me.

Unless Harvey had loused up cleaning the car and they'd got a set of my fingerprints. But they wouldn't know they *were* mine—I'd never been arrested in France. Or had the *Deuxième Bureau* taken the trouble of getting my prints when I was "attached to the Embassy" in Paris? They'd known about me, of course. And if they knew about me now, they might think of the old Resistance routes across the Geneva frontier . . .

I shook my head. You can get too clever with any police force, as well as too stupid. You've got it all worked out that they must have heard of X so they'll have stopped watching Y. And you roll up at Y, straight into their loving arms—all because the report about X has been sitting on the Superintendent's desk for three hours and nobody's remembered to tell him about it.

It's the same as systems at roulette: the wheel ain't heard of them. I'd decided to cross at Geneva. That was still the number to put my money on.

The night droned past us. Beside me, Ginette swung the big flat wheel like a *routier*, her face now and then lit by the reflection of the headlights. I lit a cigarette and watched her, serene and controlled, as the van buzzed up the steepening road into the Savoie.

"If you get stopped," I asked, "what's your story?"

"I shall deliver some wine in Geneva, anyway: two restaurants there take Pinel. And there is a good one in Gex. I will try to sell some there first, after I have had breakfast."

"Why did you have to arrive there so early?"

"Because, *Monsieur le Gendarme,* I have an appointment at Pinel soon after lunch."

"And have you?"

"I told Maurice to fix one—a safe one."

"And you still think you need a manager?"

She smiled faintly. "I need somebody to look after the wine while I look after the old Resistance friends who come through."

"Touché."

Soon after that, I fell asleep. I woke up as we came into the *zone franche* and started skirting round, with the frontier a kilometre or two on our right, to approach Geneva from the north-west.

She should have woken me: I'd missed my turn at the wheel. But it would have been hypocritical to complain. Liechtenstein was still nearly four hundred kilometres away; it could be a long day yet.

Ginette said: "I think we are close, Louis."

She'd turned right a few kilometres before Gex and was heading down towards Ferney-Voltaire, just about on the frontier.

"Don't get too near," I said. The cops were likely to be prowling well inside the frontier, not just on it. And I didn't want them to wonder about a van that they heard come close, stop, and go back.

She said: "Here, then," and drew up. She kept the engine running. I swung down, ran round and opened the doors at the back. Somebody started pulling the crates of wine aside. Maganhard stepped down, then the girl. Then Harvey.

He was like somebody who'd been dragged out of the rubble of a bombed building. Weaving and staggering and shaking his head and then obviously wishing he hadn't. As a gunman, he looked just about fit enough to tackle a rather tired kitten.

I shut the doors quietly and went back to the cab. "Thanks, Ginette. On your way."

She reached across to my window. "Look after yourself, Louis—please."

"I'll let you know. Probably tonight."

"Please."

We touched hands, and then the van was growling off into the night. I waved a hand at the roadside. "Over there, into the field. Quick."

"Quick" was a pretty optimistic word for this crew. It took us a full minute to get through the hedge and up to our shins in long, dew-soaked grass. The only thing you could count on in this job was getting your feet wet every twelve hours.

I'd insisted on leaving all the luggage except my briefcase back at Pinel—and I'd only hung on to that because of the Mauser and the maps. I took it in one hand, grabbed Harvey's arm with the other, and led off along the hedge.

The van's engine died in the distance. The night was cold and thick, without stars. The weather we'd left behind in Brittany had caught up with us again, but at least it seemed to have dropped all its rain already. Ahead, there was an intermittent glow, alternately white and green, reflecting on the low clouds. The Geneva-Cointrin airport beacon. I headed towards it.

It was a quarter to five; three-quarters of an hour to first light.

For a time nobody said anything. We weren't walking very quietly, but you can't teach people to make no noise just by telling them not to. It takes practice. But the heavy damp air meant that sounds wouldn't carry far.

The girl said softly: "What's that?"

I snapped my head around, but *that* was just a big dark house on the horizon a few hundred yards away, with a line of trees leading up to it.

"Voltaire's château." I wished I'd remembered it myself: it was a useful landmark.

She lifted a foot from the grass, shook it, scattering drops of moisture. "How about a pithy quotation from the master?" she said softly but sourly. "Such as 'All's for the best in this best of all possible worlds'?"

"Or *Dieu est toujours pour les gros bataillons.*"

"Somehow, I don't find that very encouraging."

"Jesus," Harvey said thickly, "are we on a literary coach tour or crossing a frontier quietly?"

"You mean you'd notice the difference?" I said, and started moving again.

Right then, Harvey wasn't my best friend. Awake and without his hangover, he could have looked after Maganhard—telling him when to move, when to stay still—leaving me just to do the same for Miss Jarman. As it was, I had to worry about all three of them—and particularly about how Harvey would react to trouble. For all I knew, he might be dopey enough to pull a gun and start shooting down gendarmes.

What I'd thought had been a hedge ahead turned into an orchard of small neat apple trees, growing just over head-high. And a fence of plain wire strands. The leaves weren't out yet—we were back in the northern spring up here—but the branches had been pruned so that they grew in close tangles, and the trees themselves were crowded together to make the most of the ground. In the dark, they gave plenty of cover from view.

But that works both ways. If I'd been commanding a frontier guard, I'd have posted a squad in that orchard. Spread them out a bit, tell them to stay still and quiet, and we could walk over them before we knew they were there.

And if I was commanding a real frontier-running party, I wouldn't be leading them through any orchards. We'd go round, and we'd do it on our bellies. What I *was* commanding—if that was the word—was a middle-aged businessman, a girl in a sealskin coat, and a gunman with a five-star hangover. I was dreading the moment when I had to tell that sealskin coat to get down and crawl in the mud.

We were going through the orchard.

I turned to the girl and asked softly: "Were you ever captain of the school?"

"No." A surprised whisper. "I wasn't good enough at hockey or anything."

"Congratulations. Well, you're captain of those two now. Bring them about ten yards behind me—keep me in view down the line of trees. When I stop, you stop. If I turn off, you turn off immediately—don't come up to where I turned. You see what I mean?"

"Ye-es. But shouldn't it be Harvey——?"

"It *should* be," I said grimly. "But as things are, I'd rather it was you. All right?"

She nodded. I stood on one strand of wire, pulled up another, and they climbed through without much more noise than a bad car crash. I moved out ahead and started through the precise files of trees.

I made twenty yards, then thirty, then forty. In among the trees, it was lighter than I'd expected. And when I looked back, the girl had used the light, and her head, and was keeping them further behind than the ten yards I'd specified.

I made fifty yards, and guessed I must be in the middle of the orchard by now. I looked ahead for the skyline between the trees that would mark the next fence, but all I could see was the regular glow of the beacon.

I stopped. It took me a moment to think why, and in that moment the three behind me sounded a stampede of wild elephants. Then they stopped. And I knew why I had: a faint scent of tobacco smoke.

The sergeant would have told them not to smoke, of course—but that had probably been back around midnight, five hours ago. Cold, wet, dull hours. So you lie down on your side and strike a match under your jacket, then keep the burning end hidden in the grass, leaning down to take a puff. But you can't hide the smell.

But where was it coming from? I licked a finger and held it up to test the wind, and, as usual, it felt cold all the way round. I breathed out, but it wasn't cold enough to condense my breath. All I knew was that there hadn't been much wind out in the field and there was even less among the trees.

Next move, please.

I tried to remember the voice of an ex-sergeant of the Foreign Legion who'd instructed on small arms to the Resistance in the Auvergne, and bellowed: *"Il y a un idiot*

140

qui fume! C'est comme un bistro, ici! Où êtes-vous?"

There was a startled rustling ahead on my right, then a hush that was almost as loud.

I tiptoed gently away to the left. When I looked back, Miss Jarman was moving them parallel to me.

I let out another shout of: *"Où est l'idiot qui fume?"* in the hope that if they realized I was moving away from them the last thing they'd do would be to answer or come and find me.

We moved sideways almost to the edge of the orchard, then I turned back towards the airport beacon. After another forty yards, I could see a hedge. I turned back to bring up the other three.

Miss Jarman whispered: "I thought *we* were making a noise—until I heard you."

"We nearly walked into a squad of gendarmes. Sounding like the sergeant is a good password." I nodded at the hedge. "There's a road there, and a French customs post just down on the right. It's a straight road and we've got to cross without being spotted." I turned to Harvey. "How are you feeling?"

"I think I died. Does God know you're starting the Resurrection early?"

I grinned and began to feel a bit better myself. His voice was still thick, but it had lost the dull petulant tone. He was beginning to think again. I led the way to the hedge.

When we'd found a place we could crawl through, I stuck out my head. The customs post was there all right, hardly more than a hundred yards away. A small bungalow flooded with light, with a couple of parked cars, and several people just standing around.

At that distance they wouldn't hear us—but we'd be crossing straight into the glare of the airport beacon, throwing out its several-thousand-candlepower only a few hundred yards away by now. And some of the men at that bungalow would be there just to keep a watch up this road.

I pulled my head back. "Sorry. We're going to have to move a bit back up the road before we cross."

Behind us, somebody called softly: *"Qui va là?"*

Miss Jarman whispered: "It looked as if your password's worn off."

She was right. By now it must have struck them as odd that the sergeant *hadn't* found them. By now they were looking for him. Now, we had to cross where we were.

Up the road, in the opposite direction from the customs post, an engine hummed. Then something coming fast, its headlights blazing, rushed past us. The girl ducked: Harvey and I froze. Maganhard just went on being Maganhard.

When it had passed, I hissed at the girl: "If there's a light on you, stand still; they notice movement more than anything."

She straightened up slowly. "And when it gets a bit quiet, give a shout. Yes, I'm learning the rules."

Harvey said: "D'you see what that was? Your girl-friend's van. The Clos Pinel truck."

I rammed my head through the hedge again. The van was just pulling up at the customs house, people running out to yank open its doors.

The damn fool! Why was she taking this risk? But I knew why. I'd told her the route I planned, and she'd known this road would be the difficult place. So she'd waited somewhere until we'd had time to reach it—then come charging up.

They'd be pretty suspicious of her: a van that could easily hold four passengers, from a place not far from yesterday's shooting, coming on an odd route at an odd time. But she'd known that, of course—and was deliberately using it to distract them.

"Through the hedge," I snapped. "Quick!"

Harvey piled through, without asking questions. I shunted the girl after him, then Maganhard. Then myself. Long before Ginette was clear of the customs we were safe on the other side.

I wanted to stay and make sure she got through okay, but that might waste everything she'd gained for us. We had to move on. It was an old rule.

We went crouched, along a hedge towards the airport. Now the beacon was flashing straight in our faces. The high fence was only two hundred yards ahead.

Miss Jarman asked: "We're going to come up against the airport, aren't we?"

"That's the idea. They had to borrow some French

144

territory to lengthen their runway a few years ago; now the frontier runs along the fence, here. Once we're in the airport we're in Switzerland."

Harvey said: "Airports don't have the sort of fences you can just climb through."

"I know. I borrowed some wire-cutters off Ginette."

A couple of minutes later we reached the fence.

It was seven or eight feet of strong wire mesh strung between metal posts. I got the long-handled wire-cutters out of my briefcase and chewed away at a strand. It snapped with a loud click. I tried the next one more carefully, but still got a click. It was going to be a slow job: the mesh was only two inches wide and I had to cut a vertical slice about three feet high to give us a flap I could bend back.

Suddenly light poured over me. A searchlight, coming— impossibly—from the middle of the air. I froze. Then, behind the light, the soft whistle of throttled-back jets. An airliner on the approach had switched on its landing light.

I stayed still. The pilot would never see us, but the light could silhouette us for anybody in the fields behind us.

The airliner hit the runway with a squeak of rubber, then a sudden roar as the jets went to reverse thrust for braking. Under that noise, I snipped up the fence as fast and silently as scissors going through chiffon.

I turned to Maganhard. "Welcome to Switzerland."

From there it was fairly simple. Geneva-Cointrin is just one long runway with narrow grass areas on both sides. The airport buildings and workshops were all on the far side; on ours, there were just heaps of building materials, banks of bulldozed earth that somebody hadn't got around to smoothing down, little brick huts that had something to do with power or radar or somesuch. Plenty of cover.

We walked half a mile along between the runway and the fence and then, when it was Switzerland on the other side as well, just cut ourselves out again. In both places I jammed the wire back into place and it might be a few days before anybody noticed the cuts. And even when they did, it wouldn't prove anything about a man called Maganhard.

We walked out into the suburb of Mategnin—tall new

blocks of flats standing in the sea of mud that one day somebody was going to turn into a green lawn, unless he got another contract first, of course. It would have been dawn except for the clouds and the mountains, but the streets were still empty.

Maganhard asked: "How do we reach the city now?"

"We walk round to the airport front entrance and pick up a bus or taxi."

He digested this, and then said: "We could have walked across the airport—it would have been less distance!"

"Of course—and pretended we were passengers? And shown our passports and explained how we got our feet wet on the plane?"

After that, he saved his breath for walking.

20

IT was after six, in a dull dawn twilight, when we reached the airport buildings. The lights were still on inside, but were beginning to look pallid in the mauve light seeping over the mountains on the east.

There were a few cars parked opposite the entrance, and a smallish bus towing a luggage-trailer parked alongside. Its lights were off.

"We'll go inside and clean up," I said. "Meet back at the door in five minutes."

Miss Jarman headed off in her own direction. Even in the bright lights, she didn't look as if she'd been driven for nearly five hours in the back of a van and then gone for a two-mile hike across wet fields and through hedges. She had the natural glossiness which mud won't cling to. Just a little pale around the face and wet around the feet.

Maganhard looked as if he'd just lost a serious argument with a wildcat. His neat bronze raincoat was rumpled, smudged, and torn in two places; his trousers were wet and muddy, his hair was shaggy. He just stood there, looking ruffled and unhappy and determined to go on looking that way. He still thought I'd brought him across an unnecessarily rough route, and was damned if he saw why he should make the best of it.

We hustled him into the washroom, shielding him on either side. Harvey and I didn't look so bad, but mostly because our clothes had never looked so good. Harvey was pale, his eyes sunk in craters and the lines on his face deeper, but he looked alive again.

I'd hardly got started cleaning myself up when Maganhard said: "You have not forgotten that we must ring up Monsieur Merlin."

I had managed to forget it, of course, and would have been happy to keep it that way. But he was still paying for the trip. I brushed down my raincoat, washed my face,

145

hands, and shoes, combed my hair, and was out looking for a telephone inside four minutes.

I rang Merlin's hotel, told them it was *très important*, and finally got Merlin himself.

"*Mon Dieu!*" he exploded. "What has happened to you? I have heard nothing—not since Dinadan. For more than a day! All I get is the radio, the newspapers—all about shootings in the Auvergne! What is——"

I said: "Shut up, Henri. We've got here now. If you want to see us, we'll be at Cornavin station in about twenty minutes."

There was a pause, then he said: "I meet you there."

"Just walk through the booking hall up to the buffet."

Somebody slipped into the telephone box next door. I glanced casually through the glass—and then said quickly: "Cornavin in twenty minutes, then," and slapped the phone back.

I was out and into the next box before she'd finished dialling. I smashed a hand down on the phone, breaking the connection, and jerked her out with the other hand.

She turned on a look of innocent, babyish surprise. "Now why did——"

"You were doing well back on the frontier," I said grimly. "Don't spoil it all now. I told you phoning was out."

"But only at the Château."

"You could have asked me."

I had one hand under her elbow and we were doing a twosome across the hall that couldn't have looked like a honeymoon at any distance.

She said sweetly: "I thought you might say no."

I just looked at her.

We reached the door at the same time as Harvey and Maganhard. Outside, the bus's lights were on and people were climbing wearily aboard. From the number of beards and guitars, it looked as if they'd come off a cheap night flight from Paris or London. I'd hoped for something classier —for reasons of camouflage, not snobbery. However rumpled, Maganhard still didn't look like a student on an Easter fling.

But at least students don't read the crime pages. We climbed in and paid our fare without attracting any interest.

I sat beside the girl, Harvey and Maganhard just behind us. I leant my head back and said: "We may be meeting Merlin at the station."

"Station?" Maganhard asked.

"Cornavin, the railway station where the air terminal is. When we get there, we split up. Harvey with me."

Harvey said: "No." Rule One: the bodyguard sticks with the body.

"I know." I nodded. "But nobody's going to try any shooting in a station. The danger's being picked up by the cops. I want you back with me, to make sure nobody starts tailing Maganhard—or up ahead to see if anybody's waiting for him."

He saw the sense of it. "All right. I guess so."

Maganhard asked: "What do we do then?"

"Catch a train to Bern."

"I thought we were going to hire a car?"

"Well, we're not—just yet. And anybody else who thought so is wrong, too."

Miss Jarman said coldly: "I suppose you mean me."

"I mean anybody."

The bus filled up and people started sitting too close for safe conversation.

At that time of the morning, the bus belted through to the terminal in ten minutes. We came out under Cornavin station at half past six.

The other passengers trampled each other down in the rush to get their guitars. I turned to Maganhard and said: "Go ahead with Miss Jarman. Get two second-class tickets to Bern—let her buy them. Then go up to the platform. Don't recognize us."

The girl said: "If I'm buying tickets, I need some Swiss money."

"You've already got some. You were making that phone work, remember?"

She gave me a look, and led the way off the bus.

Harvey and I let them get ten yards ahead, then sauntered after.

The booking hall was a tall, sombre art-nouveau affair, the sort of place that's built to look grimy and cold and no amount of cleaning and heating will ever change it. Railway stations specialize in it.

There were a few building workers going to out-of-town jobs, a few families coming off the overnight sleeper from Paris and London, but all wearing the same aimless, hopeless expression that you see in concentration-camp pictures. They didn't look as if they could remember their own faces in a mirror at that time of day, let alone spot a wanted man.

Harvey and I did a quick circuit, then he shook his head briefly. I agreed: nobody had smelt like a plain-clothes man.

Only one ticket window was open. Maganhard hung back, while the girl went up to it. I nodded to Harvey and he went out up the long dim tunnel ramp that led to the platforms. If you were going to stake out the station, you'd wait up there at the top, at the *buffet express* counter, where everybody had to come past you and you'd have an excuse for just standing and watching.

I went up behind Miss Jarman to get our own tickets. As she turned away, she stared straight through me.

Out of the corner of my eye I saw her rejoin Maganhard, and start for the ramp. Then they stopped. I grabbed my tickets and turned around.

Bouncing across the hall like a big white rubber ball in his natty raincoat came Henri Merlin. He had seen Maganhard, but missed me. Instinctively, I looked behind him.

A slight man in a grubby trench-coat and narrow-brimmed green trilby shoved through the main doors, started to hurry, then checked and turned quickly off to read a timetable poster. *Damn!*

I'd meant to tell Merlin to make sure he wasn't being followed—and also not to speak to any of us until I'd had a chance to make doubly sure. But I hadn't had time. Blast that girl and her telephoning!

Merlin and Maganhard were talking rapidly. I turned my back and sidled away towards the doors, keeping an eye on the trench coat. He looked round and gave them a stare that was far too bright and beady for 6.45 a.m.

I had to do something. I had to get Maganhard away before the trench-coat realized who he was. Except that he'd probably guessed already. As I watched him, he suddenly hauled a folded newspaper out of his pocket, opened it, and riffled quickly through it as if he was searching for something.

I walked back past Merlin and Maganhard and the girl, still standing at the bottom of the ramp. A few yards inside it, I was out of sight of the trench-coat but not of them. I waved furiously.

The girl came up to me. "Merlin was being followed," I said quickly. "Get Maganhard away, and up to the platform. And you still don't know me or Harvey. Right?"

She nodded. I turned and walked up the ramp. Harvey drifted out of the little crowd sipping coffee around the brightly lit buffet counter, and said: "We're clean up here, too."

I jerked my head at the ramp. "Merlin's got here—and he was tailed. I've told them to break it up."

Harvey said: "Christ!" and started for the ramp. The bodyguard's place is beside the body. But I stopped him. "If it's a cop it's too late, and if it isn't there still won't be any shooting down there. Just see if he's spotted Maganhard." I hustled him back towards the buffet crowd. He gave me a stony look, then shrugged and let himself be hustled.

Maganhard and the girl came up the ramp, passed the buffet, and went to consult a timetable. The man in the trench-coat drifted up behind them, half-checked when he saw they'd stopped.

I didn't need to point him out. He couldn't have been all that dim, so perhaps he was just unlucky in having to tail people who were moving briskly through a crowd that was walking like the awakened dead. But to anybody looking for him, his changes of pace were as obvious as a scream in the night.

Harvey said grimly: "So he knows. We can't risk a train now."

"We've *got* to take a train now. If he follows us on, at least he won't be doing any telephoning."

"Something in that." Maganhard and the girl turned and went up the steps to platform three. The trench-coat followed. Harvey moved casually into place a few yards behind.

I was about to go back down the ramp when Merlin came up it, a lot less bouncy now. He glanced at me, then left it to me to approach him. I did.

"Caneton—what is happening?" His fat face looked white and worried.

"You were tailed, damn it. Now he's after Maganhard."

"Pas possible!" His face clenched in misery. "I am a fool! I have forgotten too much. What can I do?" Then he decided. "I come with you. I help get finished with him."

He sounded as if he were ready to heave our new friend under a train. I said quickly: "No-you-bloody-well-don't. I've got trouble enough. Is there anything useful you can tell me? D'you know anything about this man Galleron, the Belgian who's supposed to be after us?"

"I have tried. My friends in Bruxelles. But"—his shoulders lifted in a delicate shrug—"but nobody knows him. I think it is not his real name. And for the bearer shares, he needs no name at all."

I nodded gloomily. "That's about what I expected. Well, he knows the business, all right." A train rumbled in overhead. "See you in Liechtenstein tonight. Don't get followed all the way there."

As I ran for the steps, he was still waving his hands in remorse, misery, and despair. French lawyers are good at that.

21

It hadn't been our train. Up on platform three, there were twenty or so people standing around in silent clumps under the dim underwater light that seeped through the frosted glass roof. Harvey was near the steps, Maganhard and the girl twenty yards along, the man in the trench-coat studying his *Journal de Genève* in between.

I asked: "When's the train?"

"Should be in now." He jerked his head at the trench-coat. "Who d'you think he is?"

"I'd guess a cop. The other side can't have enough men to stake out every station and airport."

"If he's a cop, where's his pal?"

He had a point. Policemen go in pairs when they can't go in packs. Even a tailing job really needs two or three people. But perhaps they'd been caught off balance by Merlin dashing out so early; they might have left just one man to watch the hotel at night.

I shrugged. The train, labelled for Lausanne and Bern, pulled in.

Maganhard and the girl climbed into one carriage; the man in the trench-coat got into the next back from them. Harvey and I walked up and got in behind him.

We all ended up in the same second-class non-smoker. I should have warned Maganhard to take a smoker. It was an open carriage with double facing seats on either side of the aisle, the top of the seat backs high enough so that you couldn't see over them without half standing up.

Maganhard and the girl sat down facing each other. Once they'd made that choice, I knew exactly where the trench-coat would sit—and he did: the next set back on the same side, so that he was hidden from them, but would see them over the seat back when they stood up.

Harvey and I sat a couple of rows back, on the opposite side. When we were moving, Harvey asked: "Well—what do we do about it?"

I wasn't very sure. As I'd said, as long as the man was on the train then he wasn't ringing up and spreading the word —so perhaps the longer we stayed on, the better. But if he was really a cop, then he might start passing messages to the ticket collector or chucking notes out at stations. So perhaps the sooner we ditched him, the better.

"I'd like to get off at Lausanne," I said slowly. "If we can pass it on to Maganhard."

He looked at me thoughtfully. "You haven't got a plan," he said. "You're just counter-punching. That's all."

"There are worse plans. At least it's flexible."

He gave me another look, then relaxed slowly. The smell of trouble had done a lot to wake him up. He might have been feeling like hell's ashes—and probably was—but he'd been a gunman a lot longer than he'd been an alcoholic.

But it wouldn't last. As his hangover wore off, his thirst would begin to wear on. If hangovers lasted as long as thirsts, there wouldn't be any alcoholics.

The train had the early-morning feeling, too. It crawled out along the lakeside, stopping whenever it got the chance. We'd started with about half a dozen other people in our carriage; most of them had gone by the time we got to Nyon.

The ticket collector, wearing a cash satchel slung down around his knees, came round and said *"Bern, ah?"* to Maganhard's tickets, good and loud. That suited me fine, since I'd changed my mind.

The trench-coat had to buy a ticket. I bent my ears hard in that direction in case he was passing messages as well as money, but was certain he hadn't.

Soon after Nyon, Maganhard came back down the aisle, towards the lavatory. While he was gone I scribbled a note: *The man just behind you is following you. Don't talk out loud. Get off at Lausanne. Wait until everybody else is off.*

When he came back I just held it out to him and he took it without stopping to argue, and without stopping to read it before he got back to his seat, either. Now all we had to do was wait to see if he'd obey it.

At the next few stations, people started to get in again. I

152

hoped there wouldn't be too many; I wasn't looking for an audience.

As we rounded the last curve into Lausanne, most of the people in the carriage stood up. Harvey said quietly: "Are you going to try and lose him by running all over town?"

"No."

He nodded. "I'm not offering to *shoot* any cops, but——"

"My own thoughts exactly."

He smiled. "You or me?"

"Me. You block the light."

The train stopped gently. People jostled their way off. I began to sweat. Maganhard could still wreck it by getting off too soon; I wished I'd remembered to tell him the train stopped for several minutes.

He got it right. The last people got off, a few more got on and sat down. Then the doorway was clear. Maganhard stood up and strode out, the girl a few paces behind him. Harvey took my briefcase and we started moving.

The trench-coat bounced suddenly out in front of us, snapped: *"Je m'excuse"* without looking at us, and hurried down the aisle. I took several quick steps and was right behind him when he went through the glass door into the little cramped space beside the lavatory and before the steps down. The girl was just ahead of him.

At the last moment his mind must have caught up with events: the fact that Maganhard had suddenly jumped off meant he knew he was being followed; and what were we doing getting off so late, as well? He slowed, stiffened, and his head started to turn.

I jabbed my fist, first knuckle extended, in under the brim of the Alpine trilby. He gave a little whistling sigh and folded up. I caught him and leaned us against the lavatory door. Latched.

Harvey's hand snaked under my elbow, and twisted the handle; the trench-coat and I fell inside with a rush. The door slapped shut behind us.

I hardly bothered to look at his face: it wouldn't tell me anything. I dumped him on the seat and ripped open his coat. He had a small Walther PPK in a shoulder-holster, a bunch of papers and passes in his inside and outside breast pockets, a wallet on his hip, a purse of coins, and some keys. It took me just over ten seconds to grab the lot, and I was sorry to have to leave the holster itself.

I wasn't being vindictive or money-hungry. It's just that a man without a franc on him takes more time getting his hard-luck story believed than one who can flash a roll of notes and start hiring help.

We stepped off the train not twenty seconds later than Maganhard.

I led the way down off the platform, along the passageway, and up to platform one and the station buffet. I'd still have liked to keep us in two separate parties for as long as we were travelling by train, but now it was more important to brief Maganhard and the girl again.

We sat down at a corner table, where he could keep his back to the world, and ordered coffee and rolls.

"Who was that man?" Maganhard wanted to know.

"I'm not sure, yet." I was taking one piece of paper at a time out of my pockets, looking at it, and putting it away before I got out the next.

Miss Jarman asked: "Did you kill this one?"

"No."

Harvey chuckled. "You hope. I didn't know you knew that Karate stuff—the knuckle punch."

She said: "What's Karate?"

"Ju-jitsu played dirty."

Finally I found something: a French identity card. "His name's Griflet, Robert Griflet. Policeman."

Harvey frowned. "French?"

"Sûreté. I thought it was something like that—him being alone, and so on. I think this explains it." It was a letter of the to-whom-it-may-concern type, explaining that the bearer was an agent of the Sûreté and asking everybody to give him all the help they could, if they would be so kind. It was tactfully phrased, but for me the gun under his arm had rather spoiled the effect in advance.

I passed the letter round. The rest of the papers were a French driving licence, an international one, and normal everyday junk. Nothing to show what job he was on.

The waiter brought our coffee. Maganhard read the letter,

154

grunted, and passed it back. I put it back in my pocket and said: "Well, I hope that ends the episode of Robert Griflet, policeman. With luck, he might not wake up before Bern. But I'm afraid it means we've got to change our line again. We daren't take a train on through Bern now."

"I hope we will not take any more trains," Maganhard said stiffly. "They seem to get us into more trouble. We can hire a car here."

I shook my head. "I don't want to do anything in Lausanne. Remember, that bloke Griflet's going to wake up and start spreading the word sooner or later—and the last place he saw us was Lausanne. He'll try and pick up our trail here. No—I think we'll take a train round to Montreux and start from there."

Nobody seemed to like the idea much. Maganhard said: "I am not on a guided tour of Switzerland, Mr Cane. We have only come sixty kilometres from Geneva, and Montreux is a dead end. It is round the end of the lake. Even if we get a car there, we will have to double back to reach the main road."

"True. So I hope they won't expect us to be fools enough to go there. And there's a man there I rather want to meet."

"We are not here for your social life, either!"

"It's only thanks to my social life that we've got this far. We're going to Montreux."

22

WE didn't reach Montreux until after nine; the train
service isn't good, and if you've ever been to Montreux in
April, you know why. Nobody who spends the winter there
ever uses the train; if the Rolls-Royce has developed the
staggers, they hire a Mercedes and bleed with shame.

Montreux is one of those places where English money goes
to die. It's for people who think Bermuda and Nassau are
vulgar and American, and besides, the natives are getting
uppity. In Montreux the natives never get uppity; from
September to May the hotels serve nothing but roast beef
and curry and take good care not to cook it too well. The
dining-rooms are full of sweet little old ladies with cold eyes
that can cost you down to your last half-dozen Shell Oil
shares. Anybody wearing a beard or carrying a guitar is
sentenced to be run over by massed wheelchairs at high
noon.

All this was another good reason for us being there. Unless
the airmail edition of *The Times* was running anything
about us, nobody in Montreux was likely to have heard of us.

Since we were still in fairly public places, I'd bullied
Harvey into going back to the two-by-two system, covering
Maganhard and the girl from fifteen yards back. I thought
we were fairly safe: the Swiss police hadn't been covering
Geneva station, so it looked as if they hadn't been asked to
pick Maganhard up yet. Griflet would spoil all that when
he woke up, but it would take time to get the word around.

Maganhard sat down in a café a couple of hundred yards
up from the station, as per my instructions. Harvey and I
took a table nearby, and I started sorting through some
newspapers I'd bought at the station.

The *Journal de Genève* gave it me: it must have been
what Robert Griflet, policeman, had been looking up.
They'd finally dug out the eight-year-old photograph of
Maganhard. It was obviously a passport picture, but Magan-

hard looked very much like a passport picture, anyway. And he hadn't changed much in eight years: it was the same square face, angular glasses, thick, black swept-back hair. People with a ten-million holding in electronics and a yacht in the Atlantic don't age fast.

The story alongside the picture reassured me a bit: it had been handed out by the French police on the Geneva frontier. They were blocking the border so that even a mouse couldn't cross. There was no reason why Geneva citizens should fear this rapist monster. He probably wouldn't get anywhere near the Swiss frontier, with the *Sûreté Nationale* hard after him.

On the question of who was with Maganhard, the cop had sounded honestly vague; all he knew was that they didn't scare *him*. The story meandered off into the reporter's account of his tour of the frontier posts and the questions he'd got asked at each.

Harvey said: "And I don't like *that* guy, either."

I looked up quickly. An elderly party was just getting up from a table against the wall on the far side, carrying a newspaper with him. At the door he stopped to fiddle with his newspaper and, reckoning that made him invisible, threw a stare like a searchlight back at Maganhard.

He was a squat, solid man of at least sixty, and starting to develop a stoop. He had dark eyes and a long gingery moustache that was beginning to turn white. But his clothing was the thing that rocked me; up to his eyebrows he was the perfect chauffeur: shiny black leather leggings, black raincoat, black tie with a stiff collar. But on top of it was a vast hairy, orange tweed cap.

Probably, in his mind, that put him out of uniform and helped his invisibility. He was as invisible as an airport beacon.

He suddenly switched off the stare, fiddled with his newspaper again, and then went out with a determined military strut that, with him, had aged to the plodding of a dinosaur.

Harvey and I stared at each other. "Well," I said, "he's no professional."

Harvey said: "If he knows Maganhard, he's trouble whatever he is."

I nodded. "Get them out of here. Get up to the next café on the same side, so I'll know where to find you." I stood up and tossed him a ten-franc note. "And get Maganhard to get his glasses off and comb his hair differently." I passed him the *Journal* open at the photograph, and slid out of the café.

Anywhere but in Montreux the streets would have been full of Swiss dashing resolutely about making watches or money. Not here. Here was just about finishing its second cup of China tea and wondering whether to have one or two boiled eggs this morning. The streets were almost empty, and my man was easily in sight, fifty yards up on my left, heading deeper into town.

I crossed the road. There wasn't enough traffic to make it a problem crossing back if he dived up a side road, and he didn't look the type to think you could ever be trailed from the opposite side of the street. Twice he stopped, swung round, and gave the sergeant-major's stare at somebody behind him. It made him as conspicuous as an alligator in a bath, but it seemed to reassure him that the Black Hand Gang wasn't on his tail.

I slowed up to keep behind him, and we pressed on.

Montreux is a series of terraces around the end of the lake, with the main road and the railway criss-crossing at the middle level. We went through the shopping area and out of the centre towards the last row of big hotels on the lake front. It was staying a cold, grey morning and too early even for the old girls well wrapped up in rugs and Rolls-Royces. I dropped further back as the town began to thin out.

He gave one last sweep of the evil eye behind him, crossed to my side, and ducked into the side road above the Quai des Fleurs. We passed the Excelsior and then he turned into the Victoria.

I reached the door in several quick strides, a uniformed flunkey swung it for me before he noticed I was under seventy, and I nodded and headed across the lobby towards the lifts.

The whole place was furnished with a rich gloom that would have made an undertaker's parlour seem like a milk bar: heavy square columns covered in dark wood, brown-

and-cream carpets, big rubber plants, and dark olive drapes trying to creep across the windows to keep out the light. I speeded up: in a hotel like that, the lifts work efficiently. They have to. Nobody is young enough to use the stairs.

I slid into the dark-panelled lift just behind the man I was following. The lift-boy flicked the doors shut, and asked me what floor. I bowed to the black raincoat, as a gesture of politeness to age, and he said: "Sank." I'd just got that figured out as the English for *Cinque* in time to say: "*Quatre*."

In his suspicious mood, the old boy tried to catch my eye, but I wasn't having any. You never look the man you're trailing straight in the eye.

I bailed out at the fourth floor and took a few resolute steps to convince the lift-boy that I knew what I was doing, then doubled back as soon as the doors closed. I had half an eyeball poked around the next corner of the stairs by the time the lift stopped again. The black raincoat stomped past the top, and I tiptoed on up.

The corridor was long, tall, and plastered with shiny cream paint that had darkened to a smoky orange. He went about twenty yards down and stopped at a door on the left. I ducked back a step down the stairs: I'd seen him in action enough by now to know that he was going to swing round and stare down the corridor before he opened the door.

I waited twenty seconds, then walked after him. The room was number 510, and there was nobody else in the corridor. I rapped on the door.

After a pause a voice quavered: "Who's that?"

I hooted: "*Service, monsieur*," in cheerful, confident tones.

There was another pause. Then the door opened six inches and the gingery moustache peered out suspiciously.

I rammed Griflet's little Walther PPK against the black tie at his neck and marched in behind it.

23

IT was a long room, with big windows on to a balcony over
the lake. If the windows had been opened in the last six
months, it hadn't caught on: the temperature was at steam-
bath level. That apart, it had a dark-red carpet, a load of
furniture that looked too valuable to belong to the hotel—
and another man.

I kicked the door shut and leant on it. The man in the
raincoat took a couple more steps backwards and put up a
hand to straighten his tie. I waved the gun towards the
second man, in a chair beside the fire.

He said calmly: "All right, Sergeant, don't do anything
hasty." He looked at me. "And who are you, sir?"

I said: "Somebody who scares easily," and then gave him
a second look.

He was old—so old that you didn't even think of an age
when you looked at him. His face was long and withered to
a dry mask ending in a ruin of sagging flesh under his chin.
He had a big nose with a big white moustache under it, stiff
with the brittle stiffness of a dead plant clinging to the cracks
in a crumbling wall. His ears were decayed white leaves and
his scalp a few forgotten strands of white hair. The whole
face looked as if it had been six months in a dry tomb—
except for his eyes. They were damp blobs so pale that they
looked almost blind, and it must have cost half his energy
to keep the hoods of his eyelids from flopping closed.

I had the creepy feeling that if I breathed on that face it
would fall to dust, leaving the white skull underneath.

He was wrapped in a gold-and-black dressing-gown, with
an invalid table shunted in over his knees, carrying a coffee
pot, a cup, and a bunch of papers.

He opened his mouth slowly, and his voice came out as a
dry death-rattle, but it still had a crispness that expected a
fast answer. "If you've come to kill me, you won't get away
with it—will he, Sergeant?"

The man in the raincoat said: "No, sir, he won't get away

with it." There was a rhythm, rather than an accent, to his voice that I couldn't identify because it seemed so much out of place. Then I had it: Welsh.

"You see?" the old man said. "You won't get away with it."

I got the point: I wouldn't get away with it. I leered at him. "Maybe I didn't come to kill you."

"You've got a pistol," the old boy pointed out. "Even if it's only a Walther PPK—a pop-gun. Still, it's the man behind the gun that counts—isn't it, Sergeant?"

The Sergeant said smartly: "Yessir. That is what counts."

"You see?" the man by the fire said. "It's the man that counts."

I was getting that floating feeling that comes with an influenza fever or trying to understand tax laws. I groped around for a chair. "All right," I said, "let's just take it that I can count."

The old boy let out a rasping gurgle that could have been a chuckle. "You know, Sergeant—I don't think he knows who I am."

I sat down. "I just guessed. You're General Fay." The man I'd come to Montreux to see.

In my line of business, the General had been a legend for a long time, but I hadn't realized just how long. He was some relic of the First World War who'd somehow got himself running a business intelligence network. If you wanted to know whether a company was going bust, was ripe for take-over, or was about to raise new share capital, the General would find out for you—at a price. His prices were something of a legend, too; that was why I'd never had any dealings with him before. But if you were in his price bracket —and a lot of people in Montreux were—the legend said he gave good value.

He gave another rasping chuckle. "Right. And this is Sergeant Morgan, me driver." Once you got used to the sheer age in his voice, you could spot the out-of-date British upper-class accent that uses "me" for "my" and says "orf" for "off". "And who are you?"

Sergeant Morgan said: "I think he followed me from the

café where I saw Mr Maganhard, sir." He was standing in a
stiff at-ease position, hands behind his back, and lowering at
me. It was going to take him a lot of work to learn to love
me, and so far he wasn't even trying.

"Ah." The General's half-hooded eyes fixed on me again.
"So you're something to do with that damn fool Maganhard,
are you? Who are you, boy?"

"Call me Caneton."

"Ah—then I've heard of you. Special Operations Executive, eh? Good, tough, tricky bunch. Thought you couldn't
have been real army—wouldn't have had the gumption to
point a gun at an old man like me. Lot of old women in the
last war—weren't they, Sergeant?"

Morgan said smartly: "Yes, sir, they were that."

"Lot of old women. You know they pulled a regiment out
of the line when it had less than twenty per cent casualties?
In our day, it had to be eighty per cent."

I nodded vaguely. The cross-talk act was getting me dizzy
again, and the jungle temperature of the room wasn't helping. I could have done without my raincoat, jacket and shirt,
and still been sweating. But I'd already pointed a gun at
him, then sat down before being asked. Even Special Ops
manners don't allow yanking off all your clothes, unless
there are ladies present.

I shook my head and tried to get back to within shouting
distance of reality. But the General did it for me. "All right.
So you saw the Sergeant see Maganhard, and followed him.
Not difficult. Morgan's a damn fool at this slippery-secret
stuff. Very good. What's your offer?"

"For what?"

"For not telling the police, you damn fool."

I must have been wearing my dazed look. We were back to
reality with a thump. Now I had a nice little case of black-
mail on my plate. I was beginning to see how the General
managed to maintain a permanent suite of rooms with his
own furniture in the Victoria—and why his first thought
had been that I'd come up to kill him.

I stalled: "Have the police been asked to pick up Maganhard?"

162

The half-hooded eyes watched me steadily. Then he husked: "Good question. No fool, this man. Police can't arrest and extradite without an official request from somebody abroad. Can't act just on a story in the *Journal de Genève* alone. Unless"—and the hoods lowered just a fraction—"unless he crossed the frontier illegally. That would mean he'd committed an offence in Switzerland, wouldn't it?"

"If they could prove it."

"You're more of a fool than I thought, boy. Maganhard must have crossed illegally: he was seen in France only yesterday."

"You mean by somebody who's still alive?"

He just looked at me—"stared" is too strong a word for what those wet, pale eyes could do, but it was a steady, straight look. Then he grunted. "Ah. Wondered if that shooting up in the Auvergne yesterday was something to do with you. So I was right first time. You're a killer but not a fool. Sergeant! Knock 'illegal entry' off the bill. We'll let you have that free. Back where we started: have the Swiss police had an official request? Sergeant!"

Morgan took a couple of heavy steps towards the white telephone on the far side of the fire. I said: "Hold it."

He stopped. Both of them looked at me.

I said: "Let's get my position clear. I'd like that information, and I'm ready to pay for it. But let's forget any idea of you selling out Maganhard to the cops if I don't play your game."

There was a silence. Then the General said calmly: "And why shouldn't I? I sell information for a living. I'm just giving you a chance to bid against the police, as it were. I'm a businessman."

"So am I. And I agreed to get Maganhard to Liechtenstein, for a fee. I'm going to do that."

"It won't be your money, lad. Maganhard will pay. Just tell him there's a special toll for coming through Montreux."

I took a deep breath and said: "General, you don't get the point. *I'm* running this trip, not Maganhard. I won't even ask him to make a decision on this: making decisions is my job. I've decided that if your sergeant picks up that phone and says anything dangerous to the police, I'll kill both of you."

There was another silence. Then the General said: "Waste of time threatening an old man like me. Only one flicker of the candle left in me, anyway. Could be snuffed out by natural causes tomorrow, so I haven't got much to lose."

I nodded gently. "Only as much as anybody else: the rest of your life. I don't mind how short it is."

The silence grew long and thick, and the cloying heat of the room began to crawl up my back on wet, prickly feet. But I had to sit still and watch that crumbled ruin of a face and guess at the foxy mind behind it, counting the last of its shares in a company called Life.

I knew I was going to win. Point a gun at a young man and he'll jump you because he can't believe in himself dying. But an old man has thought about it. He's seen the crack in the door widen and felt the draught come through.

I shook my head and tapped the little gun impatiently on my knee. "Well?"

The General raised his head slowly and the pale eyes looked into mine. "Damn you," he said. "All right—you can keep your Maganhard."

Then the sides of his mouth began to crawl slowly up, and up, into the faint memory of a smile. "Damn you," he rasped again, "the Special Ops people would be proud of you."

I leered weakly at him. I wasn't proud of anything.

He jacked his head round to the man by the telephone. "Sergeant! Get out a bottle of the Krug. My friend and I have things to discuss."

Morgan looked at his watch. "But, sir—"

"Sun's over the yard-arm in the Tibetan navy," the General squawked. "Get me my champagne, dammit."

Morgan shook his head severely, said, "Very good, sir," and went through to the next room.

It had all had an odd, practised sound, as if it were a little ritual they went through at this time of every day. Probably it was.

The General turned slowly back to me. "I hope you drink champagne in the mornings, sir?"

"Rather than at any other time."

"Quite right. After lunch, it becomes a drink for little girls." His eyes closed slowly, then opened again. "Not that I used to mind little girls, after lunch. Not too soon after, of course."

I nodded feebly and stood up and took off my raincoat and jacket, opened my shirt neck, and took another look around the room. There was a big, oval dining-table surrounded by expensive-looking antique chairs at the far end, a number of small writing-tables and tall brass lamps, and, hung over the fireplace, about a dozen antique pistols.

I don't know much about old pistols since I've never had the money to spend on them or the sort of wall to hang them on, but even I could see that these came off the very top shelf. If there was anything as cheap as wood and iron in them, it was well covered up with mother-of-pearl, gold, silver, brass, or merely engraved steel panels. One had a butt of ivory, carved as a head of a Roman soldier and the hammer shaped like an Imperial eagle. The rest weren't far behind.

"Probably the best collection for its size in the world," the General said contentedly. "Eighteenth-century flint-locks, as you must know, sir." I just nodded again. I hadn't known anything of the sort. He went on: "I've got a Cazes there, and a Boutet, and——"

Morgan came back with a bottle and a couple of tulip glasses on a silver tray.

He'd taken off his raincoat and was down to a plain black uniform with a row of 1914-18 medal ribbons. As he bent over to pour the champagne, he developed a hard bulge in his hip pocket, so the General's collection of pistols hadn't stopped at the end of the eighteenth century. I decided to let him keep it: if I took it off him, he'd only find something else and be a lot more tricky hiding it.

Morgan passed me a glass. The General stirred his with a gold swizzle stick and explained: "Old tum can't take the bubbles these days. Your health, sir."

We drank, and I remembered not to tell him I thought it was good stuff; he belonged to the days when everybody served only the best and to remark on it would suggest you'd expected something worse.

Instead, I said: "How did you come into this work, General?"

"Ha." He put his glass down with a careful, shaky hand. "Shall we tell him, Sergeant? Give him our credentials and experiences before we start dealing? We might frighten him off."

Morgan grinned back at him. I had an idea he'd have liked to see me frightened. He resented my threatening his master a lot more than the master himself did.

The General said: "Well, no matter. We've been here since 1916, and we've only gone up one rank since. We were Colonel and Corporal then. I was on Haig's intelligence staff, and he sent us over to start our own spy ring. He didn't trust the civil secret service. Damn fool didn't trust anybody —didn't trust us as soon as we were over the border. Did he, Sergeant?"

Morgan shook his head gravely.

"Damn fool," the General said again, and I assumed he still meant the Field-Marshal, not the Sergeant. "I gave him Ludendorff's artillery plan *and* his idea of using picked stormtroopers for the 1918 push. And he didn't listen. So that's why he got surprised in March. Damn fool never forgave me being right about that. Gave us both new ranks and kicked us straight out. We must have been the first people demobilized, weren't we, Sergeant?"

Morgan grinned again. "Just about, sir."

"Ha. So we just took up being what we'd been pretending to be—a retired old fogey and his chauffeur looking for a quiet life and good investments. Used the spy ring we'd started and switched it over to business information."

He picked up his champagne again and gave a long, careful sip. "Now, we'd better earn our lunch, hadn't we, Sergeant? I think we need some little pink cards here. You know which ones."

Morgan said: "Yes, sir," and stumped out.

The General and I watched each other across our champagne glasses.

After a while Morgan came back with a handful of pink cards each about twice the size of a packet of cigarettes. The sort you use in little desk-top filing drawers.

The General dealt himself what looked like a patience hand on to the top of his invalid table, then jammed a pair of gold-rimmed pince-nez on his nose and started sorting it over. Morgan poured me some more champagne.

Then the General looked up at me. "At least I know who you are, now." He read off one of the cards: "Lewis Cane. Wartime codename, Caneton. Ha. I see we're in rather the same sort of business." He shoved the card aside.

I frowned. I should have dropped the Caneton years ago.

He was looking at me again. "Well, Mr. Cane—have you decided what you want to buy?"

The phone rang.

Morgan picked it up, said "Yes?" and listened for a moment. Then he turned and nodded to the General. The old boy reached down beside his chair and picked up a second receiver.

He said a few words in perfectly good French, but mostly just listened. Then he put the phone down and turned slowly back to me.

"Pity I didn't make you buy sooner, Mr Cane. Your friend Maganhard's just been arrested."

I thought of asking something stupid like "Are you sure?"—then started thinking what sort of profit the foxy old pirate could be making from tipping the police off to Maganhard. I couldn't think of anything. The local cops wouldn't pay much for a mere tip-off, and the General was far too much of a solid successful citizen, in a town which exists for such citizens and no others, to need to give them something free.

I gave up and asked a sensible question: "Where did they pick him up?"

"In the Café des Grottes. That was the proprietor who rang me."

Morgan said: "That wasn't where I saw him, sir."

I asked: "Would it be the next café up, on the same side?"

He calculated. "Yes, that'd be it."

I nodded. "It sounds like Maganhard, all right." Harvey must have moved them, as I'd told him to, but probably hadn't managed to get Maganhard to degrade himself by combing his hair differently. So he'd got nicked.

"That settles one question," the General growled. "Have the police been asked to arrest Maganhard? Yes, they have. Pity. I'd planned making some money by finding out that for you."

"You still can," I said. "They just might have got the idea out of the *Journal de Genève.* Can you find out—without tipping them off that you know he's been picked up?"

The General just looked at me. Then: "Sergeant, I don't think he was listening when I told him we'd been doing this since 1916."

I grinned. "Sorry. Anyway, I'll buy that. Did he say if anybody else had got arrested, too?"

"Only Maganhard."

"Okay. I'll be down at that café. I'll ring you from there."

I dived out of the room before he could start haggling over prices.

24

IT took me about five minutes to reach the Café des Grottes. Harvey and Miss Jarman were still there. I sat down beside them.

Harvey said: "It's the end of the line, Cane. Maganhard's——"

"I know. Just tell me how it happened."

He shrugged. "I got them up here. He didn't buy that idea about changing his hair-style, but I got his glasses off. Lot of damn use that was."

I nodded. "Go on."

"I stayed by myself, playing American tourist. A cop came in for a quick coffee, and I guess he spotted Maganhard then. Then Helen"—he nodded at Miss Jarman—"she went out to do some shopping. Ten minutes later the cop and a sergeant came back, picked Maganhard up, and carted him off."

"What did you do?"

His face was quite expressionless and his eyes were staring at me but not seeing me.

"Nothing," he said calmly.

He had enough self-respect, and enough respect for my intelligence, not to offer any explanations.

Miss Jarman looked at me. "And where were *you* all this time?"

"Drinking a morning glass of champagne. Come to that, what had happened to you?"

"If you recall, Mr Cane, you made us leave all our luggage behind in France. I had to buy some things."

"And maybe make a few phone calls, too?"

She stared at me. After a time, she said in a small voice. "Perhaps."

Harvey slumped back in his chair. "I could use a drink," he said, softly but very positively. The girl jerked a scared look at him.

I said: "Not here. Get on up to the Victoria—just above the Quai des Fleures, you know? Get up to room 510, and say I sent you. You'll find a character who looks as old as the Devil's grandfather, and about twice as crafty. Name's General Fay, and I'll tell him you're coming."

"What are you going to do?" Harvey asked.

"See if there's a chance of bailing Maganhard out."

When they'd gone, I walked over to the counter. Seeing me coming, the proprietor went through a mime of never having noticed me come in. He'd been watching the three of us like a nervous cobra.

I tossed a hundred-franc note on to the counter. *"C'est de la part du Général, avec ses remerciements."*

He looked blank at me, and hungry at the note. I smiled reassuringly, but it wasn't the smile which convinced him.

I nodded at the telephone on the end of the bar and asked: *"Vous permettez . . . ?"*

He smiled and bowed. *"Monsieur . . ."*

I dialled the Victoria's number and asked for General Fay —good and loud. I was sure he must have a private line as well, but any man whose work is collecting and selling information could never refuse any phone call.

The proprietor glanced at me and I held a finger alongside my nose and he did the same, both of us sharing a big secret and neither of us having the faintest idea of what it was.

The old voice whispered tinnily down the wire: "Must be losing me grip. Occurred to me after you'd gone that I could have sold you the information that Maganhard was in the coop."

"Well, I've just done you a good turn, too. I tipped the chap here a hundred francs."

"Far too much. Don't expect me to refund it. D'you want to know what I found out?"

"Go on."

"How much?"

"Put it on the bill. There'll be more yet."

"All right. There's been *no* official request to arrest Maganhard. So they did it off their own bat. So we may be able to——"

"I'll do it. I want you to ring the duty inspector in ten minutes: say you've heard he's nicked Maganhard and you want to confirm it. Then let slip you know the French haven't asked for it. Say you've heard rumours they're dropping charges. Just get him worried. By the way—who's the duty inspector likely to be?"

"Camberet or Lucan. It's all on the bill, Cane. What are you going to do?"

"Take a long shot. Oh—and I've sent a couple of people up to see you. Look after them until I get back, will you?"

"Damn you, Cane, I'm living in a hotel, not running one."

"One of them's pretty."

There was a crackle on the line that might have been his aged chuckle. "All right, Cane. In ten minutes from"—he paused, obviously looking at his watch—"now."

"Now," I said, and looked at my own watch. I hadn't meant it to be as precise as this, but at least it gave me a timetable.

I rang off and ran.

Four minutes later I was telling the police sergeant that my problem was extremely important, highly confidential, remarkably delicate, and exceptionally urgent. That made it normal; he'd have thrown me out as a practical joker if I hadn't said something like that.

Which still left me with the problem of getting in to see Inspector Lucan—he was the one holding the fort, I'd learned—inside four minutes. I'd need the last two for softening him up before the General rang.

But at least I knew that if Lucan was busy, it could only be on the Maganhard problem. It was Montreux's slack time: mid-way between the ski tourists and the summer tourists, with no traffic troubles and, since there were no tourists to give them cover, none of the con men and jewel thieves who work the hotels in season.

The sergeant sighed, picked up the phone, and asked me my name.

I said: *"Robert Griflet. Sûreté Nationale."*

Lucan was a thin, neat man with a dark moustache, dark

hair greased flat, and bright, beady eyes. He was naturally a brisk, suspicious man, but trying hard to be what he thought a Montreux inspector should be: slow, courteous, and inscrutable.

I liked his phoney character best. If he got brisk and suspicious about Robert Griflet, I wasn't likely to have any choice about how I spent the next seven years.

I dealt him my to-whom-it-may-concern letter and followed it up, horse, foot and guns. I wanted him on the defensive, in the hope he'd forget to ask for my *carte d'identité*. The photograph of Griflet was pretty old and didn't look much like him now—but it looked a damn sight less like me.

I understood he'd arrested Maganhard? Splendid. Could he find a couple of charges to hold him on, while my bosses at the *Sûreté* made up their minds to ask for extradition? I was sure they would—eventually, anyway. Well, probably.

He frowned suspiciously at me, but went hastily back to looking inscrutable. Then he asked about the rape charge. Surely——

I shook my head with what I hoped was a look of weary despair. We'd been trying to find the woman who'd laid the charge, and she seemed to have skipped. Which led one to suspect that *perhaps* . . . and one couldn't be too careful when arresting multi-millionaires, could one?

He smiled, but only with his teeth. He knew all about being careful with multi-millionaires—any Montreux cop would. And he'd probably been getting the same song-and-dance from Maganhard for the past half hour.

He asked me what I expected him to do?

I sneaked a glance at my watch: if the General was on time, I had about fifty seconds left. I explained that I just wanted Maganhard kept on ice for a couple of days. Dream up a holding charge. What about illegal entry into Switzerland?—I could bet Maganhard didn't have an entry stamp on his passport.

He reminded me, coldly, that no court in Europe would take that as proof: too many frontier posts didn't bother to stamp passports at all. And legally, Maganhard was a Swiss resident, which complicated matters.

I got a bit huffy. Well, let him dream up his own charges.

Hell, he'd done the arresting, not me. I presumed he had *some* reason for that——

The phone rang.

He looked at it, then me, then picked it up and said: "Lucan." Then: *"Ah, bonjour, mon Général . . ."*

I turned away in my seat and pretended I was pretending not to listen.

At first, Lucan didn't say much more than *non,* a cautious *oui,* and *C'est possible.* Then he asked who had said that Maganhard had been arrested?

I gave up my pretence and hissed that he mustn't tell anybody that he'd got Maganhard—that Maganhard's lawyers must never know—that we'd both be ruined . . .

He flicked a hand to keep me quiet, but perhaps he went a little pale. He ended up saying rather stiffly that he couldn't say anything official. I hoped the General had ended up saying that he was going to start spreading the news as from now.

I demanded an explanation, and got a brief run-down on the General's history, status, and prestige. I shrugged it off: obviously, he must go and arrest the General, as well. *That* should keep things quiet.

He laughed in my face.

I let Robert Griflet lose his temper and played my fifth ace: he, Lucan, would do as I said or I, Griflet, would bring down the wrath of the Republic of France on his head and squash him like a bed-bug. Montreux cops had better learn to jump when a *real* policeman from across the frontier said so, or By God . . .

It was the one thing the real Griflet would never have done; Swiss officials blow up automatically at any hint of their big neighbours saying Or Else. Three minutes after they threw me out, they threw Maganhard after me. Whether it was mostly because Lucan was scared that he'd made an expensive mistake, or mostly to annoy me, I never asked and haven't bothered to guess.

I tailed Maganhard for a quarter of a mile to make sure nobody else did, then caught him up, and told him to head for room 510—and *now* part his damn hair differently. He did it without arguing. I took the taxi behind him.

25

WE ended up back in room 510.

Harvey and Miss Jarman were already there, tucking into the champagne, and with coats off in that heat. The General was still in his fireside chair. Morgan raised his eyebrows at me as he let us in, but left it at that.

Harvey stood up. "Christ, how did you do it?"

"I just said Please."

"Well, I'm damned." Then he suddenly looked at the champagne glass in his hand.

But I wasn't worried—yet. For him, champagne would be about as strong as British beer. Still, it wasn't a bad thing for him to remember that getting Maganhard back meant we were still in action.

I turned back to introduce Maganhard to the General— but it looked as if they'd met. Maganhard was glaring down at the long, shrivelled face with a look as friendly as a welding torch.

The General broke the ice: "I suppose you're that damn fool Maganhard?"

"Don't mind the old-world courtesy," I reassured Maganhard. "He thinks the world's divided into two: himself, and the damn fools."

Maganhard swung round on me. "Why did you involve *this* man?"

The General snorted. "Don't like dealing with tradesmen, heh? I've done some good work for you in your short life. You and those damn fools Heiliger and Flez. Don't you think I give value?"

"The information you supplied us with was valuable enough," Maganhard snapped. "Now I am wondering what value you will get from information about me."

"You could always buy it for yourself," the General suggested.

I said quietly: "We did that deal already—remember, General?"

He swivelled his head slowly towards me. "All right, Cane, I remember. Just thought it worth trying. The damn fool might have paid up. All damn fools, him and Max Heiliger and Flez. Only sensible thought they had in all their lives was that electronics was going to become big business after the war. Then they went off and started playing hole-in-the-corner with Liechtenstein registration and bearer shares and whatnot."

He picked up one of the pink cards, held up his pince-nez, and started reading: "Caspar AG. Formed 1950. Issued capital forty thousand Swiss francs." He turned to look at Maganhard. "Has to be above twenty-five thousand by law and if you go above fifty thousand you have to have a controller in. Wouldn't like that, would you? Always want to play secrets." He looked back at the card. "Controls thirteen companies in France, Germany, Austria . . ."

Maganhard was giving me the steely glare. "Have you been talking about my business?"

The General said calmly: "Most of that information is on file at the Public Registry in Liechtenstein. I know the rest because it's my business to know."

Maganhard hadn't finished with me. "Why did you get *him* involved? Now he will spread the news of us all over Europe."

"You mean there's somebody who doesn't know already?"

That stopped him.

The General chuckled. "Young man's quite right, Maganhard. I couldn't make a wooden centime out of you that way. Well, perhaps there's other ways." The pale, half-hooded eyes swung at me. "I suppose you got him out of jail because the Sûreté hasn't asked for an arrest yet. What happens when they do ask for it?"

I shrugged. It was going to come, all right—just as soon as the real Griflet borrowed a few francs and got on the phone to France. Well, the first thing to happen would be that Inspector Lucan had a heart attack. But the second thing . . . I shrugged again.

"By then we'll be on our way."

"You're joining the damn fools, Cane. How d'you plan to do it?"

"I think we'll classify that Secret, General."

"Now I'm sure you're a damn fool. D'you think I could sell that? Nobody wants to know. They all know you're going to Liechtenstein—and that's enough." He lifted a glass of flat champagne, tucked it in under his moustache, gave a long loud *slurp*, and put it carefully down again. "What d'you know about Liechtenstein, Cane? It's a small country. Frontier with Switzerland's only fifteen miles long. And d'you know what that frontier is? The Upper Rhine. And d'you know how many ways there are into Liechtenstein? Just six. Only six. Five bridges, and the south road through Maienfeld to Balzers. All they'll need is eighteen policemen to watch that lot. They won't waste hundreds of men trying to catch you before that. They'll wait for you there."

There was a long silence.

Then Harvey was on his feet, looking at me curiously from under his pale eyebrows. With his coat off, the gun at his belt looked very obvious.

"I've never been to Liechtenstein," he said slowly. "Have you, Cane? Is he right?"

"I've been there," I said. "And he's right."

He twisted his head at me in a little, quizzical look. "You sound kind of calm about it. What had you figured to do about that frontier, anyway?"

I shrugged. "If we hadn't stirred up any fuss, we'd have whistled across. Normally, those bridges aren't even watched." No customs, no guards—nothing. For customs purposes, Liechtenstein's part of Switzerland, so they just don't bother with that frontier: the real one comes between Austria and Liechtenstein. And we couldn't cross that without first crossing into Austria. I couldn't see any point in doubling our problems.

Harvey said: "So they can close the bridges. What about the south road? Can we get up close, then get off the road and walk across?"

At the southern end of Liechtenstein, Switzerland stretches

across the river, so we could cross the river down there without meeting a frontier post. But then there was only the one road, heading north into Liechtenstein.

I shook my head. "It's a fortified zone. The road's the only way through."

Just there, the valley narrows down to about a mile wide, between sheer mountain walls. This is the St Luzisteig Pass, a natural defensive position against an invader driving south up the Rhine. Personally, I can't see why any invader would come up the river: all he'd capture in the end would be the ski resorts at St Moritz and Klosters, and I'd have thought the prices they charged there were defence enough.

But for all that, they've spent nearly two centuries fortifying the St Luzisteig, right up to the Liechtenstein frontier. Most of the old stonework is just grassy humps by now, but some time in the 'thirties they added what looks like a film set for the First World War. Trenches, pillboxes, dragons-teeth tank traps, gun and mortar pits. And barbed wire: hedges of great rusty barbed wire coils. The whole zone a mile wide and several hundred yards deep: a huge cork rammed tight into the bottleneck of the valley.

Harvey was still watching me, still with the curious look on his face. "You know, Cane—this might have been something worth planning for."

I nodded. "I thought about that. The trouble was, I couldn't think of any plans."

"Christ." He looked down at his empty champagne glass. "I could use a drink." He looked up at Morgan. "Have you got anything stronger?"

I said: "Stick to champagne for the moment."

He said: "You *still* sound calm about it."

"Of course. The General's got a plan. He's going to sell it to us."

After a little while the General said: "Have I, Cane?"

"Oh yes. You haven't made any money out of us yet, General. And it was you brought this problem up. Yes, you've got a plan."

"Ah." He gave a gentle sigh. "Perhaps I have. But can you afford it, heh?"

177

I shrugged. "That's up to Mr Maganhard. Still—he knows Liechtenstein. He knows the problems."

I looked sideways at Maganhard. He was staring down at the General with a look that suggested he was prepared to bid about two pfennigs—and stick there.

I said quickly: "I think we need this plan. But you can make most of the payment on results—it may not work, after all."

He got the iron filings back into his voice and said: "I agreed to pay you a certain amount to get me to Liechtenstein. Now——"

"And expenses," I said.

"Yes. The expenses are more expensive than I had estimated," he said thoughtfully. "We have crashed one of my cars; my yacht is in custody in Brest, my luggage is somewhere in France, and now you want——"

"Sure," I said soothingly. "It's getting to be hardly worth your ten million quids'-worth of Caspar, isn't it? I'd just jack the whole thing in and catch a train down to Como for a few days' holiday."

He gave me the steely stare. "Do we need this plan? Have you no ideas of your own?"

I spread my hands. "I've got a few. And we can try them if you say so. But they won't be as good as the General's." I was just trying to keep down his price. I wanted his plan, all right.

Maganhard swung round on the old man by the fire. "All right. How much? I will pay you one-third now."

The General said: "Ten thousand francs. And half now."

Maganhard said: "Five thousand and I will give you half."

"Ten thousand. But I'll take one-third."

"I'll pay you one-third of seven. What plan is it?"

"A damn good plan. I'll take a third of nine."

I said: "Give him a third of seven-and-a-half."

The General said: "I'll take a half of six."

Maganhard said quickly: "Right. Three thousand now and the same if we get through."

The General's head moved in a fractional nod; he closed his eyes and sighed. "I'm getting old. All right, Maganhard.

Give me a cheque on one of your Swiss banks, and make it cash. Sergeant! I want the file on the Upper Rhine."

Morgan stumped off into the next room. Maganhard hauled a sheaf of cheque-books out of an inside pocket, and started sorting through them. "Geneva?" he asked. The General nodded again, and Maganhard started writing the cheque.

Harvey was looking at me curiously. I winked at him, and he turned away and stared out of the window down across the grey windswept lake.

Morgan came back with a green folder, and the General started sorting through it. Finally, he came up with a large sheet folded double. He opened it, stared at it, then carefully tore a corner off it.

Maganhard finished writing the cheque and dropped it on the General's table. The General gave him the paper in exchange.

"Show that to Cane. He may make some sense of it."

For a moment it seemed unlikely. It was a large photostat of a drawing: a number of wavering, curling lines, overlaid by hard geometric lines: zigzags, rows of little triangles, lines with crosses every half inch. And wandering across the whole thing was one red ink line.

I stared at it. Then it snapped into place: a plan of the modern St Luzisteig defences. The wavery lines were the contours, the geometric ones the trenches, barbed wire, tank traps. And the red line——

The General said: "Well? D'you know what it is?"

"I think so. We follow the red ink and find the end of the rainbow. Just what *is* that?"

"Patrol path. To let out the patrols."

I waggled my head and kept a slightly doubtful look on my face. "This plan's probably twenty years out of date——"

"Damn fool. They haven't changed those defences in twenty years. Why should they?"

Maganhard was peering over my shoulder. "Is it worth anything?" he asked suspiciously.

"It's genuine, all right. Why should he keep a faked one lying around? He's probably had this on file since 1940, waiting for somebody to sell it to."

The General let out his rasping chuckle.

Maganhard fingered the torn corner of the plan. "What did you tear off here?"

"Name of the man I got it from," the General said.

I folded the plan up and shoved it in a pocket. "Okay," I said briskly. "So we can get across once we're there. But how do we get to the frontier?"

He leant back in his chair with his eyes closed. "All in the same price. Morgan drives you there."

"Yes? And what's so wonderful about that? I could hire a car down the road."

His eyes stayed closed. "And tell them exactly what car you're in. They'll check up on that first thing. But they'd never stop *my* car. And they all know it."

Harvey said: "Must be some car." He was looking suspicious. So was Maganhard, but with him it was congenital.

The General said calmly: "It is 'some car', as you put it."

I was ready to believe him. And even if I wasn't, we still stood a better chance in his car than in any one we hired. Switzerland's a small country, and the area you can drive across before the southern passes melt is even smaller. Whatever we did, we were going to have to drive down the central valley which includes almost all the big cities—Fribourg, Bern, Luzern, Zürich—and that gave us a choice of only about three main roads.

Harvey said slowly. "Look, I'm not sure I like the idea——"

"I'm running the ideas department," I snapped. "Shut up and look at the pretty pistols!"

He stopped as if I'd slapped him in the face. Then he turned slowly away, and went back to staring at the guns over the mantelpiece.

Miss Jarman glared at me.

Maganhard said: "Shouldn't we be starting?"

I looked at my watch: nearly noon. Three hundred kilometres to go. Say five hours' driving.

"We're not in too much of a hurry," I said. "We can't cross the frontier until it's dark, after half past eight. And we don't want to spin out the road journey—we're safer sitting here."

"Then you'll join me for lunch?" the General asked.

Maganhard said: "We will not be in Liechtenstein until nine o'clock, then? We are cutting it very fine. What if the car breaks down?"

"Sergeant!" the General called. "When did the car last break down?"

Morgan stiffened and started considering. "We had the silencer trouble in 1956, sir. But that wasn't a real breakdown. I think the last time was the electrical problem in— that would be in '48."

I grinned. "All right. Lunch up here?"

"Of course," the General said.

The lunch arrived on the table at the other end of the room. Morgan took the trays at the door and handed round the food—presumably so that the waiters wouldn't set eyes on Maganhard. My first idea was that this would make them doubly suspicious, but then I remembered the General had been in this hotel over forty years. Forty years isn't enough to stop waiters being suspicious, of course, but it's time enough for them to learn to be forgetful when the police come asking questions.

We had trout *au bleu* and a straightforward veal escalope that was as soft as butter: the General obviously didn't belong to the overdone-roast-beef movement that most of Montreux's English guests insisted on. He went on with his glass of swizzled champagne, but the rest of us got a crisp cold Ayler Herrenberg.

It was a quiet meal, except for the General's eating. Maganhard was worried about the time factor, and annoyed that the right thing to do was just wait. Harvey was quiet and morose. He drank a glass of wine—no more—but he took it in three big gulps, and fiddled with his glass a lot, counting the seconds until he could take the next gulp.

Just before half past one, Morgan was pouring coffee. The General asked if we'd like a liqueur and I said No, fast, to pass the hint to Harvey. He gave me a twisted little smile and said No in his own time. No customers for liqueurs.

I tried to think of something to say to spin things out a

bit—and to stop Maganhard and the General insulting each other and cocking up the whole deal.

Before I could think of anything, the General looked at Harvey and said: "Understand you're a bodyguard. What d'you think of me collection?"

Harvey glanced back at the guns over the mantelpiece. "Pretty expensive, I'd guess."

"One of the best collections in the world. For its period. But"—and the old face dragged itself into the ghost of a smile—"I thought perhaps you'd see another value in 'em."

Harvey shrugged. "As pistols, you'd be better off throwing rocks. As art, the trouble is they're pistols. Junk like that stopped gun development dead for two hundred years. And I don't suppose it helped art much, either."

I said: "Hold on. You could never get handcrafting like that on a gun these days."

"Thank Christ for that. Or somebody, anyhow." He jerked his head at the display. "Take a real look at them: with all that carving the butts are lousy grips, and I'll bet most of them are muzzle-heavy. Sure, some of the cheaper stuff was better—duelling pistols had real grips and a good balance. But when the top men were doing this sort of stuff, the rest were trying to follow. So they spent two hundred years putting more engraving and gold wire on pistols. If they'd known their jobs they'd have learnt a bit of chemistry and invented percussion caps and cartridge loading two hundred years earlier.

"But they weren't interested: that was too damn practical. They wanted to be artists. Wanted to forget they were making pistols." He stared across at the General. "So they ended up making your stuff. It's an expensive sort of wall-paper—but the wall's where they belong."

I'd been half expecting the General to burst into flames the moment Harvey gave him the chance. But all he did was nod very slowly and rasp: "A refreshingly new point of view, young man. Why d'you hold it so strongly?"

Harvey shrugged and frowned and said slowly: "Pistols are for killing people. Nothing else—there's no other point to them. Maybe I just don't like to see that wrapped up in fancy dress."

The General chuckled softly and the damp eyes fixed on Harvey. "If you get to my age—which I doubt, in your job —you'll know that everybody has to wrap it up somehow. You must have your own way, already."

Harvey went very still.

I shunted myself to my feet. "If we rehearse much longer, we'll start overplaying our parts. Let's get started."

Morgan began helping people into their coats. The General sat where he was, and I stood where I was. The eyes swivelled to me. "Well, Mr Cane," he said quietly, "was I right about Mr Lovell—the way he wraps it up? I saw him with his glass . . ."

"You were right."

"Difficult, Mr Cane. Difficult." The old head trembled on its stalk. "And how do you do it?"

"Me? I go around believing I'm in the right."

"Ah. You know—I'd say that was even more difficult. One so easily comes unwrapped."

I nodded. "And how do you do it, General?"

He sank carefully back in his seat and his eyes closed slowly. "As Mr Lovell said: with gold wire and fancy engraving. I find it lasts."

"I hope so, Brigadier."

The hoods slid open. "You noticed my little conceit, did you?"

"One rank up from Colonel is Brigadier-General—in your day. They dropped the 'General' from it in the 'twenties some time."

"True. But the 'General' was still there when I got it, so . . ." The eyes closed again. "It helps the wrapping."

"Good-bye, General."

He didn't say anything. I nodded and picked up my jacket and raincoat and followed the rest out. Morgan led the way to the back lift. We went straight down to the basement garage.

26

THE moment I saw the car I knew we were safe as far as the frontier. To forget a car like that, the cops would have to be a lot more stupid than even I was ready to believe. Apart from anything else, they must have had over thirty years to get to know this car.

It was a 1930 Rolls-Royce Phantom II 40-50 with a seven-seat limousine-de-ville body. I didn't know all those names and numbers right then: Morgan told me. All I could see then was something like the Simplon-Orient Express mated with a battleship and on four wheels. It was sharing the garage with a couple of modern Rolls, a new Mercedes 600, a Jaguar Mark 10, and a Cadillac. It made the whole bunch look like mere transportation.

It had one little distinction: the damn thing looked as if it was made of engraved silver. In the dull basement light it glowed like next Christmas.

At a second glance, I saw it was just aluminium: unpainted aluminium, milled in small circles so that it caught the light from every angle, and studded with lines of ground-down rivet heads. Five minutes before, I'd have said aluminium hadn't got quite that Rolls touch. I'd have been completely wrong. It had exactly the Rolls touch: it looked expensive, simple, and tough, the way the best fighter planes look, the way a good rifle looks, the way the first real space ship will look.

Beside me, Harvey said softly: "Jesus." Then he nodded at the rear door. "I guess he was worried it didn't look individual enough."

I hadn't noticed it before: a painted crest, about the size of a spread hand, on the door. At first I couldn't work it out, then it clicked. The green-and-white shield of Vaud canton, with the rose and laurel wreath of the Intelligence Corps painted on top—the "rampant pansy resting on its laurels" as the rougher Departments of the Army used to call it. I grinned. It was the only fancy thing about the whole car; the General hadn't been able to resist wrapping it up a little.

Morgan stepped forward and swung open the door. By now he had a black, peaked cap on his head instead of the orange tweed accident. He looked the perfect chauffeur.

Maganhard and Miss Jarman climbed in—and I mean climbed. The bottom was high off the ground, and the top was high off the bottom: you couldn't see over it without standing on the running board.

Harvey walked past and up to the long square-cut bonnet, rapped on it, and called: "You down there in the engine-room—this is the Captain speaking. I want flank speed on both engines." He walked back and got a look from Morgan that you normally only see at bayonet practice.

Harvey nodded to him, said: "And damn the torpedoes, too," and climbed in.

I asked: "Will we have to stop for petrol?"

Morgan did a little mental arithmetic, then said: "I don't think so, sir. We have twenty gallons—and another two in a tin in the boot, if we need it."

That reassured me. I didn't much want to start showing our faces at petrol stations. I climbed in after Harvey and the door closed behind me with a small solid click.

We rolled up into the daylight with all the stately dignity of the *Queen Mary* going down the Solent. Or a hearse heading for an expensive funeral.

The time was half past two.

We turned north, back through most of Montreux, then right into a zigzag up the hillside to Blonay and over to meet the main road for Fribourg, across the corner of the mountains.

Harvey sat beside me on my right, sharing a jump seat that folded down from the partition between us and Morgan. We faced forwards and the back of our seat almost restricted Maganhard's leg-room. But not quite—not in that car.

As soon as we were rolling, Harvey started a careful check-up on the inside of the car: the plate-glass partition between him and the back of Morgan's neck, the roof, the door beside him.

I wasn't worried about the local citizens seeing it wasn't the General in the back seat: where Maganhard and Miss Jarman were sitting, it was too dark to recognize your own wife, even if you'd wanted to. There were no side windows behind the rear doors, and the car went back nearly four feet from there. The small back window was heavily smoked glass, and even the rear door windows were tinted. The car had the atmosphere of the smoking-room from one of the richer London clubs, and it was furnished to match.

The seats were of thick brown leather, the woodwork was dark mahogany, the handles and knobs of scratched, worn brass that looked much more solid than brand-new brass ever did. The carpet and the silk panelling on the roof had the same tone: a dull gold. None of it looked smart and new, but it had never been intended to. It was supposed to look worn—and as if it would never wear out.

After a while, Maganhard said: "This seems a very distinctive car for a man like the General. He must be a man who makes enemies; I would have expected something less obvious." He was obviously feeling smug about his own idea in choosing a Citroën.

I'd been trying to work that out for myself, and reckoned I had. "It's protection—of a sort," I said. "Once somebody's really trying to kill you, you can change your car every month and it won't fool them. This way he attracts as much attention as he can—and a pro killer won't shoot at a man in a spotlight. I suppose it's the same thing as living in one part of one hotel for forty years: anybody knows where to find him but they *don't* know how to get through five floors of a big hotel once they've blown his head off. In a private house up in the hills, he'd be a pushover."

Maganhard said: "I seem to remember some famous political assassinations that worked in public places."

"Political killings are by cranks—and they get caught. The point of a pro killer is that he can count the odds; he won't shoot unless they're on his side."

"Amateurs are hell," Harvey said absently, still looking carefully round the inside of the car. "You can set up something that's watertight for the professional—you're playing the same rules. Then some amateur walks in and blows the whole thing. The trouble in our business is, we only fire the second shot. You get a guy who doesn't care if the second shot knocks his head off—what can you do?"

I turned and smiled reassuringly at the dark shape that was Maganhard. "You see? Just be glad people like you and the General don't attract cranks—only real killers."

Maganhard said: "I'll try and remember to be thankful."

Harvey just grunted and went on exploring the door at his side, and the partition in front.

I noticed we were going up a steep hill, but the car didn't. It would have taken a hopped-up Mercedes a lot of work with the gearbox just to keep us in sight. Morgan only changed down from top a couple of times. But you hardly need gears with a seven-litre engine that turns slowly enough to have started the old crack about "it fires once at every mile-post". That period of Rolls doesn't have much top speed—and never did have—but it'll go up a vertical slope like fire along a fuse.

We didn't even slow down for the corners. I got a hasty flashback of my past life the first time Morgan slammed that great chariot into a hairpin bend, but it just sailed round. The springing was as stiff as a five-day corpse. We got to know that springing better once we were over the crest and opened up down the straight on the other side. It felt very solid and stable, but when you hit a hole in the road your backside knew about it by special delivery.

Harvey finished his tour of inspection, swung round on me, and said abruptly: "Okay—the car's secure. There's no microphones and that partition's soundproof. He can't hear a word." He nodded at the back of Morgan's neck, a few inches away through the thick glass. "So now tell me, Cane: why the hell are we riding in this heap?"

I smiled in a friendly way and said: "It's a nice car. And as far as you're concerned, it's a free ride. Enjoy it."

His eyes were cold and steady. "A piece of cheese," he said softly, "just a big piece of Gruyère—and four blind mice sitting around in the holes thinking how nice somebody's left it lying around just when they felt hungry. *Why are we riding in this car, Cane?*"

"It's still a free ride."

Miss Jarman said: "Do you think the General——"

"Yes-I-do-think-the-General," Harvey said, still watching me. "Okay, Cane—I know you've been right before. But just think of this: for the first time on this trip, somebody knows where we'll be—*exactly* where we'll be, within a few inches—when we're crossing that frontier. If that's a trap, it's a very damn good one."

"I know," I said. "But look at it this way: *we* know exactly where *they'll* be waiting. And that hasn't happened before, either."

"You mean it *is* a trap?" His eyebrows had that half-degree slant on them.

"Hell, of course it's a trap. What else d'you expect for three thousand francs in this business?"

Maganhard came awake at full volume: "General Fay is working for—for this Galleron?"

I smiled over my shoulder at him. I liked the way he said "this" Galleron, as if the world was full of Gallerons, all trying to lift his ten millions' worth of Caspar AG, but only this one likely to do it.

"Well," I said, "if the General wasn't working for him twenty minutes ago, I'll bet he is now. But I think he always was. It was always likely, wasn't it? There's damn few big deals in this part of the world where the General isn't working for one side or the other. And you and Flez hadn't hired him."

"You guessed this?" he shouted. "And you let me pay him three thousand francs?" He was glaring at me as if I'd grown two heads, and neither of them friendly.

"Well, I *did* suggest you paid a third of seven-and-a-half," I said soothingly. "That'd have saved you five hundred. *He* knew he'd never collect the rest, but he wouldn't have dared refuse it."

He wasn't soothed, of course. "Why should I pay anything to be betrayed?"

"He did help get you out of jug—and you're still getting what he sold you: a cop-free ride to the frontier. He wasn't fooling about that. If he wanted us caught by the cops, he could have left you in the pen in Montreux. Anyway, we know they don't want us caught: they want us dead. You must have noticed *that*."

"And we're driving into a trap," he said harshly.

"Let's just say we've conned them into giving us a free ride past the cops. And telling us where the trouble's coming."

Harvey slanted his eyebrows again. "You were planning this?"

I shrugged. "I was spinning a coin. Either he wasn't working for Galleron, so he could have sold us some genuine help, or he was, and he'd try to steer us into a trap. When he came down, I just had to know if he was heads or tails."

Miss Jarman said curiously: "How *did* you know?"

"He didn't make enough money out of us. Three thousand is nothing in this game; he didn't even charge for getting Maganhard out of jail. Then he tried to fool us over the fortifications."

"You mean the map's a fake?" Harvey said.

"No. What good would a fake do them? And, anyway, why should he have one lying around?—he didn't know we were coming. No—when I sounded worried about walking through the fortifications, he backed me up. *He* knows all about fortifications, but he didn't think I would, seeing they weren't much used in the last war.

"In fact, a fortified zone's one of the easiest things in the world to walk through; trenches are just a lot of paths sunk seven feet down. They're planned just so that you can rush up reinforcements or retreat down them or whatever. But he wanted us to think it was difficult—so he could steer us into just one place. That's why he called that map a 'patrol path'. There's no such thing: a patrol would go up through the communications trenches, if it didn't start from the front line itself."

"So what's the map?"

"A tank path. A fixed line's also a base for the counter-attack, and you've got to be able to send up your tanks: *they* can't go through the trenches. You'd have to have a path for them: bridges over the trenches and so on. That's what he tore off the bottom of the map: the title."

Harvey nodded slowly. "And a copy of the map's on its way to Liechtenstein by train right now?"

"I hope so. They should have plenty of time to get ready for us."

"That's great." He eased down comfortably in his seat. "So we know they'll wait till then?"

"They're professionals."

He closed his eyes. "That's always nice to know."

27

WE rolled past the last of the big cuckoo-clock style chalets of Montreux residents who don't like living in hotels or don't have bad enough consciences to make it necessary, and came into open farmland. Children at the roadside tried to sell us bunches of wild narcissus by waving them at us, but we steamed on past. On this trip, no flowers by request.

Beside me, Harvey was dozing, which wasn't typical for him. Maybe his short night and the long hangover had caught up. Behind, Maganhard settled down to reading the *Journal de Genève* which he'd picked up in the General's rooms, and muttering things about share prices to Miss Jarman. I stretched my neck and caught her writing them down. I suppose it mattered.

About half past three we burbled through the outskirts of Fribourg, the great cliff of the old town hanging over us until we were on our way out on the other side. I did a bit of work on the Michelins with my watch and reckoned we were well on time.

I felt sleepy, despite the jolting and creaking of the car, but I wasn't sure I ought to be asleep. I tried to convince myself that the last thing the General would do was set up a gunfight for when we were still in *his* car with *his* driver. I convinced myself, all right, but by then I wasn't sleepy any more.

Just before Bern, Harvey woke up. He did it slowly, like a man climbing out of mud, or out of an hour's sleep when what he needs is another six. He lit a cigarette, still moving slowly, and coughed several times.

Then he asked: "Where are we?"

"Bern."

"How far now?"

"About four and a half hours."

"Jesus." He wiped a hand over his face and then looked at the hand. I tried not to look as well, but I was as interested as he was—and for the same reason. The fingers were quivering.

I waited, but he didn't say anything.

We sailed majestically through the middle of Bern, sprang past the national Parliament, across the river, and out along the Thunstrasse. We got a lot of interested looks from the citizenry, and a couple of cops gave us half-official salutes. They knew the car, all right.

We ran out of the city and the road surface turned rough again. The Rolls gave out a faint squeaking and creaking of wood rubbing on wood. It was an oddly reassuring noise, perhaps like being in a cabin of an old tea-clipper under full canvas.

I turned and peered into the shadow of the back seat. "You say you haven't heard of this man Galleron?"

Maganhard said: "Never."

I nodded. "He's turning out quite a boy, isn't he? He knows enough to employ the General, to hire a gunman like Bernard, maybe enough to frame you on a rape charge— and he gets hold of Heiliger's shares."

"To me," he said, "that is the most remarkable thing. Max believed in personal possession. He carried everything with him."

"A big black briefcase," Miss Jarman said softly. "Chained to his wrist. And full of bearer shares, bonds, deeds. It must have been worth millions."

"So?" I looked at her. "Then why wasn't he carrying it when he crashed?"

She smiled in the gloom. "Nobody seems to know, Mr Cane."

Maganhard said suddenly: "You said *maybe* this Galleron arranged the—the charge against me. Is it not obvious it must be him?"

"Not quite. If he fixed that charge, then he gave himself a system for keeping you away from Caspar meetings: getting you pinched by the cops. He could have put the cops on to you several times in the last two days—but every time he tried to kill you instead. I don't see why. He doesn't need you dead to be able to out-vote your partner Flez. He only needs to stop you coming to the meeting."

Maganhard said: "He dare hardly leave me alive if he proposes to try and destroy my company." And he sounded rather smug about it.

I shook my head. "I don't buy that. What could you do to him, once he's forced the decision to sell Caspar out? He isn't stealing anything, he's just turning the company into cash. He gets his share—but you get yours. Where's your complaint?" Before he could start telling me, I added: "I mean legal complaint."

Miss Jarman said: "Are you trying to tell us that this Galleron person is not really trying to kill us?"

Harvey chuckled quietly.

"No," I said. "But if he was going to the trouble to hire people like Bernard to kill you, I don't see why he needed the French rape charge as well." Then I got another bright idea. "Maybe it's all a stunt by Flez, trying to get control of Caspar. Maybe there's no Galleron, maybe Heiliger's certificate *did* go up in the crash. You've never met Galleron."

"No, but Monsieur Merlin has. As soon as I heard from Herr Flez, Merlin flew out to see them."

"He saw Galleron?"

"Yes."

"Why the hell didn't he kick Galleron's teeth in and grab the certificate?"

"That is not the way *lawyers* work, Mr Cane. And you forget—this Galleron may legally own the certificate. He may be Max's legal heir."

"Yes. I forgot there must be *something* legal about all this."

"And in any event," he went on smoothly, "Herr Flez could not hold a meeting by himself. Under the rules, there must always be two shareholders present."

I nodded. "All right. Now we know Flez is a Good Guy. So why isn't Galleron killing him instead of you? He can out-vote either of you as long as the other isn't there—but you're skidding all over Europe and Flez is sitting in Liechtenstein. I'd've thought it was a lot easier to knock off Flez instead."

Maganhard chewed this over. Then he said: "Also under Caspar's rules, Herr Flez, as resident director, has a special responsibility. He must be at a company meeting. If he is not, and he is still alive, his vote is taken for granted on the majority side. This, you understand, is to stop him deliberately preventing a meeting by not appearing when only one other shareholder can be present.

"But, of course, I am not bound to appear. So if this Galleron killed Herr Flez, I could stop the meeting by not arriving."

I nodded slowly. "I get it. So as long as he's trying to kill you, he's got to keep Flez alive."

But I still didn't see why simply getting Maganhard in jail wouldn't have done just as well.

We rumbled through the covered wooden bridge into Langnau and across the cobbled streets. Beyond that, we were in the picture-postcard country of the Entlebuch valley; dark sweeps of pine forest on the hills, bright apple blossom by the roads, and old church spires that looked like witches' caps.

But to me, most of Switzerland is a picture postcard. Calm, arranged, carefully trimmed . . . *the weather isn't bad, the Rolls is going well, but not much excitement—nobody's shot at us in hours* . . . It's something to do with me, not with Switzerland. Maybe just that this place looked like a postcard when a lot of Europe was like something from a horror film.

I'm too old to grow out of it, but perhaps it'll die with me.

Harvey shifted in his seat, rubbed his face again, and sneaked another look at his fingers. He just spread them open in front of him—not as obvious as stretching them full out at arms' length the way doctors make you do it, but clear enough if you knew what he was up to. The fingers were shaking like a hula dancer's hips.

He turned his head slowly and looked at me. His face was blank—as blank as his face could ever be. It was still a face that would know hell when it saw it, but it didn't show what it knew now.

Except that I could guess. I said: "You need a drink."

He looked at his spread fingers again, with no more emotion than if he was deciding he needed a manicure. Then he said slowly and simply: "Yes. I'm afraid I need just that."

I'd been expecting this—but still hoping I wouldn't get it. After getting plastered last night at Pinel, he was back on the old routine: either he took a drink, or his hands shook themselves off his wrists. He'd only managed to delay it so long by the wine he'd drunk at the General's; now even that was wearing off.

The shakes would pass, all right—in about twenty-four hours. I might need him handling a gun inside five.

I sorted the maps in my briefcase and consulted one. "We should be in Wolhusen in ten minutes. You can get a couple of quick ones there."

He nodded, but went on staring at his hand. Then he said: "Or maybe a bottle."

I didn't like the idea. I wanted him to take on just enough to cure his shakes, but not so much that he slowed his reactions. It was a pretty thin line . . . I was crazy: it wasn't a line at all, only a matter of time. Once he started drinking, he wouldn't stop until he'd dissolved. That's what alcoholism's about.

But an alcoholic who's worrying about where the next one's coming from won't have time to worry about anything else. A bottle would reassure him, and all I could do was hope any trouble came before his co-ordination had washed away.

"All right," I said. "We'll stop and pick one up."

Miss Jarman said: "Must you, Harvey?"

Harvey twisted and held a hand out to her. She looked at the dancing fingers, then reached and held them for a moment. Then she opened the mahogany glove-box set into the wall beside her, and took out the biggest silver flask I've ever seen.

"I found it earlier," she said simply.

He took it and unscrewed the big cap and poured himself a shot. Whatever it was, there must have been well over half a bottle of it. He sniffed and sipped.

"Four-star, too," he said.

"Cognac?"

He nodded, lifted the cap, and toasted me. "It could be a good day yet."

I wasn't sure about that.

We passed Wolhusen and ran into Luzern. We lost time there by mixing in with the rush-hour traffic, but I'd have been far more worried to reach the frontier in daylight and dawdle around waiting for darkness.

After that we were into a series of long switchbacks: winding along on the level by a lake, then hauling up over a small range of mountains, and down to the next lake. Nobody said much. Harvey took occasional sips at the cognac: twice he filled the cap up again. But he wasn't rushing it.

I looked at my watch. An hour and a half to dark. Five hours to midnight.

Maganhard asked: "Have you worked out where we shall cross, Mr Cane?"

I grabbed to make sure the partition window was wound up tight—and found Harvey's hand on it already. He smiled easily. By now, he was just about at his brightest and best. Three cognacs had killed the shakes without clouding his reactions.

But from now, the only way he could go was downhill.

I pulled out the photostat map and spread it across my knees. "The fortifications run crossways over a small ridge—the Fläscherberg. The tank path stays on the road side, runs almost parallel with it, a few hundred yards away. So if we cross over the ridge, alongside the river, we can walk through there and nobody'll hear us."

"In all, how long will it take?"

"If we can get started soon after eight-thirty—well, we may have to get through a bit of barbed wire at the front itself. . . . Let's say we'll be at a phone on the other side by ten o'clock at the latest. We get your pal Flez to come and collect us, and we'll be in Vaduz by half past."

"We are not going to Vaduz."

I turned and peered into the gloom. "Maybe I should have asked this before: I'd been worrying just about the frontier. Right—where *are* we going in Liechtenstein?"

"Company meetings are held at Herr Flez's house in Steg."

"Steg?" At first the name didn't mean anything to me.

Then I remembered it: a little village way up on the only road that ran up into the mountains. The road itself faded out a couple of kilometres farther on, at a ski hotel right under the peaks that were the Austrian border.

"Christ," I said slowly. "It's a pretty lonely place up there." All I could remember of it was a few woodcutters' huts and a handful of chalets. "Flez must be an honest man."

"We have not had dealings with gunmen before this," Maganhard said. "And I do not think it would be wise for Herr Flez to come and fetch us. You forget: he will have this Galleron with him by then. If Galleron knows we have escaped his ambush, he may . . ." He tried to think of things this Galleron might do.

I could think of them for myself. I started to ask if Merlin would be there by then, but didn't: even if he was, the same snag applied. We'd still tip off Galleron and lose the element of surprise.

Maganhard said calmly: "So you must find us a car on the other side of the frontier."

That was all—just find a car. And a driver to get a good look at our faces—even if he agreed to go up the steep, stony road to Steg that was probably snowed-in at the top. And we wouldn't even find that nearer than Vaduz, ten kilometres beyond the frontier.

Maganhard knew Liechtenstein—and the problem. "You may have to steal one," he added just as calmly.

"That always sounds the easy way," I said gloomily. "Look —there won't be many cars in those little villages just across the frontier. And they won't be parked in the street. And even if they are, they won't have the keys in them. And I can't start opening one up and rewiring it in the middle of the village."

"Then you will have to think of something else," Maganhard said. "I hired you to get me to Steg by——"

"I know. I'm thinking." But I didn't like what I was thinking. And the more I thought, the less I liked it. But I couldn't think of anything else.

I said slowly: "We're already in a car."

Harvey jerked his head round, then slanted his eyebrows at me. Miss Jarman said: "What d'you mean?"

"The tank path. If it'll take a tank, it'll take a Rolls-Royce. We kick out Morgan—and drive across. Then we've got a car on the other side."

The girl's voice was almost breathless with disbelief. "But —but you said they'd be waiting there, expecting us!"

"They aren't expecting a Rolls. And they aren't expecting us to expect them. We've got that much margin."

"We could still get shot to hell," Harvey said thoughtfully.

"Then think of something better."

After a long time, he smiled crookedly. "Hell, you're just crazy to use that machine-gun of yours again. All right." Then, carefully and steadily, he poured himself another brandy.

28

THERE was a police Volkswagen parked up on the clifftop road alongside the Wallensee, but they waved us on past and went on stopping selected other cars. They obviously weren't taking the roads before Liechtenstein very seriously—the real blocks would come at the frontier—but it still told me something.

They didn't know we'd been in Montreux: if they'd known that, they'd have been bound to stop any car they *knew* came from Montreux, even the General's. And that meant my friend the Montreux inspector hadn't talked— and if he hadn't talked now, he probably wouldn't later. He had good reason: if he talked, he had to admit both to arresting Maganhard before there was an official request *and* to getting conned into letting him go again.

Those are two big pieces of pride for a cop to swallow whole. I hoped he'd go on chewing a long time: he was the only official who could give a good description of me. I must remember not to drop in and buy him a drink one day.

The last of the sun glittered on the snow of the mountains across the lake, and darkness closed in around us as we came down into the See Tal valley. After that, it got darker fast. Morgan put on the headlights and huge yellow beams spread all over the road and well off it.

Harvey poured himself his fifth cognac and asked: "Where do we take over?"

"May as well wait until he stops to let us out, near the frontier. You noticed he's got a gun?"

Harvey nodded, sipped, and asked: "And where d'you think they'll be waiting?"

I opened the photostat map again, lit a cigarette, and started studying.

The fortifications were some of the most careful, well-planned ever built. Three lines of firing trenches—first line, second line, reserve line—neatly laid out with plenty of corners, and connected up by zigzag communication trenches.

And pillboxes, blockhouses, dugouts scattered around lavishly. Everything to fight the Perfect War.

And why not? Generals never get things right until it's well out of date, and this lot had been built a good fifteen years after air power and armour had made it useless. Nowadays, you wouldn't attack this sort of thing head-on: you'd isolate it with fighter-bombers, flatten it with carpet-bombing . . . No. Nowadays you'd just press a button. My own ideas were a war out of date by now.

It makes you feel old. Probably that's the generals' trouble, too.

Harvey said: "Well?"

"I think they'll be coming in from Liechtenstein itself," I said. "They'll have been waiting for us there: they couldn't have banked on catching us anywhere before then, not until they knew where we're crossing. And they'll probably want to hop back into Liechtenstein afterwards. The Swiss side'll be crawling with cops—but *only* the Swiss side. Liechtenstein's only got about fifteen cops: they couldn't put two men on every frontier post for any time."

Harvey nodded. "So they'll come just across the frontier —but only just?"

"I think so. Most of the fortified zone isn't fortified at all: most of it's just headquarters buildings, artillery platforms —stuff like that. It's only the last couple of hundred yards— the battle zone itself—that's really built up. And that's bang on the frontier."

"Plenty of cover," he said thoughtfully, "and just a short step home to Liechtenstein." He nodded again. "And what are the Swiss cops going to do when they hear shooting?"

"Come running. But they'll be half a mile away, up on the road, and they'll be running through trenches. I think they'll miss the big picture."

Maganhard said sharply: "They will know I am in Liechtenstein."

"They'll guess it. But they can't come chasing across that frontier. The *Sûreté*'ll have to start all over again, asking Liechtenstein to extradite you. You—or Flez—should have enough pull to hold that off for a few days. By then——" I shrugged.

The girl said quietly: "I think that's Liechtenstein."

It was the lights of Mäls and Balzers, the two little towns —villages—down just inside the frontier. Still miles away, across a river we hadn't yet reached, but somehow very bright and close. All we had to do was be in those towns; by then, our troubles would be behind us.

The Rolls trundled steadily on, angling away, turning its back on the lights as it ran down to cross the river where both banks were Swiss territory.

We crossed at the first bridge, turned back north through Maienfeld, and started the climb up to St Luzisteig. The tank path would begin there.

On our right was the steep mountain wall, turning to snow a couple of thousand feet up: that was the right wing of the St Luzisteig fortifications. Ahead on our left was the long dark bulk of the Fläscherberg, the ridge that was the central anchor of the defences. By now, out there, the defences would be beginning: the old overgrown humps of the hundred-year-old stonework, mixed with the modern first-aid dugouts, artillery locations. But soon the real trenches, pillboxes, wire. Too dark to see. But there.

It wasn't easy to think of cold, waterlogged trenches and rusty barbed wire, not from the back of a Rolls Phantom II. It was too solid, warm, and imperturbable to imagine anybody stopping us. All I had to say was "Drive on, my man", and we'd bluff our way through at the frontier easily. Why bother with barbed wire?

I was learning how the rich can get to feel—and why they suddenly wake up in such trouble. Maybe they wrap themselves up warm in Rolls-Royces, in mahogany and dark leather, and say "Drive on". It couldn't happen to them. And that was why it did.

Both kings and fieldmice would be showing their passports on the frontier tonight.

We passed a handful of lights, the last village before St Luzisteig itself. Morgan slowed down, searching the roadside carefully. There was a notice saying that stopping and taking photographs was highly *Verboten*. We were in the right place. The Rolls drifted to a stop.

We were just before the high point of the road; from a couple of hundred yards ahead, it sloped down to Liechtenstein, three kilometres away. The plan would be that tanks could get to here on the road itself, out of sight of the enemy over the crest. Then they'd swing off on to the tank path.

Morgan switched off the lights, climbed down, and opened the left rear door. I had my hand on the Mauser, down in the briefcase, but he was still being the perfect chauffeur. It wasn't his job to swing the axe; he just led us politely up to the chopping block. I climbed stiffly out and looked up at the sky.

Inside the narrow valley the light had seeped away quickly, but the sky was more opaque than really dark. It was a stampede of broken, lumpy cloud hurrying south-westwards, jumping from peak to peak, and letting through flares of thin, nervous moonlight. A cold wind nibbled at me and I buttoned my raincoat. But there was another cold wind nibbling inside.

Harvey came up between me and Morgan, took out his revolver, and checked the load. I'd never seen him do that before: a gunman always knows exactly how many rounds he's got left.

"Congregation will sing three choruses of *Wir fahren gegen Liechtenstein* and we'll roll," he said. He turned to Morgan and pointed the gun. "Don't try for that gun."

In the quiet, Morgan made a small sucking noise between his teeth. Then he looked past Harvey at me. "I never did trust *you*," he said.

"That makes it even." I walked round behind him and lifted a huge ·45 Webley service revolver from under his raincoat. It must have given him ten sorts of rheumatism driving with that cannon back there.

"You'll be taking the Rolls, I suppose?" he said gloomily. "You know they'll arrest you, anyway, man."

"Not if we go down that tank path."

"But—after that they'll think the General is involved!" He sounded honestly outraged.

"Wrong answer, Sergeant. Don't you remember?—we're not supposed to know it's a tank path—or that something's going to happen down there. And the General's already involved up to his moustache; if he gets a bit of it up his nose, well—he shouldn't have sold us out."

He just glowered at me, a little bent man searching his little bent brain to save the reputation of a crumbling old crook back in Montreux. Nothing to give three cheers for, but maybe nothing to sneer at either.

Then he said: "He's sold out better men than *you*."

Behind me, Maganhard said: "I hope I'm not expected to take that as evidence of General Fay's kind heart."

Morgan glanced contemptuously at him, then walked off back down the road to Maienfeld, moving with the last remnants of a military strut.

I watched him out of sight, round a bend, then walked across to the left-hand side of the road and started looking at the fence.

Twenty yards up I found what I was looking for: a thin place in the wire fence, guarded by a couple of barbed-wire strands. I waited for a flare of moonlight, then picked out a faint track beyond it leading off at the right angle.

I found Miss Jarman just behind me. She asked: "Is that the path?"

"That's it." I hauled out Morgan's big revolver, broke it open so that it couldn't fire accidentally, then caught the top wire strand between the hammer and the breech, and started twisting quickly side-to-side. Not as good as wire-cutters, but it works in the end.

The girl said: "It won't be easy without lights. And it might be overgrown by now."

"They probably clear it every few years—and anything a small tank'll knock down, so will a Rolls."

"Can you drive a Rolls?"

I shrugged. "They're rich men's cars, not wild men's. They can't be difficult."

"You're used to the ignition retard-and-advance and mixture controls?" she asked sweetly. I stared at her. She said: "I'd better drive."

"Don't be——" The wire strand broke. "Don't be crazy. In case you didn't know, you're not even coming on this trip. You walk back to Maienfeld and get picked up tomorrow."

She said quickly and tonelessly: "My father had a Phantom II as official car when he was Governor-General. I learnt to drive on one. So I'd better drive."

I thought of asking where he'd Governor-Generalled, then decided I believed her, anyway. And she had a point about the driving; whatever I'd said about a Rolls not being difficult, this one had been built for a style of driving more than thirty years old.

I started to work on the second wire.

She said: "It would let you and Harvey keep your hands free, as well." Which was another point.

"Unless," she added, "you still think I'm on the other side."

"No." I shook my head. "I don't think that. I don't think you were trying to get yourself—and Harvey—killed. I just wasn't sure you knew the danger of tapped phones—or just people talking. Somebody says 'Maganhard's secretary rang me today from Montreux', and the word gets around. That could be just the same as selling us out." I waited a moment, then asked: "So who were you ringing?"

"A man who has a . . . a sort of hospital, in the mountains near Chamonix. For Harvey. I know he cured another man who drank too much. I thought he might help."

"Why didn't you tell me this?"

"I don't know," she said quietly. "It seemed sort of . . . private. And I didn't think you were taking me seriously."

And that was just about true. For the sake of honesty rather than tact, I said carefully: "Maybe I wondered if you were just playing at helping lame dogs over stiles."

"I can't be sure myself," she said simply. "Lame dogs are very rare in our world, Mr Cane. Most of them are either wolves or overfed lap-dogs. All I can do is try and help him—and try and find out why."

"It'll be a full-time job—even if you can get him to go with you."

"I don't suppose I can. But I can go with him. I've told Mr Maganhard I'm leaving."

I nodded. Maybe I was getting convinced, after all. But there was one thing more to be said. "He's the sort of man he is partly because he drinks. If he stops drinking, he'll be a different man. You may not like the different man."

"I know. It's a risk."

The second wire broke. She said: "Have you lost the wire-cutters we used at the airport?"

And damn me, they'd been sitting in my briefcase all the time. I was in a marvellous state for starting a battle.

She said: "So I can drive, then?"

Somebody with some sense had better do something. I kicked the ends of the wire clear. "You can drive."

We walked back. Harvey said: "What the hell's been keeping you?"

"Short exchange of views on the political situation in the Balkans. She's driving."

"She's *what*? We figured she'd be staying here."

"Changed my mind. She knows how to drive these cars. Cuts down the risk, when you think about it."

"Not for her, it doesn't."

"True."

The girl climbed in the driving seat, which put her head higher than if she'd been standing on the ground.

Harvey said: "Is this the old Resistance spirit?—equal opportunity for women to get killed?"

"Something like that."

The starter whirred, the engine began its deep burble, like a gramophone record of a voice being played far too slow.

I turned away. Harvey said doggedly: "I still don't like it."

I jerked back. "D'you think *I* like it—any of it? If I'd known this job would end up running a Rolls-Royce through the Western Front, I wouldn't have come within a thousand miles of it. But we came—so we're going the last two kilometres."

"She could get killed."

"Talk her out of it, then."

I got into the back of the car, assembled the Mauser, and then remembered Morgan's big Webley which was weighing down my raincoat pocket. I thought about it, decided I wasn't a two-gun man, and handed it to Maganhard.

He started to object. I said: "Nobody can force you to

use it, Mr Maganhard. But if things go wrong, you may just feel like it."

When I got down again, Harvey had finished his conversation with the girl.

I said: "Well?"

He said: "I still don't like it." But he swung up on the right-hand running-board, his arm wrapped around the door pillar. I climbed up on the left one. Miss Jarman shoved the lever into first gear, and we were on our way.

29

THE first few hundred yards of track were in good condition; they must have been used as a farm path. We were passing through grazing meadows, past clumps of trees, past odd-shaped grassy humps that were part of the old stone fortifications.

The girl could drive that car, all right. The engine sometimes slowed to a deep thumping like a pom-pom gun firing in a pillow factory—but she used the ignition retard instead of the gearbox, and kept in second gear. The faster, higher pitch of first gear would have carried a lot farther.

The path was angling gently away from the road above us, keeping more or less to the floor of the small valley, but wandering from side to side in a way that was meaningless until you remembered it was a military affair. Then you saw that it was taking advantage of every small fold in the ground, every clump of trees, to find cover.

Abruptly we were in among pines, weaving along just inside the edge of a forest that stretched uphill to the Fläscherberg on our left. More cover; logical. But very dark.

Miss Jarman asked: "Can I use the lights?"

I leant in through the window. "No. But if I shout for lights, I want the headlights on full, undipped."

"Is that a good idea?"

"If I don't think so, I won't shout."

We crept on. The trees had no colour; just burned, black skeletons draped in tattered black robes. And you couldn't see five yards through them.

But nobody sets up gunfights among trees. Too narrow a field of fire, too dark, plenty of cover to jump behind . . . I remembered all that.

But did they?

I said: "Push it along. Fast as you can."

"I thought you said they'd wait until the very front," she said.

"I still think so. I just got frightened."

She may have laughed to herself, but we speeded up. She was winding the big, almost horizontal wheel from side to side; either she'd been seeing too many gangster movies, or the steering was very light and high-geared.

We cleared the trees, and the cringing feeling of waiting for a bullet passed.

Then, just past the edge of the forest, there was a low, long square shape: the first of the modern fortifications. I leaned in and said: "Stop here for a moment."

She let the car drift to a quiet stop. I walked across, and Harvey came up behind me. Without saying anything, we moved to either side as we closed up on the door of the blockhouse.

He asked quietly: "What are we looking for?"

"Just studying the local architecture."

He glanced at me, then nodded and started studying.

It was a very good blockhouse, if you happened to care about blockhouses, and the people who built this one had really cared. The walls at the loopholes were eighteen inches of solid concrete; the entrance was correctly cluttered with blast walls to keep out stray bullets or shell splinters; the loopholes were horizontal fan-shaped slits, wider at the outside. And the whole thing sunk several feet into the ground, so that only the top three or four feet showed.

It wasn't brand new any more. The camouflage paint had worn off, and the concrete had a damp and spongy feel, and came off in a gritty paste on your hands. But it was still eighteen inches thick.

Harvey ran a finger down the wall and said thoughtfully: "Would have been a wonderful war." Then he looked at me. "You think the rest of it, up front, is like this?"

"Yes."

"I'd been thinking of just holes in the ground, trenches. Like that." He turned away. "Would have been a wonderful war."

After that, the fortifications came thicker and faster. An occasional pillbox in among a clump of trees; concrete platforms for guns; mortar pits gaping like open graves. The track got rougher, became just two ruts with small bushes and four-year-old trees sticking up between. The Rolls swept over them and scraped them to pieces on its underside.

I could have wished it any other colour but the one it was. In the drifts of moonlight the polished aluminium seemed to shine like a neon light.

The track flattened out on the valley floor. Half a mile away, up on our right, headlights flickered silently along the frontier road and stopped . . . *Your papers please . . . just a routine check . . . Thank you very much, a good journey to you.* A different world.

The car slowed. Harvey asked quietly: "Is this it?"

I looked ahead—and it was.

It was a bank, about seven feet high, right across the valley. It had an even, unnatural look, like the slope at the end of a lawn. Then a flare of moonlight showed me more. It wasn't a bank, but a small plateau. The generals had decided that the higher the ground, the better fighting country it was—so they'd made it higher. The whole battle zone was set on a raised platform like a well-laid-out bowling green. It was all very logical, and all a little creepy.

The girl lifted her foot and the car stopped gently at the foot of the bank. An extra advantage of the platform was that it made the land just behind it dead ground—out of sight of an enemy in front. Or anyone waiting in the battle zone itself. That must have been planned, too.

Harvey and I stepped down and walked carefully up the slope and looked out across the battle zone.

At first all I could see was an unnaturally flat plain covered with a dark sea of short bushes, waving stiffly in the wind. Then I began to see the hard, square shapes underneath. Blockhouses, pillboxes, command posts, mortar pits, and the zigzag of communication trenches.

It didn't look like a battle zone. It still had a squared-off neatness that was only slightly worn by thirty years of wind and rain and creeping grass. It looked like an old, lost city, abandoned and gradually sunk seven feet into the earth. But you could never wonder what sort of people had lived here. Nobody had lived.

But nobody had died, either. The clerks had typed out

their little lists of *Casualties to be expected*—and the war had never come, nobody had fought, no casualties. Only the ghosts of men who had never died except on the clerks' typewriters.

Moonlight rippled over the zone and the concrete shapes turned a dim bluey-white like fresh damp bones.

Harvey said: "It doesn't look good."

I looked at him, wondering if he'd been thinking the same things. Then I realized what he meant. And it didn't look good. Out in the zone, you could hide an army. It had been built to do precisely that.

I said carefully: "They'll be near the path. In this light, that means less than ten yards. So we get ourselves into the trench system and kind of creep up on them."

He thought about it for what seemed like a long time. Then he shook his head. "Sorry, Cane. If there's shooting coming, I've got to be with him." He nodded at the car.

"You'll be doing a better job if you and me get the shooting done with before he gets near it."

"Or maybe they jump us and he's sitting back here, naked. I can't do it, Cane."

I said: "We were hired to get him through. I'm going to do that."

He shook his head again. "No. *You* were hired to get him through; I was hired to keep him alive. If I don't think he'll make it alive, my advice is he don't try." He stared at me. "I *told* you at the beginning, Cane, this could happen. We'd end up wanting different things."

"Maganhard'll want to try."

"You could be surprised how people don't want to try things when I tell them it'll get them killed."

I looked at him carefully. "D'you want to call the whole thing off?"

He said quietly: "Yes. I want to call it off."

And then I knew. He was being honest—in the long, looping way that is the only way for a man like him to be honest about such things.

I said: "Let's see what Maganhard says, "and turned back to the car.

Maganhard was already leaning out of the window. I couldn't see his expression, but I could guess. "Well?" he crackled. "What's the delay now?"

Harvey said carefully and tonelessly: "The battle zone is very difficult ground, Mr Maganhard. It's built for exactly the job the other side's trying to do. I can't guarantee your safety if you go on. I advise you not to go."

Maganhard's spectacles glinted dully as he turned to me: "What d'you say, Cane?"

"I don't guarantee anything, either," I said smoothly. "I never did. But I'm ready to go. And in this light they're as likely to hit me as you."

The flat metallic voice said: "That sounds reasonable." The spectacles glinted back at Harvey.

Harvey said doggedly: "Cane and I are trying to do different jobs. He's trying——"

"He seems to be doing the job I want done," Maganhard snapped. "Why aren't you?"

There was a long, slow silence, with just the tickover of the Rolls like a tired heartbeat.

Then Harvey said: "I've drunk too much, Mr Maganhard. There's no point in saying I'm sorry. But I'm slowed up. I'm not as good as I should be."

It must have cost him blood to say that. No alcoholic ever admits it, and no gunman ever admits he might be beaten. And he had.

Maganhard looked at me again. I shrugged. "I still think we can do it."

The front door opened and the girl stepped down beside us.

"If Harvey says he shouldn't go, then you can't make him——"

"I'm not asking Harvey to go. I'm going myself. It's what I was hired for."

Harvey said dully: "You know who's up there? Alain."

"Alain?" Then I thought about it, and he was right. Alain and Bernard—the two top gunmen, the men I'd first asked for. They always worked together. Only they hadn't been together in the Auvergne—and Bernard had got killed. Yes: Alain would most certainly be here now.

I should have thought of that.

Harvey said: "You know Alain. You think you can beat him?"

"Yes." I nodded. "I know him. I can beat him."

"You're crazy."

"No—Alain didn't set this thing up—*I* did. *I* put him out there. And he's still thinking we'll come walking down not expecting trouble. No—this is going to happen my way, not his. I can beat him."

Miss Jarman said viciously: "You must really *want* your money."

"No." Harvey shook his head wearily. "It's not that, honey. He wants to be Caneton. And nobody ever beat Caneton. Yet."

I said quickly: "Bring the car through in fifteen minutes. Unless you hear shooting. Then you can decide for yourself."

I walked away down the bank to the right, looking for the entrance to the communication trench. I found it and turned in.

30

I TOOK several fast steps, turned the first corner, and the close concrete walls shut in on me. After that, I moved more carefully, testing the walls at my side, the floor beneath.

The trench was no more than an unroofed concrete tunnel, working its way forward in zigzags so that an invader couldn't shoot down the length of it. The concrete had the same gritty-soft dampness of the blockhouse farther back, and mud had dribbled down the sides into heaps that were growing tufts of grass. The floor had once had a drainage channel down the middle, but now it was a series of slimy puddles where things moved and gurgled, but never seemed to break the thick surface.

And where are you waiting, Alain? I should know. I worked with you, on your side, in the old days. I remember you: fast, cool, and ruthless. And since then, you've been practising, I hear.

I found myself walking crouched. Stupid. The trench had been dug just deep enough so that you could walk upright and not be seen from outside. Seven feet deep. Just one foot deeper than the grave. And the view out wasn't much better.

At the next corner the turn was much sharper. I poked an eyebrow round, and I was in the third-line firing trench.

It ran across square to the line of the communication trench. Again lined with concrete, but wider and with an eighteen-inch firestep on the front side for defenders to stand on. And above that, at the lip of the trench, there was an irregular humped line sprouting small bushes that must once have been a sandbag parapet.

I took a step and trod on something that crunched. The walls picked up the sound and rang it like a peal of bells along the trench, and things moved suddenly in the puddles, leaving slow swirls and soft *glop* noises.

I froze, and the sounds died. Then I lifted my foot and I'd crushed the muddy-white skeleton of a frog. I took a deep breath and a long stride across on to the firestep.

The air felt suddenly sweet and the bushes rustled gently in the wind. But I couldn't see a damn thing. Ahead of me, the whole battle zone was covered with small bushes, growing higher than I could stand from the trench.

Are you out there, Alain, and not in the trenches at all? You could hide an army out in the bushes, too, by now. And you wouldn't be alone; not you. At least two of you, one on either side of the path to give cross-fire. So if the first shots missed, whichever way we jumped, we'd be jumping into the guns. You're professionals—this job's no use if you don't live to collect your pay. You don't want a gun-battle; just a neat little murder.

I moved along the firestep, where there were no puddles but just heaps of wet sand that had spilled down from the rotted sandbags. When I ducked my head, the wind shut off as if I'd closed a hatch, and the air was close, warm, and slimy.

The firing trenches had their own pattern: the zigzags were squared off, like the shape of huge battlements laid flat on the ground. The front parallels were where you were supposed to win the war from; the rear ones (what the hell did they call them?—yes, "traverses") for having a quiet smoke while somebody else won it.

I walked round several corners, from traverse up to front and back again. Almost every front wall had something in it: dark, foul-smelling entrances to deep dugouts, or steps up to a squat pillbox sunk into the parapet. The pillboxes were always on the front parallels.

Then I saw the tank path. It crossed on a culvert built into a traverse: a heavy concrete affair to support the weight of a tank above, yet leaving a three-foot tunnel for crawling through underneath.

I stayed where I was. I knew now that if Alain was in the trenches, he wasn't in this third line. He'd have somebody on both sides . . . I shivered as I remembered how cheerfully I'd walked up round those corners.

I walked back more carefully, found the communication trench leading to the second line. As I turned in, I looked at my watch: I'd used six of my fifteen minutes.

The lines were supposed to be seventy yards apart, but

the zigzag of the trench turned it into a hundred-yard trip. And at one point a barbed-wire entanglement laid across the top had collapsed into the trench itself. I slid through with no more than three or four injections of blood-poisoning off the rusted spikes.

But at least it told me how far I'd come: barbed wire should be laid just outside grenade-throwing range of the trench it protects. Rules of War—before people started throwing dive-bombers and armoured columns instead of grenades. . . .

Grenades. Would Alain have grenades? Yes—if he was expecting a car. But he wasn't. Just several people in the open—and there grenades are useless. All that time waiting for them to go off, and after the flash and bang, you don't know if they're dead or hiding in the ditch. So—no grenades.

So what instead? A burst of Sten-gun fire. Just waiting until we were close enough to chop us down with one burst . . . And where had I thought of that idea before? Yes—in Quimper, the man in the car, the dead man. Resistance Stengunner. 9 mm. cartridge on his key-ring—probably from the first time he killed with his nice new Sten. Sentimentalist. Realists fight for money. Like Alain. Like Caneton.

I stopped at the corner, lowered my head, and peered carefully around three feet off the ground. Nothing. I hadn't expected anything. But I'd remembered I was in a trench system built to have as many corners as possible for men with guns to wait behind . . .

Was I here for twelve thousand francs? No. I'd insisted on being told that Maganhard was in the *right*—that he hadn't raped anybody, that he wasn't trying to kill anybody but people were trying to kill him. That made him in the right—and me too. Just an old sentimentalist.

Or because I was Caneton?

I looked quickly left-and-right into the second-line firing trench, stepped across on to the firestep, and started moving left, towards the tank path.

Suddenly it was a long, cold bright way to the next corner. I got there, but it cost me something that I wouldn't have left to get me round the next. And the next after that.

I moved carefully, feeling with my foot for obstacles before putting it down, keeping my eyes and the gun on the corner ahead.

Put "He died for twelve thousand francs" on a man's tomb and nobody'll sneer. They'll reckon he knew what he was doing. Twelve thousand francs is something you can count; you can say it isn't enough; you can change your mind and not earn it.

But you can't count being Caneton; you can't back down from that. And for that, maybe you'll do things you'd never do just for twelve thousand francs . . .

Then the next corner was a long way off and horribly close, and I was moving towards it far too fast and much too slowly. And my time must be nearly up—but I daren't look at my watch. I had to look at the corner. And the corner looked steadily back.

I froze, with the Mauser up and aimed and the trigger a fraction away from loosing a bright, noisy, friendly blast of fire. And the quiet corner watched me.

But Maganhard is right and Alain is wrong . . . And me? Then I knew that nothing I could do would ever change either of those things. All I could do was fix the cost—the cost of being right or wrong. And perhaps who paid.

Slowly, very slowly, I lifted my left wrist and laid it across the barrel of the aimed gun and flicked my eyes for an instant at the luminous dial of my watch.

Three minutes. Just time to go back, to say the hell with twelve thousand francs *and* being Caneton. To tell Maganhard he'll still be in the right whether he gets through or not, and that what matters is the cost . . .

But still time enough to fix the cost, to make that right. Because it was still the fight I'd planned and not what Alain was expecting. Because I *was* still Caneton—and nobody else was that. *And I could get round that corner.*

I took three quick soft strides and was around it, pointing the Mauser into the long, dark loophole of a pillbox, staring down at me from the next front parallel.

Nothing happened.

I walked very carefully towards it, up a few yards of fore-and-aft trench without a firestep. There was another corner just before the pillbox, but I knew nobody would be around it. If they were anywhere in this trench, they were up behind the loophole. At the corner, I stopped and studied it.

It was a six-sided affair sunk into the front parapet, with loopholes around five sides. The sixth was the way in from the trench: you climbed three steps and in through a low doorway. I didn't climb anything. I just looked. Beside the pillbox the parapet had rotted and sand had poured down on the steps . . .

If anybody had got into that pillbox in weeks, he'd done it in a flying upwards dive. The sand on the steps hadn't been touched. I scuttled up and inside.

Like the blockhouse, you had to walk in around a blast wall. And inside, there were a lot of complicated bits of internal wall so that nobody could sneak up, shoot in through an unoccupied loophole, and hit everybody else in the back. A lot of thought had gone into this pillbox. I stepped quickly across to the rear left-hand loophole.

It looked half-backwards: above and across the bushes— and just twenty yards away, there was the square outline of another pillbox. And running between, across another culvert over the trench, the tank path.

I saw the pattern now: the two pillboxes placed like gate-posts to guard either side of the tank path, the one weak spot in the whole defence.

And now I knew where Alain was—where he had to be. In the same twin pillboxes up on the front line; the only places where he could stand up to see above the bushes without being seen. And where he could catch us in the only place where a bunch of people on foot could be straggled out to make a difficult shot: crossing on the culvert.

Behind me I heard the distant heartbeat of the Rolls. My time was up.

I jumped the steps down into the trench and ran. The corners didn't matter any more; now the corners were *my* protection. Nor did the noise; the steep sides of the communication trench would channel my crashings and splashings straight up in the air. In a concrete pillbox, already intent on the throb of the Rolls, Alain would never hear me.

I burst into the front line, turned left, rounded a couple of corners, and jumped on to the firestep. The sound of the car slapped at me.

Over my shoulder, I saw it: a dim grey cloud drifting gently over the ground maybe seventy yards back. And perhaps a dark figure walking beside it: Harvey, herding it along like a ghost elephant.

But across the bushes, I could see the pillbox on the next front parallel.

Alain must have seen it by now, know something had gone wrong. Would he shoot sooner—or later? Wait until the car was on the culvert, ten yards off, or fire at long range, knowing the Rolls daren't swing off the track?

I ran along the firestep, turned left, turned right . . .

Would Alain use lights? No—never. Why did I think that? Because we'd never used lights in the old days—lights meant throwing flares that would light us as well, would stop us pulling out if things got too tough . . .

I jumped on the firestep below the pillbox and screamed: "Lights!"

The Rolls paused, then the headlights came full on. Light, glaring blazing light, slammed against the pillbox like a silent explosion. Inside, a Sten fired into the blinding glare—but in the long wasteful howl of a man shooting at something he isn't certain about and is scared of.

I ran up the steps, threw the little Walther pistol in around the blast wall and yelled: *"Grenade!"*

He must have been thinking about grenades already—wishing he had some, maybe. He came around the wall like a kicked cat.

I pulled the trigger at a range of four feet. The burst lifted him, smashed him against the wall, hung him there. Then he pitched slowly forward and I stood aside and watched him fall past me into the trench.

It was the man coming out behind him who shot me.

31

It was dark and my mouth was full of slime and there was a distant rattle like a large-tooth file dragged across my raw brain. And deep inside, pain. The sort of pain you don't want to disturb, that you want to leave sleeping—but you know it won't sleep. But *you* can sleep. Just lie there. And sleep. And maybe die.

The idea jerked me awake. If I was dying, at least it meant I wasn't dead yet. I spat and tried to roll up on to my side—and that hurt. A flare of pain like a lighted fuse ran clear through me.

I kept very still and it died to a dull red ache around my stomach and a heavy feeling in my legs. *God, not a stomach wound, not a bullet in the guts and living on milk the rest of my life. And you can bribe a doctor into patching up a bullet scrape and calling it a road accident, but a hole in the belly is going to get reported . . .*

At least I was thinking like Caneton again. And come to that, why should a stomach wound paralyse my legs? I screwed my head around and saw the dead man lying across the back of my knees.

I looked carefully around. I was lying at the bottom of the pillbox steps, and just ahead of me was the body of the man I'd shot. The Rolls' lights were out.

The rattle started again, and this time it didn't feel distant. Bullets crunched and screamed at the lip of the trench and somebody dropped into it with a heavy splash. I groped in the mud for the Mauser, found it, then Harvey said: "Cane—are you alive?"

"Christ, *I* don't know," I said crossly. The shock was beginning to wear on and it was making me angry. Mostly at myself.

He rolled the dead man off my legs. I asked: "Did you get him?"

"Yes. You seemed to be busy standing up in the spotlight taking a bow."

"You were fifty yards off," I said, still angry. "You couldn't hit him with that little gun."

"If you stopped being surprised at what other people can do, you wouldn't get your head shot off so often."

I said: "Stomach, damn it, stomach." But he walked straight past me and turned over the other dead man. It occurred to me that I'd better find out just where I *had* been hit.

There was a messy hole just about the bottom of my ribs on the left-hand side: that would be the exit wound. For my cleverness, I'd got myself shot in the back. I groped round and found a smaller hole, higher up, round under my shoulder-blade.

I decided it probably hadn't got my stomach, and since my breathing didn't seem to have any leaks, it hadn't got a lung. I found Harvey squatting down beside me.

"I've got a busted rib or two," I said. "I think it ran around outside them."

"Probably. He was using a 7.65 Sauer." He tossed a small automatic into the mud by my face. "Peanut gun; you were lucky. Can you walk back to the car?"

"We've got so far. It's not much farther."

"*You've* got so far," he corrected, "and you ain't no advertisement. In case you want to know, neither of these guys is Alain. He's holed up in a pillbox across the track with a Sten."

I hadn't really expected we'd killed Alain, but I'd hoped. "Alain won't stay," I said. "Not if he knows we're still trying. The odds are against him now—he's a professional."

"Still playing Caneton, hey?" He stood up and back. "All right, let's see how you look on your feet."

I took a deep breath—which was a mistake—and started. It took time and blood, and it was climbing a skyscraper with little green men swinging axes into my side. But after a while, I was up on my two feet and leaning hard against the wall.

Harvey said: "Me, I'd say the wall was doing the work."

"I'll chase him out," I snarled. I was breathing in fast shallow gasps, to keep the strain off my ribs. "Get me the petrol tin out of the car."

"Recommended procedure for knocking out pillboxes."

220

He went on looking at me. Then there was a distant shouting. We both looked back up the trench, to where the dark slope rose up above it to the frontier road and the mountain wall beyond. Light flickered, like men running with torches.

"I'd forgotten about the cops," Harvey said thoughtfully. "If we go back, we're still in Switzerland." He swung back to me. "You've kind of committed us, haven't you?"

"Get me the petrol."

"Where'll you be?"

I nodded towards the culvert. "Far side of the path."

He nodded and hurried back towards the communication trench.

Crawling through the culvert started the little axes chipping away at my ribs again, but I made it. Then I had an eight-foot stretch of trench wall before it turned a corner leading forwards to the parallel where the pillbox was.

I knelt down carefully and took a quick look round the corner. The narrow dark eye of the pillbox stared back at me.

I jerked back. The pillbox wasn't only to cover the tank path—but also the trench itself. To stop an enemy spreading along it if he broke in. Just what it was going to stop me doing—if Alain was still there.

"*Alain,*" I called softly. "*Voici Caneton, C'est tout fini, Alain.*"

The pillbox stayed quiet.

I climbed up on the firestep, found a place where I could peep through the bushes and the wet sand-heaps, laid the Mauser down, and waited. Moonlight washed over the pillbox, turning it to a dirty bone-white—and as cold and quiet as the far side of the moon.

Are you still there, Alain? Don't you remember that a fixed position can turn into a trap? Damn it, you're a professional —you must have crept out and away. Given it up as a bad job, decided you wouldn't earn this twelve thousand or whatever you're getting paid . . .

Then the loophole spluttered flame and noise, Short, fast burst, as when a man knows what he's firing at. Harvey must have reached the car.

I fired two single shots and ducked, swearing angrily. Behind me, the shots had started more shouting among the cops weaving their way through the trenches from the frontier road.

But damn you, Alain—you shouldn't still be there. You've forgotten everything. You should never cling to a fixed position when the odds turn against you; it can kill you. It must kill you—because now we must go on.

There was a clatter in the culvert behind me, and a few moments later Harvey whispered: "I've got it—where do I throw it?"

"*I'm* throwing it. Cover me as I go round the corner; he can see down that stretch."

He hung on to the tin and said coldly: "What's the matter —one medal isn't enough for you?"

"*I'll* get him. Give me the petrol."

"Listen, hero," he said softly. "We don't have time for you to stagger bravely on and get your head blown off. Cover me."

I'd committed us all right. And he had to dig us out.

I nodded. "Don't go until he shoots at me."

"Okay. Where do I throw it—over the top so it drips down and blocks the loophole?"

"That wouldn't stop Alain. Chuck it inside."

He looked at me, then turned away. Then he turned back and said: "Can you really light gasoline off a gun-flash?"

"Yes."

He walked carefully up the firestep to the corner. I waited until he was there, then raised my head and started firing careful single shots at the loophole. The first one raised dust just below it; the second didn't—it must have gone straight in. With a Mauser on a butt at eight yards, you can place shots the way a brain surgeon places a scalpel. The third shot didn't raise dust, either.

The Sten blared at me, throwing gobs of wet sand and bullets clattering against the back wall. Harvey went round the corner with a rush and splash.

Alain had forgotten another lesson. He'd let himself be distracted. I flicked the Mauser on to automatic and let go a burst that scattered dust around the loophole and then climbed uncontrollably off the roof. But the Sten had stopped.

Harvey didn't pause. He must have had the top off the can already. He jumped up the steps; I saw his head and shoulders rise above the parapet, holding the big can upside down to lay a petrol trail.

He ran smack into Alain coming out.

For a moment they hung together, so close that Alain couldn't use the Sten—and Harvey's gun was in his belt. Then they bounced apart. Harvey dropped the can and grabbed for his waist; Alain slashed with the Sten, knocking him back off the steps.

I stood straight up, shoved the Mauser out to arm's length, and squeezed the trigger. It fired once and was empty. Alain ducked, then calmly straightened the Sten in his hands and aimed down into the trench.

Harvey fired.

I saw the reflected flash—and Alain became flames.

You can have seen petrol fires before—have lit them before—and you never remember how fast they light because you just don't believe what you see. Alain must have been soaked in the stuff from bumping into the can, and the steps were flooded. Together, they turned into fire.

He didn't shoot at Harvey. He turned, a man of flames standing in a hedge of flames, tried to wipe the fire out of his eyes with a burning arm, then started to shoot careful bursts across my head at the Rolls. He had forgotten a lot— but not what he was here for.

Harvey fired again. The figure toppled off the steps with the Sten still going, and hit the bottom of the trench with a hiss.

I laid my head down on the wet sand of the parapet and started to feel very sick.

Harvey met me at the tank path; he was moving slowly and wearily, and he looked singed, dirty, and damp. Behind him, the flames still flickered in the trench, and behind me the waving torches of the police were only a few hundred yards off. But somehow they didn't seem important; nothing to hurry us.

Harvey said: "We seem to have won the war." His voice was flat, numbed, without any expression.

I said: "Yes," and braced myself for anything he had to say about my bright ideas.

But all he said was: "I could use a drink."

"Me, too."

We walked slowly towards the Rolls, which had come across the culvert and stopped just past the front-line trenches. When we got there, I said: "Take the wire-cutters out of my case. There's probably some front-line wire ahead."

He took them and started out in front of the car, then stopped and said: "Bernard. And now Alain." But his voice was still dead. He wasn't feeling anything about it—yet.

32

FIVE minutes later we were in Liechtenstein and turning on to the main road which we'd left on the other side of the frontier, three kilometres back. The Rolls had taken a thumping, but Rolls's are built for that, and fifty yards in the dark is a long range for a Sten—particularly if it was like most Stens I'd known and the single-shot button didn't work. One headlight was shot out, there were bullet-holes through the windscreen and both left-hand doors, and one through the big radiator grille. I didn't know if it had punctured the radiator itself—but we'd certainly find out on the mountain road to Steg.

I sat at the back alongside Maganhard, wincing at every jolt and slopping cognac down my shirt. Harvey was up front with the girl.

Maganhard hadn't said a word, but he didn't look much more dead than usual, so perhaps he was thinking.

After a few miles, Harvey turned round and said through the partition: "D'you want us to leave you down near Vaduz?—find a doctor?"

Maganhard woke up and looked at me. "You are wounded?"

"I'm not dying. And I don't suppose you know a doctor who's ready to call a bullet-hole a mosquito bite. And, anyway, there's still Galleron to come."

"Think we'll have any trouble?" Harvey asked.

"Not much. He can't have every gunman in Europe under contract. And if he had, he'd have put them down in the battle zone."

After a time, Maganhard said: "When I told you I wanted to get past the frontier, Mr Cane, I did not understand that it would be necessary for a man to be burned as that man was."

I said wearily: "Nobody knew it would be necessary, Mr Maganhard. It just happened. In this sort of job, people don't always die with a brave smile and a kind word for mother."

"I thought you knew him!"

"I did. And I'm sorry he got burned, if that helps. But nobody forced him to be down there with a Sten."

He thought for a moment, then said: "I suppose they came to kill or be killed. Perhaps it was fair."

"You're still sentimentalizing them. They came to kill—full stop. If they'd thought there was a chance of getting killed, they wouldn't have come." I shook my head. "Alain didn't become St Francis just by dying rather nastily."

Miss Jarman said: "All the other times, you didn't have a choice about shooting. They started it. But this time—you planned it. You started it."

"I could have stuck my head out of the trench," I growled, "and given them the first shot—if that would have made me more moral. It would damn sure have made me headless."

"I didn't mean that." Her voice was cold and a little shivery, and not just from the wind coming through the bullet-holes. She'd seen Alain burn, too. "I mean perhaps we could have done something else that. . . ." He voice trailed off.

"Perhaps we could," I said heavily. But I was trying not to think what.

We turned right at Triesen and on to the twisting road up to Triesenberg and, beyond it, Steg. We were going to find out about that radiator now.

Miss Jarman said: "The engine's getting warm."

"Keep going. Don't slow up."

She didn't. We slammed into a series of hairpins as fast as Morgan would have taken them—and on just one headlight. But she had an open road for it: Liechtensteiners don't believe in doing much but sleep outside the money-making hours. We'd only seen a cyclist and a tourist coach since the frontier.

As we came up to the lights of Triesenberg, it started to drizzle gently. Harvey leant across almost into Miss Jarman's lap to read the radiator temperature. "The needle's practically off the clock," he reported. "We won't get much farther."

"Keep going."

"Christ, we'll blow a cylinder."

"That engine's full of cylinders. Keep going."

The girl said flatly: "We won't get as far as Steg unless we stop to cool down."

"If we don't get there quick, there won't be any point in going."

Maganhard turned to me. "We have nearly an hour and a half."

"D'you think so? Didn't you tell me that Galleron wouldn't kill Flez as long as he was trying to kill you? Well, perhaps now he knows he can't kill you—so his only hope is to knock off Flez and then out-vote you."

He went quiet. Then he asked suspiciously: "How could he know I am not dead?"

"By now Morgan's probably rung the General and the General's rung Galleron. And there must have been some arrangement for Alain and Co. to ring Galleron to say the job was done. Either way, nobody's told him you *are* dead—so he must be getting pretty jumpy by now."

We ran clear of Triesenberg and the road became a gritty track winding up through the steep mountainside pastures. A faint smell of hotness began to drift back from the engine —and a small, harsh clattering sound.

Miss Jarman said: "I think the engine's going to seize."

"Not yet. Just the valves getting hot. Get above the snow-line and we can stuff some of that into it."

Maganhard said: "If Herr Flez *is* dead, then it would be a mistake for me to go on."

"More of a mistake not to be sure."

We wound on up. The rain got stronger and colder, and as the headlight swept the mountainside on bends, I could see fragments of cloud crawling in among the pines above us.

And by now the engine was sounding like a convention of Spanish dancers. Harvey turned to say something.

Headlights blazed in our faces. The girl tromped on the brakes.

The other driver must have reckoned our single headlight for a motor-bike, because he kept on coming. Then his brakes screamed like a new soul in Hell and his lights zig-zagged as he skidded. There was a long tearing *crunch*. The Rolls shuddered delicately and stopped.

Harvey was out on the running-board, gun in hand. I grabbed the empty Mauser, tried to jump to my feet, got a flare of pain in my rib, and sat down again.

Jammed at an angle across our left front bumper was a big black German saloon, ripped open like a sardine tin from front wheel to rear door. The Rolls' bumper probably had a couple of scratches on it.

In the sudden silence Harvey said clearly: "Come out slowly and with the hands empty."

The driver got out fast, waving his hands furiously and swearing like a pirate's parrot. It was Henri Merlin.

I climbed carefully across Maganhard's feet and said: "Calm down, Henri, the Marines are here."

He shoved his head forward and peered through the drizzle. "Caneton? *Pas possible!* But it is! You are superb!" He reached to clout me on both shoulders. I dodged gingerly.

Maganhard stepped down behind me. We were standing between the cars, just outside the headlight beams, lit by a soft underglow reflected back off the rain. I saw Merlin's huge damp grin—and then his face collapse into despair.

He spread his hands. "But now—it does not matter. He— they——" He stopped to sort and translate his thoughts.

Maganhard said: "Good evening, Monsieur Merlin."

Merlin turned to him. "I came—to Monsieur Flez—a quarter of an hour since. And I find no Galleron—and Flez is dead."

It went very quiet again. Something that wasn't quite rain brushed my face. Several somethings danced like moths in the headlights. We hadn't quite reached the snow-line, but as the freezing level slid down the mountain, the snow-line had reached us.

Maganhard looked at me and said quietly and bitterly: "It seems this Galleron took your advice."

"He could afford better advice than mine."

"He is not a fool," Maganhard said. "An hour ago he was

228

counting on me being dead. Now, he is counting on me being alive. So—we must not go."

"We could just sneak up and view the body," I suggested.

"Galleron must be waiting nearby for me to come."

"But it isn't midnight yet. We could still go and view the body."

There was a clatter as the girl opened the bonnet of the Rolls, and a long hiss as the snow hit the hot engine.

Maganhard said with stiff patience: "Under Caspar's rules, the time set for a meeting is the *last* possible time. If all shareholders are present before that, a meeting is automatically convened. With Herr Flez dead, all the shareholders will be present if I am there and this Galleron walks in. Therefore——"

"But he won't convene any meetings," I said cheerfully, "on account of me having a gun stuffed down his throat. So let's go up and view——"

"Christ," Harvey said, "anybody'd think you were running for election, that way you say the same thing every ten seconds. So you want to go see the body?—okay, let's go see it, if it'll keep you quiet."

"All right," I said. "All right, if you insist." The girl came up beside me. "How's the engine?"

"I've got the radiator cap off, but we need something to put inside. The snow isn't lying yet."

"Drain off Merlin's car."

Henri started to look horrified, remembered all the other things that had happened to that car, and just shrugged.

Harvey and the girl went away. The snow, in bigger and slower flakes, drifted slowly around us.

Merlin coughed and said: "Caneton—I am sorry, but—" He turned to Maganhard and said in a legal voice: "Monsieur, as your lawyer, it is my duty to advise you against risks. To go to the house would be a risk. *Donc*—I must advise you not to go."

Maganhard frowned.

I said: "As your illegal adviser, I'd say it would be nice to meet Galleron after all this."

Maganhard looked at me sharply. "I do not want any more shooting!"

I shrugged one shoulder. "Whatever you say. You're the boss." He looked suspicious. I went on: "But there's no need to rush a decision. Let's just get the issues quite clear."

He shook his head impatiently, throwing off the clutching snowflakes. "It is cold out here."

"Be a lot colder without your share of Caspar," I said soothingly. "Let's see now: Caspar's got a share capital of forty thousand Swiss francs, right? I suppose it's in ten— or hundred-franc shares?"

"Ten."

"Making four thousand shares in all. How many d'you own?"

"You know already. Thirty-three per cent."

"Not the question I asked. How *many*?"

It was very quiet in the slow, swirling snow. Harvey and the girl passed as dark ghosts beyond the lights, draining Merlin's car into the empty brandy flask, then pouring it into the Rolls.

Maganhard hunched his shoulders against the snow and said: "I would have to work that out. But the percentage is the important factor."

"Sure—but share certificates only show how *many* shares. Now, you two have met Flez; I haven't. Tell me if I'm reading him right. Galleron walks in a week ago, slaps down his share certificate, says: 'I've got Heiliger's shares—let's have a meeting and sell out the whole company,' and Flez remembers the trouble you'll have getting there—and goes into a galloping panic. Am I right?"

Maganhard and Merlin looked at each other. Merlin spread his hands and murmured: "*C'est possible.*"

Maganhard said slowly: "He would probably do that. But——"

"Maybe he panicked a bit too quickly. Still, he knew the certificate could *only* be Heiliger's, could *only* be worth thirty-four per cent—and so it out-voted him. But a bearer certificate doesn't show either of those things: no name, no percentages. Only the number of shares held. And Flez would be used to thinking in percentages, too. So maybe he didn't stop to work it out. Have you worked out your holding yet?"

Maganhard said stiffly: "If you please . . ."

I found I was waving the Mauser at him for emphasis. It was still empty, but I'd shoved home the bolt, so nobody would know by looking at it. "Sorry."

He said: "I own 1,320 shares."

"Correct. Thirty-three per cent. And thirty-four per cent is 1,360 shares. Pretty easy numbers to confuse, aren't they? —when you're used to thinking in percentages. I wonder if Flez didn't do just that—and Galleron's certificate showed just 1,320 shares, same as yours, same as Flez's."

He stared at me. "You mean—it is a fake?"

"Why would you fake one with the *wrong* number of shares on it? No, it's genuine—but it isn't Heiliger's. That burned up when he crashed. No, it's yours. Right now, you don't own a centime of Caspar. How does it feel being poor?"

There was a long hush.

I said quietly: "I suppose when you got hit with that rape charge you couldn't get around so easily, so you increased Merlin's power of attorney. I'd guess you even lodged a lot of important papers with him, or maybe gave him power to get them out of a safe deposit for you. I'd even guess one of them was the Caspar certificate."

I grinned at Merlin. He went on watching the Mauser which was watching his stomach. "Any Frenchman could do that heavy Belgian accent, Henri—hell, I could do it myself. Well enough to fool a Liechtensteiner like Flez, anyway. Now give kind Mr Maganhard back his ten million quid— Galleron."

He looked up slowly, and after a time he smiled a little sadly. "Legally, of course, a bearer certificate belongs to whoever bears it. But possibly we are not being strictly legal." He sighed and reached inside his coat. A gun blasted three times beside my elbow. Merlin's face was lit by the flashes, his expression frozen in the moment of changing. Then he was pitched away into the swirling snow.

I whipped round and clouted the big Webley out of Maganhard's hand.

Harvey came cat-footed out of the curtain of snow, gun in hand. "What in hell happened?"

"We met Monsieur Galleron." I nodded at Merlin. "Meet Monsieur Galleron."

Harvey looked at me, then walked across and peered carefully down at him and shook his head.

Maganhard was standing with his eyes clenched shut, melted snow streaming down his face and glasses and glinting in the backlash of light from the headlamps.

I said: "Welcome to the Murderers' Club?"

He opened his eyes slowly. "Is he dead?"

I nodded. "It's not so difficult really, is it?" But I wished I had remembered he still had that damn revolver.

Harvey came back. "Was he really Galleron?"

"Yes. D'you want to stand around talking about it in a snowstorm, or can it wait?"

"Can wait. But what about him?"

"Strip his pockets and stick him in the Rolls. We're going to have to dump that car before morning, so he may as well go with it."

Merlin's car had a Liechtenstein registration, so it must have been hired. So perhaps he'd hired it in the name of Galleron. But it didn't much matter.

Harvey said doubtfully: "He'll get found."

"Christ, we've left dead men spread from here to the Atlantic," I snarled. "One more'll just screw things up so the cops never work it all out."

And that was just about true. Beyond a certain point, a crime can get so complicated that the cops know no jury or judge will ever understand it—even if they do themselves. On top of everything else, finding a Paris lawyer who'd been posing as a Belgian businessman dead in Liechtenstein in the car of the distinguished British resident of Switzerland would just be a ten-aspirin headache.

Harvey grinned sourly and bent over Merlin and came up with a handful of papers and a small automatic. I took the biggest of the papers: a stiff, folded document that opened out into a spread of fancy lettering and a big seal like a "wanted" notice for Robin Hood. The Caspar certificate. For a few seconds I was a very rich man. The snow went on falling on me.

I gave it to Maganhard. "Yours, I think. Let's get up the hill for that meeting."

"But Herr Flez is dead," he said faintly.

"Don't be silly. Saying that was just Merlin's last chance to stop you coming; he could have killed you off later, before you caught on. But using your certificate, he always needed you dead and Flez alive. It makes sense now."

Harvey dragged Merlin's body into the back of the Rolls. Maganhard kept his eyes front and walked carefully in after it. I picked up the Webley, rubbed it clear of fingerprints, and threw it into a field.

And now perhaps we could go up and have a quiet company meeting.

33

"So you were all really working for the same person," Miss Jarman said. "Harvey and you, and those—Bernard and Alain and the others. All working for Henri Merlin."

I nodded. "Just like the Christians and the lions down in the arena. All really working for old Emperor Nero."

"I don't imagine," she said sharply, "that the Christians thought of it that way."

"I don't suppose the lions did, either."

We were sitting drinking whisky around a big log fire in Flez's living-room. It was a long, wide wood-panelled place that would have looked expensive if it hadn't looked like a Swiss souvenir shop. Every time Flez had made another million, he'd celebrated by buying another dozen cuckoo clocks and carved brackets full of china and painted-wood figures.

Flez himself was a fussy little man who'd nearly gone catatonic when we'd marched in bristling with pistols and started bleeding on his rugs. Miss Jarman had done the real work of fetching hot water and antiseptic and starting temporary repairs on me, while Maganhard had taken Flez into a corner to explain the True Life Story. But I don't think it had registered, even in Schwytzer-Deutsch. Flez just couldn't believe there was that much wickedness in this big, beautiful, coloured postcard of a world.

Maganhard came out of his corner and planted himself in front of the fire. "Do you say, Mr Cane, that Monsieur Merlin planned this whole thing from the beginning?"

"No, he can't have done. He must have set up the phoney rape charge in the hope that you'd give him more power of attorney. After all, he'd know how you'd react: that you'd prefer to stay away than fight the charge. Then all he had to do was wait for a chance to turn his power into cash. When Heiliger flew into a mountain and you were stuck out in the Atlantic, that was his chance. The rest of it all came from that.

"What *I* don't understand," I added, "is why you lodged a bearer certificate worth ten million quid with him."

His voice got a touch of the old stiffness. "Since I was liable to arrest it would have been foolish to carry a document like that on me. And of course I made arrangements that if anybody appeared at a Caspar meeting with my certificate, certain precautions had to be taken to ensure that he truly owned it."

I nodded. "But as he was pretending it was Heiliger's certificate, none of the precautions applied. I get it."

Miss Jarman asked: "But if Merlin was going to kill us, anyway, why did he send you and Harvey? Or why didn't he send those two—Bernard and Alain—and let them pretend to guard us, then kill us?"

"The risk—to his Merlin personality. Remember, everybody knew Merlin was Maganhard's lawyer and that he'd be arranging this trip. So when you ended up dead, Merlin would get some blame anyway. If it then came out that he hadn't arranged an escort, or had sent one that somehow stayed alive while you got killed, it would have looked suspicious. Since he was guilty, he couldn't risk *any* suspicion.

"That's why he rammed Harvey down your throat: made you take him along even when Maganhard didn't think there'd be any shooting. That way, when it was all over, it'd look as if Merlin had done his best—and all the blame was on Galleron. He didn't mind that: Galleron hadn't got a traceable past and was going to vanish, anyway, once Caspar was cashed in. Probably he hired Alain and Bernard in the name of Galleron, so they never knew who they were working for and couldn't give him away." I looked up at the girl. "I told you the lions might not know they were working for Nero, either."

She raised her eyebrows. "And that makes us the Christians, does it? I hadn't known Christians ate lions."

I gave her an insincere smile and said quickly: "So all in all, Merlin could go back to being Merlin with just an extra ten million in an anonymous account in Switzerland. No need to run off and be Joe Smith in Brazil." Then I thought of something and turned to Maganhard. "Aren't you supposed to be having a company meeting, after all this?"

"Yes. But Herr Flez has been good enough to remind me that we do not have proof that Max's certificate was destroyed. It is still possible that his heir may appear with it before midnight. Therefore we must wait until then." He gave Flez a heavy sideways look that showed what he thought of the possibility.

Then he remembered: "Herr Flez could have identified Monsieur Merlin as this Galleron."

"He could, but it wasn't so much of a risk. By Caspar's rules, I believe Flez can't get away from Liechtenstein much, so he wouldn't be likely to meet Merlin again. And when the deal was complete, in a month or two, I imagine Flez would have got quietly pushed off a mountain."

Flez went as white as new snow and dropped his glass. Maganhard smiled a stiff satisfied smile.

Miss Jarman said: "Who killed that man in the Citroën at Quimper, then?"

I shrugged my good shoulder. "Merlin, I'd say. Harvey's got Henri's gun, but it looked the right calibre."

Harvey seemed surprised for a moment, then dipped into his pocket and brought out the little automatic and peered down the muzzle. "Six-point-three-five," he said. "That's right."

"But Merlin wasn't at Quimper that night," the girl objected. "You rang him up in Paris at four o'clock or something."

"He *shouldn't* have been there," I said. "Probably the driver spotted him and that's what got him killed. And I didn't get through to him in Paris. I rang there, and he had to ring back a few minutes later. There was time to ring from Paris to Quimper to tell him to get on to me. After that, we didn't talk to him until past noon. He could have got back to Paris by then."

She nodded thoughtfully, then said: "So the telephoning that was getting us into trouble——"

"Yes. I was doing it all myself."

She just looked at me.

Harvey got up and helped himself to another whisky without being asked. The girl watched him, expressionless.

Maganhard said: "And what will happen now?"

I lifted one shoulder in a half-shrug. "The French police'll be jumping; the Swiss police'll be jumping. And you'll have the Liechtenstein cops up here first thing tomorrow. But as long as you swear you were here since before they closed the frontier . . . they won't convict a live millionaire on the evidence of a few dead gunmen. They won't even try."

The girl said softly: "Poor old lions."

Maganhard said: "But what about the . . . the charge against me in France?"

"It'll fall down. The woman in the case is going to get a letter from Merlin, back-dated a few months, saying he'd arranged for it to be sent if he died. And it'll tell her to drop the case."

He frowned. "Do you believe he has arranged such a letter?"

"Of course not. But I'll get Ginette to write it—I told you she was a good forger, remember? Just send me the woman's name and one of Henri's signatures."

He stared at me while he chewed this over. Then his face moved slowly, piece by piece, into his version of a smile. "Considering everything, Mr Cane, you appear to have done an efficient job." The voice got official. "I would consider having you work for me on a permanent basis. I might pay——"

"No."

The smile vanished. "I have not said what I might pay!"

I shook my head wearily. "That's nothing to do with it, Mr Maganhard. Don't you see what Merlin proved? I'd been going around playing Caneton: the big professional, the man who couldn't step aside when a job like this came up. Now—now we know Merlin picked both sides: Harvey and me against Alain and Bernard and the others. So he chose *us* as the two most likely to fail."

There was a silence. Then Harvey said mildly: "Wrong, wasn't he?"

"Only just, chum, only just. And at least he tried: he picked an Englishman who made a reputation back in the war—and an alcoholic gunman. To guard a man worth ten million quid. And we weren't even bright enough to see that."

Maganhard put on a stiff frown. He hated the idea that

anybody working for him might have been second-rate; he could swallow Merlin—first-class and merely crooked—a lot easier.

He said: "I think you are being rather fanciful, Mr Cane. As Mr Lovell says, Monsieur Merlin was wrong. We were right, and we were successful."

I nodded. "Oh yes, we won the war. And *you* were right . . . I thought for a time that made me right, too. But it doesn't. I should never have taken this job. The way I do things—the way Caneton does them—too many people get killed. I don't know what else I could have done . . . but maybe that's the trouble. Maybe somebody else could have thought of something. You find him. Hire him."

The girl was looking at me curiously. "I thought you didn't care about what happened to those men down there."

"I don't, not much. Maybe I'm wrong, but I don't think it matters who kills hired killers, or when, or even how. I was thinking of Harvey." Out of the corner of my eye I saw his head jerk round. I kept looking at Miss Jarman—hard. "Harvey's no killer; don't ever think you have to cure him of that. The real killers are the ones who can do it without taking a drink. After or before."

"I hate to spoil a good speech," Harvey said slowly, "but nobody seems to have noticed I ain't dead yet."

I gave him a quick look, then stood up, finished my drink, and said to nobody in particular: "I'm going to run the Rolls down the hill and dump it, then catch a train from Vaduz. They won't be checking on who's going *out* yet." I looked at the girl. "Get him away from here before the cops come."

Harvey asked me: "Paris?"

"France, anyway. I've got to find a doctor who won't talk."

He finished his whisky with a gulp. "Guess I'll come, too. The work'll be piling up."

Miss Jarman turned slowly to face him, her face stiff and unbelieving. "*What* work?"

He seemed surprised. "My work."

Inside, I felt as cold and empty as a forgotten church. I said dully: "That was what I meant."

34

AFTER a moment I said: "He's the top gunman in Europe, now Bernard and Alain are dead. Even if it never gets out that he killed them, he's the number one man. The best jobs, the top rates."

The girl didn't seem to have heard me. She said to Harvey: "But . . . but Merlin chose you because of your—your drinking problem. He *expected* you to get killed!"

He shrugged. "So like I say—he was wrong."

I said: "He doesn't have a drink problem. Not now."

She whipped round at me.

I said: "His problem was he didn't think he could mix guns and booze. That's why he went dry at the beginning of this job. It's why he tried to keep us out of it tonight—he knew he'd drunk too much. He'd faced up to it, then: he was honest enough to say he'd screwed up his job by his drinking."

My voice sounded empty and monotonous, like the hollow thumping of a big gong. But I had to go on beating it. "Then he got into the fight—and he killed the best gunman in Europe. A man rated above him. Now—where's his problem? He's proved he can mix pistols and whisky. He won't live two months."

Her eyes got narrow. "But you dragged him into that fight —and you *knew* this could happen?"

I shook my head helplessly. "I tried not to. That's why I tried to kill Alain myself. I thought I could do it—the element of surprise, creeping up the trenches . . . being Caneton." I smiled a little stiffly. "Caneton used to be pretty good at that sort of thing. But maybe Merlin was right."

She said quietly: "About both of you."

Harvey lifted himself on to his feet. He was perfectly steady; several of Flez's whiskies on top of the flask of brandy hadn't touched his balance. But you need a lot more than balance, and a lot less whisky, to be Europe's best gunman.

He said: "So let's get to Paris."

I nodded and turned for the door. The girl said clearly and bitterly: "Thank you, Monsieur Caneton."

And perhaps she was right. Perhaps I was still Caneton. And perhaps——

I looked at her, then at Harvey; at the haunted, lined face that was, in an odd way, so innocent because it showed its guilt so clearly.

I said: "How're the shakes?"

He stretched his right hand towards me, fingers spread. They were as steady as carved stone. He smiled down at them.

I said: "Pretty good," and then swung the Mauser over and down. I heard—and felt—the fingers crack.

In the shocked silence his dragging breath was like a scream. He arched forward, hugging his hand against his stomach, his face clenched and white. Then he toppled back and crashed into a chair.

The girl was at his side, cradling his head, stroking his hair, murmuring to him.

Maganhard said coldly: "I hardly think that was——"

"I saved his life," I said. "For another month. It'll take three months for his hand to heal well enough to use a gun again."

Miss Jarman looked up at me, her eyes hard and bright. "You didn't need to do *that*."

"It was cheap, simple, a bit nasty," I said dully. "What Caneton would have done. If I'd been somebody else maybe I'd've thought of something better. But I'm not."

Harvey half-opened his eyes and whispered hoarsely: "You'd better hide good, Cane. Real good. Because I'll spend a long time looking."

I nodded. "I'll be at Clos Pinel—or they'll know where."

"He'll kill you," the girl said.

"Perhaps. It could be up to you. It could even be something for him to stay sober for."

I walked out and nobody tried to stop me.

It was still snowing gently. Halfway down the mountain I remembered that I'd never collected the balance of my pay —four thousand francs. I kept on going, but looked at my watch. It was a minute after midnight. Ahead of me, the mountain road was a dark tunnel without any end.